This book is dedicated to my loving parents.

BLEEDING FOR THE WRONG CAUSE

YOUNG LIFE IN "HITLER'S GERMANY"

Thomas awoke from a sharp pain in his right lower leg. It felt like a lightning bolt had hit it! Sweat was running down his face. His body was drenched! He sat up in bed and threw the blanket to the side. His eyes fell on his right leg. It was... gone! In shock, he stared and shook. How could this be? His right leg had been cut off! Then it all came back to him. The doctor had amputated his leg a couple of days ago because of a serious sepsis that had developed due to the gunshot in his right shin bone. This was now his first phantom-pain. The doctor had told him about it. You don't have the leg anymore, but you get the pain instead! How cruel! He looked around the room with the twelve beds in it. One was empty. The fellow with a high fever had died last night.

The door opened, and nurses Olga and Lidia entered the room. Olga spoke, "Hi Thomas, what is going on with you? You are totally drenched in sweat! What happened?"

Thomas replied, "I had my first phantom-pain! It wasn't good, to say the least."

"I am so sorry, Thomas! I heard from other patients how painful it can be! I hope you don't get them too often! Why don't you change your clothes and go on the balcony in the warm sun? Lidia and I will put new bedsheets on your bed during that time. We have to get the other bed ready for the new patient anyway."

Thomas got out of bed, changed his clothes, and grabbed the two crutches that were leaning against a chair. He asked, "Are we getting a new patient today?"

"Olga is adamant that you and the new patient are related!" Lidia said. "She wants to move his bed right beside yours. His last name is Wenzel, just like yours."

"Ha-ha" Thomas laughed, "People with the name Wenzel are all over the Riesengebirge, where I am from. It would be a real miracle if the new guy would be related to me! Ha-ha."

Olga replied, "You never know!"

Thomas made his way towards the balcony. He had learned to get around with his crutches. He opened the door to the outside, where the warm air from the sun engulfed him. It was May, and the trees, the meadows, and the flowers, were all in their best green. It was a wonderful, rich landscape to look at, but Thomas couldn't enjoy it! His heart and mind were too troubled with his fate of going through life as a cripple instead of reaching his dreams of becoming a pilot, emigrating to Canada, and marrying a wonderful-looking woman. None of his dreams would become reality! He knew that. He grieved. It was hard to let go. They had tricked him into the war! He would have never joined the army by himself. Never! He turned around to go back into the room again. His wonderful, warm, brown eyes were downcast, his gentle face, surrounded by thick, black hair, bent down in defeat. He opened the door to step inside.

At the same moment as he was through the door, the door at the other end of the room opened. Thomas looked at worn-out boots, a dark brown, very worn pair of pants, a checkered blue shirt, a face... that face? Thomas's face turned white! Trembling, he had to hold on to his crutches so he wouldn't lose balance. "Papa!" he said out loud. "Papa!" Both men made it to the middle of the room and met in a long embrace. Thomas thought, "Home!"

It all came back to him. He couldn't remember the day he was born, April 15th, 1927, but Mom and Dad told him it was a stormy day with lots of rain. Germany was still suffering from the worldwide economic depression. Confidence in the Weimar Republic, their government at that time, was dwindling. Many people were without jobs, especially young people, and the outlook for the future was bleak, but nevertheless, Thomas would see the light of this world.

August had to put up the collar of his overcoat and bike to the next village to get the midwife. In those days, a midwife was a farmer's wife with a brave heart and compassion for the new mom and the newborn baby. The good ones knew a bit about proper hygiene, but you would hear many reports about mothers dying while giving birth to a child. All those facts went through Dad's head on his way to the village. He had heard good reports about the midwife he was going to ask. Hopefully, they were true!

The water was dripping from his hat when he knocked on the door. A farm woman with an apron over her strong middle section opened the door. "August, it's you! I was thinking that it would be about time for Trudy and the baby! How far are the labour pains apart?"

Dad answered, "Uhm, I don't know! Trudy told me to get you! She said it is time!"

"If that's so, we better be going!" She went into the house to get her bag and tell her family where she was going. After she got her bike from behind the shed, the two were on their way. August was thankful for her eagerness to help his wife and the baby. He would pay her well, he decided.

Thomas saw the light of the world before the day was over. All went well. Dad rode home with the midwife so she would be safe. When he returned home, he marveled at the picture of the new mom, with her thick, black hair, and soft face, lying in bed beside the newborn son, with the same thick, black hair. He quietly took a blanket and slept on the sofa.

The parents of August, Milli and Otto, loved the newborn baby. The whole family lived together in one house. All of them were busy tending to their few animals and working the huge garden, except for Dad. He was seldom at home. His passion was to travel, which he combined with trading and selling goods. You could see him all over the countryside, visiting the villages in the neighbourhood, while doing his business. Everybody knew August. He tried to satisfy all their demands for special goods. He had a talent for trading and talking with people. Trudy was very busy as well, taking care of the house and all the other tasks around the home. She put little Thomas in a stroller under the fruit tree in the garden where their dog Hector, the boxer, watched over him. Mom came only to feed him. There was too much work everywhere. She and

Grandma Milli decided that it would be healthy for Thomas' lungs if he would cry.

Little Thomas was almost two years old when Mom was close to giving birth to another child. "This one is a wild one!" She told August. "He is kicking and boxing, as if he is angry at me!"

"He didn't get that from me!" August answered. "I am not angry at you! I love you!" Ludwig was born! He was a very healthy, strong boy with blue eyes and dark brown hair. Since all the adults were busy with the house and other things like the animals and the big garden, Thomas and Ludwig had a lot of time by themselves. As soon as little Ludwig was able to walk, the two explored their surroundings together. All the adults kept their eyes on them, but a lot of times, one thought that the other would take care of the boys, so, nobody was actually watching!

Ludwig was full of crazy ideas. He was almost three years old when he decided to investigate chickens. He wanted to take a look at the inside of a chicken. Thomas had a bad feeling about it, like so many times when Ludwig was up to no good, but he didn't want to argue and went along with it. Ludwig was smart enough not to take a chicken from his Mom. He stole a chicken from the neighbour instead. With a knife from the kitchen, he killed the chicken as he had watched Grandpa do and cut the belly open to look at the inside. Thomas was curious as well! Both boys found it very interesting! Unfortunately, the neighbour, who was searching for his missing chicken, did not share their interest.

With both boys pulled by the ears, he went up to Grandpa and told him the story. Grandpa was a very relaxed and understanding man! He showed a frown to the children, but had to hide a bit of a smile. His pipe almost fell out of his mouth. Only on special occasions would you see him without his pipe hanging down across his beard. One of their own chickens was given to the neighbour. Mom, however, had no mercy on either of the boys and made this clear to them by getting the stick for their backsides. She thought that they had learned their lesson.

But Ludwig had his own mind. The only lesson he learned was not to take the neighbour's chicken; a mouse was his next victim. She had to suffer the same fate as the chicken. So, the older Ludwig got, the clearer it was to Thomas that his little brother knew what he wanted, and if he didn't get it, you better watch out! His anger would be fierce!

Ludwig got stronger every year. One day the boys were sitting at the breakfast table. The old pig was no more. Pieces of it were on the table in the form of bacon. Both boys had a good helping of it and devoured it down. Ludwig had the urge to use the outhouse and made a run for it. So, Thomas was sitting all by himself with the last crumps of bacon in front of him. He knew it would be trouble, but bacon was bacon! All of it ended up in his mouth. When Ludwig came back, he wasn't amused! He didn't say a word. He turned his back towards Thomas and went calmly outside. Thomas felt sorry already! He should have kept a bit for his brother! He knew better!

After a while, Thomas decided to play outside and look for his little brother. Ludwig was nowhere to be seen! It was eery quiet! Thomas went across the yard towards the shed. As he turned the corner by the shed, he faced his angry brother, who was waiting for him with grandpa's axe swinging over his head. His eyes full of fury as he stared at Thomas, the axe coming closer to Thomas head. Thomas stood motionless! A large hand grasped the handle of the axe and pulled it out of Ludwig's grip. Grandpa was there! Just in the nick of time! Thomas almost fainted! This time it was Grandpa's turn to teach little Ludwig a lesson on his backside. He himself learned a lesson as well. The axe did not lean against the wall of the shed anymore. Grandpa tucked it away where little ones couldn't reach it.

Mother got a job outside the home in a small store. The money was badly needed. She came home one day with something new, a fruit that none of their family had ever seen before. She opened her bag and pulled out a big paper bag full of grapes. There were no vineyards in the "Riesengebirge" were they lived. A lot of people had never eaten grapes. After dinner, the family tried them out and fell in love with them. Ludwig ate the most. Everybody laughed when he showed his big tummy.

They went to bed early, like normal. Nights were short in the country! At two in the morning little Ludwig woke up with painful cramps in his tummy. He cried for his mom. Trudy put her feet onto the floor and opened her eyes slowly. She looked at the window and couldn't believe her eyes. It didn't make sense at first, but after a second, she knew what it was. Flames were coming down from the roof licking the window panes. August was on one of his trips with Grandpa, so Trudy ran to Grandma Milli's door, opened it, and fearfully told her the bad news. Grandma was already up as she was getting ready to tend to the animals. Together they gathered the boys and ran out of the house. Mother, Grandma, Thomas, and Ludwig, stood by the fruit trees and watched the house burn to the ground. Neighbours came with buckets of water, but it was of no help. The fire was very fast and way too advanced for them to make any impact on the flames.

When the sun came up, you could clearly see the damage. The house was gone! The hazelnut tree, which was very close to the house didn't make it either, but the stable with the animals stayed intact. "At least something." Trudy thought.

A good neighbour, who had a huge house, took them in until their new house was built. The cause of the fire was never determined. It started on the roof! Everybody was thankful that Ludwig had his tummy ache. Without it? You never know!

"We got a new Chancellor!" Yelled August to everyone in earshot as he entered the house.

Trudy was busy baking and asked back, "Is it this Adolf Hitler we hear so much of lately?"

"Yes! It's him! The people say he is our savior! He will provide jobs and give us a life of stability! If you join the Nazi party, he promises you a job. Hitler will even pay you a salary if you are out of work for a while. The same will happen if you are sick. You will get pay for a while. But listen to the best news. Everybody will get a holiday of three days a year! This should increase to one week a year in the future."

Grandpa took his pipe out of his mouth. "I heard he is a powerful speaker, spellbinding and big words. I hope it is not all charisma but real action for a change!" Mom and Dad had to work more hours to pay for the new house. Life was hard! Thomas and Ludwig didn't see their parents a lot. Grandma and Grandpa took over.

It was 1933, and the big day had arrived for Thomas. He had been longing to go to school for a very long time, but there was a problem! Mom was Catholic, and the only school in town was Lutheran. School was important, so Trudy left the Catholic church and joined the Lutheran church. In order to qualify for school, Thomas had to be baptized. The parents decided to let both boys be baptized on the same Sunday so Ludwig would be ready for school when his time would come. Hitler tried to be part of German families and offered them a deal. A friend of August told him the news when he heard about the baptism. The deal was 100 Deutschmarks for the children if the parents let Hitler be the godfather. This was a lot of money! They would be able to buy windows and a lot of other things needed for the new house. So, Hitler became the godfather of Thomas and Ludwig.

Sunday morning, the whole family walked to church. The Wenzel family had to sit on the first bench. Grandpa was without his pipe! This was an important day! The baptism was at the beginning of the service. The pastor asks the parents and the children to come to the front where they gathered around the baptismal bowl. The pastor said a few words and told Thomas to come closer. Little Ludwig watched carefully as Thomas had to hold his head right over the bowl. The pastor said words of blessings and let water run over Thomas's head. Thomas pulled his head away and stepped aside. Little Ludwig didn't wait a second. He pushed Thomas aside, stepped onto the stool, and without being prompted, held his little head over the bowl. The whole church had a good chuckle!

Thomas finished his bowl of milk and flour. His stomach was in knots! Today was his first day of school. He got ready to walk for a short hour to the next village to reach the school. Mom and Dad were at work, and Grandma and Grandpa had lots to do at home. He had to walk alone! He was sad about that, but excited to go to school. The way was up the hill and down the hill.

The 'Riesengebirge' (Giant Mountains), where the family lived, was a countryside with small mountains. Thomas met other kids on the way and reached the school on time. This little country school had one teacher for all eight grades. All the children were in the same room. Children in the city had a better school system with their own teacher for each grade and higher grades for those who wanted to go to university. No such luck for Thomas, but he was excited to go to school and to learn a lot.

Herr Wengel introduced himself. "Good morning, everybody! Good morning to our newcomers. You will learn our school rules in no time! My name is Herr Wengel. You should know, and this is very important to me, that I am a real, pure 'Arian'! The blood in my veins is pumping with only pure German blood! All my ancestors are pure Germans. I am proud of it!" Thomas didn't care at all! His parents didn't care about the race content in their blood. It was not a topic in the Wenzel house. The day in school went on.

Thomas came home after his first day of school with Ludwig waiting for him for hours already. He ask, "How was it?"

"Boring!" Thomas said. He was disappointed! He wondered how much he would learn from 'Mr. Pure Arian'. His mood improved when he spotted the huge cone on his chair made of cardboard and filled with lots of sweets. Ludwig was right beside him with a begging face. The cone called "Schultuete" (schoolcone). It was a German custom to sweeten up the first day of school.

One winter afternoon, Thomas, Ludwig, and the neighbour boys in their age group, went sledding down the hill. They tied the sleds together to play train. One boy went first and all the others followed on their sleds down the hill. It was fun! Over time, a group of older boys gathered at the top of the hill.

They started mocking the smaller boys. "Ha-ha, look at those dwarfs! The sleds are way too big for them! Where is your mother? Don't you have to change your diaper?" All the big boys laughed. Ludwig didn't say a word. He was a picture of pure calmness! When he and the others had made their way up the hill, he slowly, with a serious face, untied the chain from his sled. The chain was used to hold the next sled together. Holding the chain in both hands, he walked towards the big boys. Once he reached them, he swung the chain over his head and mercilessly hit the boys standing in front of him. Their eyes got big! The hits were fierce. They turned around and fled. The small children also got scared but were thankful that Ludwig was one of them.

Dad was at home the next day. He was surprised to see one of his neighbours, with his boy at his side, coming towards the house. Father greeted them, "Hi, how are you doing? Pretty cold today, isn't it?"

"I am doing fine," the neighbour replied, "but I can't say the same for my son. Show him your back!" he told his son. The boy took off his coat and pulled up his sweater. August looked at swollen, red streaks all over the youngster's back.

He said, "Oh boy, that must hurt! How did that happen?" The boy told him, accusing Ludwig in a whiny voice. Dad said, "My little five-year-old boy hit you with a chain? How old are you?"

"Twelve," the boy replied. The father of the boy told the whole story, and August understood.

He said, "I am very sorry for your pain. I will have a word with my son! But maybe next time, leave the little kids alone! Goodbye!" Dad had a word with Ludwig!

After this incident, Thomas and the rest of the smaller kids had peace with the bigger boys. Nobody bothered them again. It was a happy time with lots of fun, playing at the small river or in the yard.

Dad had a new job as a salesman of gardening tools. He sold them all over the countryside and made good money. The new house was built and had electricity. The old oil lamps were gone! They had more rooms, it was beautiful! Trudy loved her kitchen! She was well known for her amazing meals and cakes. The new oven was a joy! Her cheesecake became so famous that people ordered them for their celebrations. It was another way for her to make money. A lot of neighbours ask her for the recipe, but she kept it secret. It was her own invention;

"4 egg yolk, 250 gr of sugar, 250 gr of butter, 2 tbsp. of vanilla. Beat it all with a whisk until it gets foamy. Mix it with 150 gr. of cream of wheat, 2lb. of quark and 1 tbsp. baking powder. The 4 egg whites have to be beaten until stiff and gently folded under the mass. Bake one hour in medium heat. The cake has to come out moist."

Trudy was a very good-looking woman! Her thick, black hair was normally put away from her face and braided down her back. Her features were very soft and gentle, with warm brown eyes looking out of a wonderful oval, soft, face. People trusted her. She was well liked! Her strong bones made her look healthy. August was rather the opposite! He was skinny with a slim build. His hair was a dark brown, his eyes blue, full of laughter and mischief. He knew all the jokes. His charisma attracted people to him wherever he went. Woman especially liked him! This was a mutual attraction! He met a lot of them on his trips. Thomas got his looks from his mother's side.

A very good-looking man stood before Trudy. She knew Harold! He was the manager of the work crew in the forest. Harold's beautiful, carved face was surrounded by his full, black, very curly hair. He had a fine build, an athletic body. He was a beauty of a man. He was making Trudy an offer. "Trudy, you would make almost double the money you are earning now! How can you refuse?"

Trudy replied, "I don't want to be away from the kids and the house for that long! If I cook for you guys in the woods, I will be stuck there for weeks!"

Harold insisted, "Trudy! You will never get a chance like this! You will be able to come home for four days every two weeks! You can check everything out and come back into the woods again. August will be at home for some of the days when you are gone, and you have his parents taking care of the kids and the house. Please think about it and talk it over with August!"

"OK, I'll think about it!" Trudy talked it over with her husband and his parents. All of them concluded that the money would be needed and she should go for it.

Three days before Trudy was supposed to leave, Ludwig had an accident. Thomas and his brother got hold of two old rims from a bike. They were perfect for a game they liked to play. With the push of a stick, they had to propel the rim forward as long as possible. Whoever's rim fell to the side first lost the game. The rims went down the hill, up the hill, all over the neighbourhood. It was a lot of fun and very challenging. Ludwig's rim rolled into a more rugged area with a lot of rocks. He had a hard time keeping it turning. His eyes were glued to the rim, his stick high. He misstepped and got his foot caught between two big rocks. "Ow!" he cried. Thomas came right away to help him up, but Ludwig couldn't stand on his injured foot. He sat down on a rock and waited for Thomas to get help. Mom and Thomas came in a hurry. Mom took the little brother in her arms and carried him home.

She asked Grandma for help to check out the injury. Both women determined that it wasn't broken. He was still able to stand on it, they said. It was a cracked bone. Ludwig should stay in bed for a couple of days and would be able to run around in no time. Since Grandma would have her hands full with taking care of the house and the animals, Trudy asked a young girl from the neighbourhood if she would be able to spend time with Ludwig, and take care of him for a couple of hours a day.

Three days later, Harold was at the door to pick up Trudy, and go with her into the forest. Trudy left with a heavy heart. "I know, you are a very strong, healthy boy! That little cold and the cracked foot will be all gone in a couple of days! I baked you a lot of cookies! I will be back before you know it!" She gave both boys a warm hug and a kiss and walked out the door to join up with Harold. Thomas got ready for school, and Ludwig played with a wooden toy on his blanket. He had a cough! It really hurt, but Mother and Grandma said it was only a cold.

The girl came and stayed with Ludwig. She played with him and gave both boys something to eat when Thomas was back from school. Thomas and Ludwig liked her! Grandma was around for the rest of the day and all night. The girl came the next day and thought that Ludwig looked different. She felt his forehead and guessed that he had developed a fever. She told Grandma, "I believe that Ludwig has a fever! His forehead feels very warm!"

"Nothing to worry!" Grandma said, "It must be a high temperature as he is fighting a cold!" Ludwig didn't want to play anymore. He seemed to be tired! Grandma took over in the evening and had to admit that the boy had a real fever. This wasn't good! She filled a bucket with cold water and some rags in it. She squeezed out the rags and put them around Ludwig's legs. It was a common way of fighting a fever! "Thomas, you better go to bed! I'll stay here with Ludwig all night!" she said.

Thomas got worried. "Is Ludwig really sick Grandma?"

She replied, "Don't you worry, you know your brother! He is such a strong boy, a real fighter! Thomas went to bed but had a hard time going to sleep. Ludwig was coughing a lot. Grandma had the opposite problem. She was fighting to stay awake but lost her fight very soon.

When she woke up towards the morning, the little one's breathing was more laboured. His fever seemed to be much higher. When the girl came to help, Grandma instructed her to keep going with the cold rags and to give him lots to drink. She would go to the doctor to ask him to come. Thomas didn't go to school that day. Nobody seemed to mind. He wanted to stay close to his little brother! Grandma came back with the doctor by her side. Everybody made room for the doctor and waited. The doctor examined the boy, listened to his chest, and listened to his breathing from the back. His face was very serious. He had seen it before, actually, too many times in his career. A little child with pneumonia! There was little help for something like that! Most of his younger patients succumbed to these diseases. He turned towards Grandma and the others.

"I am very sorry! Your little Ludwig has pneumonia! Please keep going with the cold rags around his legs and put some on his forehead as well. Give him lots to drink, one sip at a time! Where is the Mother?" Grandma told him that Trudy was cooking for the forest workers in the woods. The doctor said, "Please send somebody to get her! The boy is seriously ill! If you are able to reach the Father, that would be good as well!"

Grandma gave the doctor his money, and he left. She went to a neighbor, who was willing to go into the woods to get Trudy. It would take two days for Trudy to make it home. Another friend had plans to travel into the area where Dad and Grandpa were selling their goods. He promised to find them and send them home. Thomas was sitting on the other side of Ludwig's bed. Ludwig opened his eyes. He looked so very tired! His normally, puffy, healthy cheeks had deflated into something very hollow.

Thomas had a hard time recognizing his brother. Ludwig's eyes looked scared! Thomas didn't know what to say. "You are a strong boy, Ludwig! Pretty soon you and I are going to walk to school together! The big boys will not bother us anymore! You showed them! Ha-ha" He turned to the side and cried.

The fever got higher, and Ludwig was hardly awake for the next few days. Grandma took over for the nights. She was hoping that the boy would make it, at least until his parents would be able to see him. She put the rags on that burning forehead. Ludwig had almost no strength to drink anymore. Grandma kept her watch until sleep got her.

The sun rose, and Grandma woke up still sitting on the chair beside the little one's bed. She looked at his face. Ludwig was asleep forever! His face was white! She closed his eyes and cried. "How is Ludwig?" Thomas asked as he came into the room. Grandma took him into her arms. Looking at the white face of Ludwig, Thomas knew. He cried in Grandma's arms. "Where is Ludwig now? What happens when you die?" he asked.

"Ludwig is now in heaven with all the angels! That is a good place!" She sent Thomas outside to tell the girl not to come anymore, and took care of the body of Ludwig. The animals needed her as well, she had her hands full.

It was almost nighttime when Trudy finally arrived at the house. She knew that Ludwig had gotten very sick! She was worried, but relieved to be home and able to help him now. She opened the door to the house. It was so quiet! She opened the door to the bedroom... Thomas was sitting beside the body for the death watch. His eyes were red from crying. He was so relieved to see his Mom. Trudy knew! She was too late! She took Thomas into her arms and started weeping. Her shoulders shook violently! Grandma came in from the stable, embraced them both, and said, "Sorry, Trudy, we couldn't help him! Sorry!"

"I'm so sorry!" Trudy said between sobs. "I should have never left. I am so sorry! I should have been with him and all of you! I am so sorry!"

August and Grandpa came the next day. It was a very sombre house! The funeral was three days after Ludwig died. Thomas and his family had to sit in the first row of the benches in the church. "The same like at the baptism!" Thomas thought. The baptism was fun, but this wasn't! The rest of the benches of the church were filled with almost everybody from the village. A lot of other families had lost one or more of their children. They all knew how it felt! They had to show their support! Dad and Grandpa had their only suits on. Grandpa had left his pipe at home. The woman were in their best dresses, and Thomas had on a new Lederhosen, a white shirt, and real shoes. Normally the children didn't wear any shoes during the summertime but when the snow was on the ground, Mom always insisted that Thomas put on shoes. There was no snow on the ground, but a funeral was a shoe occasion.

The small coffin was at the front of the church. The pastor came to the pulpit and started speaking. Thomas didn't really understand what he was saying. He thought a lot about what Grandma told him, that little Ludwig was now in heaven with all the angels. He thought, "I hope Ludwig will behave in heaven. With so many angels around him, if he doesn't behave himself, the Almighty God will tell him!" Thomas was sure about that.

The mood of everybody in the house after the funeral got a bit better when Trudy presented her 'Streuselkuchen'. Friends and neighbours filled the house and the front yard, sitting, talking, and laughing. It seemed like when a body is under the ground, the dirt washes all the tears away! At least for the time being. Trudy and August served real coffee, together with the cake. That made people happy and talkative as well.

The days after the funeral were sad! Mom cried a lot! She blamed herself over and over again that she was gone when her child needed her the most. A little girl, who was born at the end of the year, gave her some condolence. Regina was a healthy little girl with thick, black hair and brown eyes, just like Trudy and her big brother. Thomas fell in love with her as soon as he was allowed to see her. He promised himself to watch out for her so she wouldn't die like his little brother.

The money situation at home didn't change and Mom was working a lot outside the house. She got a job in a gardening shop in the village down the hill. You had to cross the woods in order to get there. After school, it was Thomas's duty to push his baby sister in the stroller to his Mom so she could nurse her. He didn't mind at all! He learned how to change her diaper and feed her. He loved her very much!

Regina was walking, and Thomas was able to play with her, when another little girl was born into the Wenzel home. Otilia came a bit too early and had to be packed in cotton for a couple of weeks in order to stay warm. With a lot of care, she became stronger and healthy like every other normal baby, but she looked different than Regina and Thomas! Her bones and her hair were very thin, and not only that, her hair was very curly. As curly as the hair from Harold, the good-looking guy from the woods?

GROWING UP IN "HITLER'S GERMANY"

The world for the Koster children was small and simple! Sabine, the youngest girl, had one older sister named Emma and one older brother named Emil. They lived in a two-bedroom apartment together with their father Heini and mother Otti. The building was owned by the factory, Braukmann & Rahmede, where Heini worked. Outside of their apartment, at the end of the hallway, was a toilet that the five members of the family shared with two other families. The kitchen was their largest room and had a big stove and a sink. A metal tub big enough for one person to sit in was placed in the centre of the kitchen every Saturday, where they would each take their turn enjoying a bath. It was Father's job to carry the tub from the basement upstairs into the kitchen. The hot water came from pots and kettles on the stove. The stove was fueled by coal. This was very affordable because there was plenty of coal in the ground all over Germany.

It was the morning of the 24th of December, 1938, when Sabine was watching her Father put up the Christmas tree. The tree was placed in the spacious kitchen. The kitchen was the place where the family gathered. It was more or less the living room.

The headlines of newspapers all over the world touted rumours of war. Hitler had his dream and vision of a Germany much bigger than it was. His vision was to raise up a people of greatness and of ushering in a 1000-year reign of glory. He tried to win the common German over to his dreams by providing for them with work and things like an affordable car, the 'Volkswagen'. His constant propaganda against the Jews was hard to ignore. Father tried to shield the family from it, but the voice of Hitler was everywhere.

"Otti, could you please hand me the candle holders?" Heini asked his wife. Otti, with her thin brown hair tied in a knot, and her apron wrapped around her strong middle section, handed the big candle holders to her husband.

"Heini, make sure you don't put them too close to the branches, I don't want to have a fire like the Meier's had last year!"

"Don't you worry, Otti," Heini reassured his wife. "I'll make sure of that. Sabine, you can help and tell me if I am too close to a branch?!" Sabine was very proud that Dad would ask for her help. Her small, skinny body could only reach the lower branches of the big tree. She had to stand on her tippy toes to see the next level of branches. Sabine was ten years old. Old enough to play outside by herself, old enough to walk to school by herself, and old enough to help peel potatoes for dinner. Emma was sitting on the floor next to Sabine. The older sister opened the flat carton in which was the star made out of straw, and handed it over to father who put it on the top of the tree. Finished with the candle holders, he started putting the tinsel on. The sisters turned away from the tree and tried not to watch. It was a painful sight to see him placing one tinsel on at a time. It took forever!

Heini was a man of principle, and this was the right way to put tinsel on a Christmas tree. He treated this the same way he treated his work at the factory. Every day Heini walked across the long back yard of their apartment complex to the factory, which stood just on the other side. His factory produced screws. He was proud of all the screws that passed through his hands and that he knew about the different types, those that turned clockwise and those that turned counter clockwise.

    Luedenscheid was built on seven hills. People compared Luedenscheid to Jerusalem the Holy City that was also built on seven hills. If you had to go anywhere in town you had to walk either up a hill or down a hill. It was the normal way of life. The city was full of small factories, producing small parts made out of metal. You could find knobs for anything; buttons, furniture couplers, brackets, handles and door knobs. The joke was, that every family in Luedenscheid owned their little factory. Finding work was never a problem, even during hard times.

    Heini was in love with the surrounding hills of Luedenscheid. The woods around the town were filled with a variety of trees. You could meet a deer or a wild boar, never mind all the birds and smaller creatures. His Sundays were dedicated to walking the hills around Luedenscheid and anybody that wanted to was gladly invited to join him.

    Sabine and her siblings went to the same school, the "Westschule". This Lutheran school was just a ten-minute walk down the hill. The other school was Catholic and was on top of the hill. Sabine loved to go to school. Every grade had their own classroom and special subjects like sports, hand craft, and cooking were offered. Sabine loved her teacher and easily made friends wherever she went.

Life was exciting for Sabine. Skinny as she was, with her golden blond shoulder length hair bobbing around, she used to skip on the sidewalk down the hill of the Koellnerstrasse, until she met one of her friends and they would then walk together to school. Sarah was one of her friends. They often met up at the corner store, which belonged to Sarah's parents. School was only in the morning, so the girls spent many afternoons doing homework and playing together. Sabine loved to skate and go sledding in the winter and did all sorts of fun games during the rest of the warmer part of the year.

All of Sabine's friends, except for Sarah, belonged to the Hitler Youth. Sarah wasn't able to join, because she was Jewish. Sabine and her older sister and brother were also not permitted to join the Hitler Youth. Their father didn't trust Hitler! As far as he was concerned, evil venom was spitting out of Hitler's mouth.

Sabine couldn't understand the reasoning of her dad. "They are doing all the fun stuff in Hitler Youth!" she told him. "They have swimming, outside games, gymnastics. I am really missing out on a good time if I don't go! Nobody understands why you don't let me be part of it! Even the teacher says we should join the Hitler Youth!"

Father looked down at Sabine, with his eyebrows sternly together, and said, "Sabine, you just have to trust me on this! It is best for you if you don't go, and believe me, I know of a lot of parents who aren't giving permission to their children either. You are not the only one! And I don't want to hear about it anymore in this house. Our children don't go to the Hitler Youth!" With this, he left the room.

It was Christmas Eve. Sabine was waiting for the time to open the presents. The presents were shared in the evening and it was only lunchtime. She had great hopes of getting a bike this year. Her older brother had one, but he wasn't able to use it anymore, which was Sabine's fault. She had watched her brother with envy when he was riding his bike on numerous occasions. It looked like a lot of fun and so easy! The only problem was, his bike had this stupid bar between the seat and handle bars that made it too big for her to ride.

One day she figured out how to solve that problem. When Emil was at a friend's house Sabine spotted the bike outside, leaning against the wall. This was her moment! She took the heavy bike and put herself halfway under the stupid bar. She was able to hold on to the handle bar and stepped onto the pedals. "Ha, it works!" she thought. She took a good turn in the back yard, between the building and the factory, but started having difficulty with the steering. She didn't give up though as the bike rolled along. This was fun! She was picking up speed but then it happened. The stairs leading down to the basement suddenly opened up before her! She wasn't able to avoid them, so she went riding down the stairs and crashed the bike into the wall.

Her first thought was that she at least didn't need to figure out how to stop the bike anymore. After that, she noticed her bleeding knees and bleeding elbows, on top of her bleeding nose. Climbing out of the stairway, she ran into her brother and his friend. "You look all battered up!" Both were uneasily laughing at her, with a bit of concern, looking at all the blood. "What happened to you?" Emil asked. "

"It's your bike's fault! It doesn't turn fast enough!"

"My bike? Emil asked. "Where is my bike?"

Sabine replied, "Down the stairs. It's too hard to steer!" Sabine started to get scared now. The face of her brother got white and very serious. He and his friend hurried down the stairs. Sabine waited for them to return. Emil had his bike in his hands. The front tire looked like an egg! He looked angry.

"Don't do that again! Never! Do you hear me?"

Sabine said a quiet, "Yes."

Finally, the time for the presents! Mother was cooking up a storm with the little bit they were able to get in the store, and Dad told the children to go outside into the hallway because the 'Christkind' would come. The children waited in the hallway! Their ears were glued to the door. It was always the same. Mom and Dad would pretend to talk to the 'Christkind' and after that the kids would be called inside. Today they heard that the 'Christkind' wasn't happy with Sabine this year because she took her brother's bike without permission. The other thing they talked about were the bad grades Emil got in school. But Emma was praised like always. Emil and Sabine resented that!

The kids were called into the huge kitchen where the tall Christmas tree stood with the shiny silver tinsel streaming down, the branches and the candles giving a bright and calming glow to the whole room. Sabine looked for the bike. No bike! Only a new tire for Emil's bike. Sabine was very disappointed! All she got was a new backpack for school and a new pair of shoes. Maybe next year, father told her. It was very hard to get anything in those days. War was in the air! People were hoarding everything they could, just in case. A good useful item, like a bike, was gone in no time. Father went through a lot of trouble to get the new tire for Emil's bike. Everybody knew that the stores would soon be empty because of the war.

Germany invaded Poland on the 1st of September 1939, signaling the beginning of the Second World War. Sure enough, one year later the stores were half empty! You couldn't buy anything with your money anymore. The government gave every family stamps according to the number of family members. Mother had a hard time finding enough food to feed her family. Dad had to work just as hard as in normal times. His factory was essential. Hitler needed a lot of screws for his tanks and all the other war machinery. The family was glad that Father didn't have to go to war because he was needed in the factory.

Life for Sabine remained pretty much the same as before the war. She had school in the morning and lots of play time in the afternoon. Today, like on so many days, they played hide and seek. The area they were hiding in was very large, with a lot of houses to hide behind. Sabine had the perfect place to hide. She had used it many times before. Nobody ever found her there. She was sitting and waiting. It got boring! She could hear the other kids wandering up the hill still looking for her, but getting further away from her. She had a great idea! She would run across the Koellnerstrasse towards the house, and hide in another good place, in her back yard. She stole away from the hiding spot, making sure nobody saw her. She crept up to the road, checking up the hill for her friends, then straightened out and ran as fast as she could to the road to the other side. Out of nowhere a truck came upon her and Sabine found herself staring in bewilderment at a huge tire! Bang! She landed on the pavement!

The driver of the truck hit the brakes, jumped out and ran to the front. Sabine was halfway under his truck, but not under the tire! People from the other side of the road came over to help. Sabine opened her eyes, dazed and confused. She felt very dizzy and wondered what was going on. One of the bystanders who knew Sabine's family, ran and got her dad from the factory. A neighbour told the driver not to worry, he had witnessed it all. Sabine had run right out in front of the truck! The driver was thankful that his speed had been very slow, due to the heavy load of goods that he was delivering to the factory. It could have been so much worse!

Sabine ended up in the emergency, where the doctor told her parents that she had a serious concussion. The nurse, her parents, everybody told her to look both ways before crossing the road. She knew that! But this was a different situation, when you had to hide! The doctor told her to stay home for a couple of days and rest. No school for a while! "How boring!" she thought.

Her friends visited her after school and gave her the home work for the day. Today was Erika's turn to come.

"Frau Witte told us a great story in Religion today!" She said, "I found it very interesting! I brought you the story! We have to write an essay about it." They talked a bit more and Sabine was left alone in the room with lots of time on her hands to read.

She read about the second day of July 1505. "That was a very long time ago!" she thought. The young Martin Luther was riding his horse towards the city of Erfurt. He was only six miles away from the town when a mighty thunderstorm erupted. The rain came down in buckets, the thunder was deafening. He got off his horse and tried to hide under a tree. The storm got stronger. He was scared to death! A lightning bolt struck very close to him with an earthshaking thunderclap at the same time. The 21-year-old Luther fell on his knees and cried out to Saint Anna for help! He promised to become a monk if his life would be spared. He promised to become a man of God. His life was spared and Martin Luther made good on his promise.

Sabine got ready to write her essay. "Hm, what was the message of this story? Why was it so important to my teacher? Luther could have died in that storm! The lightning bolt was just meters away from him and didn't hit Luther! Hm, Luther believed that God protected him! I think, he was right! God protected him. To show his appreciation and thankfulness, Luther gave his life to God. I have to point that out in my writing!' She took her pencil and the booklet to write in. Starting the first sentence, she paused.

"God protected Luther in the storm! Did God protect me when I ran in front of the truck? That tire could have rolled right over me, at least over my leg or arm, but I had no injuries except for my concussion. God protected me! I will spend more time with the Bible. I will learn more about God!" she decided.

It was the winter of 1940, and Thomas watched excitedly from the window as Grandpa pulled the big sleigh out of the stable. It was almost Christmas Eve. Time to get the Christmas tree out of the forest. The area in which they were allowed to cut a tree this year was deep in the woods! Thomas's friend Karl had told him the other day how dangerous it would be to go that deep into the woods.

"Don't you remember "Ruebezahl" the ghost?" he said as his blue eyes grew big. Thomas chuckled. He didn't believe this little kid's story anymore! He knew it was a story that parents told little children to make them come home before it got too dark in the evening. The folktale they told was of a ghost that lived in the mountains and would look for little children to lock them up in his cave. Thomas was 13 years old now, so he knew better! Karl's big, blue eyes looked downward. He noticed that Thomas wasn't buying his ghost story so he came up with another one.

His eyes became slits and with a very serious face he said, "This is a true story! I am only telling you this as a warning. One day a father went all by himself into the deep woods to cut a tree. A pack of wolves attacked him. He didn't survive! When the search group was looking for him the next day, they only found what was left by the wolves!"

Thomas ask, "What did the wolves leave behind?"

Karl's eyes looked downward at first and after a pause he looked right into the eyes of Thomas and replied, "Bones, bare bones!" Thomas shuddered inside. This was a bad story!

Thomas and Grandpa were on their way into the woods. The snow was almost one meter deep. Grandpa, with his ever-present pipe in his mouth, went ahead to make a trail for Thomas. It was a long walk! Once in a while Grandpa let Thomas sit on the sleigh and pulled him, but only for a short stretch. Thomas was a big kid now! On top of the sleigh was the shotgun and grandpa's saw. Thomas felt safer as he looked at the shotgun. Karl's story kept going through his head, he just couldn't shake it off, but he knew that Grandpa was a good shot! He assured himself of it over and over.

It took a good two hours walk for the two to reach the area where they were allowed to cut down a tree. The two looked around.

"What do you think Thomas, will this be a good tree?" Grandpa pointed to one. Thomas wasn't sure about it. They walked around some more and found themselves standing in front of the perfect tree.

Thomas said, "This tree is perfect, just made for us! It will be a beauty in our house!" Grandpa agreed. He took the saw from the sleigh and started cutting at the trunk of the tree.

"Timber!" He yelled, and the tree fell over. Together they put the tree on top of the sleigh and tied it down.

"Lunchtime!" Thomas said. This was the reason why he loved to go with Grandpa into the woods. Lunchtime was the time for good food and great stories. Out of Grandpa's backpack came the sandwiches, made from sourdough bread with smoked ham and cheese on it. Oh, it was good! Sitting on a tree stump, Grandpa started his first story;

"One day, when I was on the road with your father, we had to walk for many kilometers through the forest, pulling the cart with our goods on it. Because of all the roots from the trees sticking out and crossing over the trail, it was very difficult. Your Dad pulled at the front and I pushed at the back. There was not one house in sight where we would be able to sell anything! The sun was ready to go down, when----" They heard a loud howl.

Thomas got up from the tree stump and looked around. Another howl! This one was a bit louder than the first one. Grandpa got up as well and went to the sleigh to get the shotgun.

"We better be on our way!" he said. Thomas couldn't agree more! This time Thomas walked right beside Grandpa. The walk back out of the forest was a lot faster than their way into the woods. They made it home safely.

Waking up in the morning, Thomas couldn't wait to tell Karl the story of the howling in the woods. Finally, at recess, he got his chance. Karl was keenly listening to everything Thomas told him. The odd thing was, his face, instead of being stunned, was rather very much amused.

It dawned on Thomas, "It was you and your dad in the woods! You were there to cut a tree as well! I know your dad is famous for imitating animal sounds! You tricked us!" Karl had to hold his belly! It was too good! Thomas felt really stupid, but he had to laugh as well. It was a good story! Now he had a story to tell Grandpa.

Grandpa's pipe fell out of his mouth. He had a good laugh about the story with Karl and his Dad. The joke was better than if it had been a real wolf. He and Thomas put up the tree in the living room. It was Christmas Eve, the second Christmas during war time, the second Christmas without dad. When August had heard the war was on, his eyes had lit up with excitement. He was one of the first who volunteered to join the army. He was a true adventurer who dreamed of foreign countries! The war was his chance to get out of Germany and discover the world. He didn't care about politics or the reason Hitler started the war. He was able to travel, that was all he knew! The family had heard that France had declared war on Germany in September, and they wondered if August was on his way to France. Trudy knew that her husband would cherish every minute of it. To be able to see France was above anybody's dream in their little village they lived.

Thomas wondered about the presents this year. Nobody could buy anything with money anymore. Shopping for everything was done with stamps, even for clothes. Of course, there was also the black market in which the Wenzel family was heavily involved.

Mother trusted Thomas to buy the groceries for the family with the stamps. On a lot of days, Thomas had to walk to the neighbouring village to get what they needed. During the summer it was every day. Trudy had started a summer guest house in their home. The new house was beautiful and big enough to host a couple of guests. She was a great cook and baker and served all three meals to the guests with joy.

Now, during the war the guests had to hand over their stamps, so that Thomas would be able to get the extra supplies they needed for them. The cow gave the milk, the chickens the eggs. All the bedrooms of the family were taken by the guests. The family slept in the attic under the straw. Thomas and his sisters loved it!

"We did a wonderful job this year with the Christmas tree, don't you think, Thomas?" Grandpa exclaimed.

"Yes, we did! Too bad that Dad can't see the tree this year! It is beautiful!"

"You wonder where he is and what his Christmas Eve looks like?" Grandpa said. "I hope he doesn't have to fight on a day like this! OK, every child has to go into the hallway! The "Christkind" is coming!"

Thomas' little sisters screamed with delight! They had no idea what war was all about and why Dad wasn't at home. Dad wasn't at home most of the time anyway.

"My best Christmas ever!" Thomas thought, holding a train car close to his face. He had wished for this train set for many years. Now he had it. The set was used, but that was OK. Grandpa was very lucky on the black market and was able to get a real electric train set for Thomas. Thomas would use it a lot this year! Next year was Thomas's final year in school. After that he would enroll as an apprentice at a train factory, to become a technician. Being a technician would bring him closer to his real dream of becoming a pilot. He wasn't able to go to a high school like the kids in the city. To get his dream job he had to do it this way.

Another very important part of getting closer to his dreams was the 'Jungvolk Dienst' (Young People Service). This group was for boys in his age, created by Hitler, in order to instill his ideas and propaganda. Here they learned the ideas of the 'Third Reich', discipline, and obeying orders without asking questions. Most of all, they were supposed to learn to love their Fuehrer Hitler himself. One had to say

"Heil Hitler" as a greeting in that group while standing up straight with one ankle put together.

Outside of the group none of the kids cared about that stuff. You didn't say "Heil Hitler" when you met your neighbour. People knew each other like family in the village. The city was different however, because you never knew if the one you met was an SS man, or a special guard from Hitler. raising your right hand and giving the required verbal tribute could keep you from getting into trouble. The reason why Thomas was in the 'Jungvolk Dienst' was so he could fulfill his dreams. One had to be part of Hitler's Youth in order to learn any trade or to do other things in life. Hitler wanted to be part of everybody's future, especially the young people. They were the future of his "Third Reich".

You had better be on time when the group started. Punctuality was one important lesson the boys had to learn, especially when Herr Hartmann the leader of the group, was in a bad mood. Today was a bad day. His mood was miserable. Karl and Thomas were on time like everybody else, except for young Gustav. His family owned the bakery in town, where he helped out a lot. It was very hard for Gustav to get out of the store on time. Gustav was also more on the portly side, which didn't endear him with Herr Hartmann either. A German boy had to be in excellent shape, hopefully blue eyed with blond hair. If you looked like that, you were the favourite of all the authorities. A bigger person was seen as a disgrace to the German race. "Gustav why are you late this time?" Herr Hartmann asked.

Gustav's face was red and in a quiet voice he said, "We had a very difficult customer in the store. She bargained with me, trying to get more bread for her stamps. I couldn't just leave."

Herr Hartmann said in a quiet voice, "You know what you have to do! You are late! Do your push ups!" Gustav started his 25 push ups. He knew the routine. The rest of the group had to jog around the outside of the hall ten times, as fast as they were able to. Gustav joined in, after he was done with his push-ups. His shirt was glued with sweat to his body. Drops of sweat were dripping down his face. All the other boys were done, while he still had to do another two laps.

"Gustav, you are the last one again! You are in terrible shape! You are a disgrace to the German Jungvolk! 25 more push-ups, but fast." Herr Hartmann got a red face himself by yelling his orders. Thomas and Karl felt sorry for Gustav, who was doing his push-ups, almost getting a heart attack. His sweat formed a pool underneath him on the ground but Gustav worked hard to finish his punishment. He had his dreams like all the other German boys and didn't want to be stuck in his parent's bakery. He had his own goals!

There were other people in Hitler's Germany who were seen as a disgrace to the German race. Disabilities of any kind were a huge problem. German people had to be perfect! One boy in the village had a mental impairment. He was eight years old and his mother cared for him as good as she was able to. She tried hard to teach him to read and write but without any success.

Nobody knew how the government nurse found out about the boy, but the nurse showed up one day in order to talk to the mother.

She said, "Frau Hermann, we heard about the good care you are giving to your son. We heard about your tireless effort to teach him how to read and write. Those tasks are very difficult for a person like you, without the proper education. You must be so tired! We want to offer you some help. There are new treatments for people like your little boy. Our Fuehrer Adolf Hitler is giving a lot of support for research in this area. We have a wonderful hospital in the beautiful southern region close to the Alps. This place is managed by people who studied mental disease and have helped so many children like your boy already. Please let us help you! I could bring your son tomorrow by train to the hospital and you will be informed of his progress."

The mother got a shock. "I can't just give him to you! He will be very scared! He will miss his mother!"

The nurse said again, "I know exactly how you feel, Frau Hermann, I am a mother myself but I have seen the remarkable changes in those little lives. Their condition improves so much. He will have a real future! It will only take a couple of weeks for starters and if he improves with the treatment, we will be able to evaluate him more and see if he should stay a bit longer. You will be able to visit him and for sure, we will keep you posted on his progress. Frau Hermann, you don't want to stand in the way of your son's healing and of becoming a normal person!"

The mother had tears in her eyes. "Of course I will not stand in his way! Please let me talk to my husband and if he agrees you can pick my son up in the morning." The nurse said her goodbye and left.

The parents had a sad talk that night. Neither of them wanted to stand in the way of their son's wellbeing. The nurse picked up the boy the next morning. She had to pull him out of the tight embrace of his mother. The nurse and the boy climbed onto the train to the south. Coming home, the house of the Herman family felt empty. Every night the mother cried herself to sleep. After three weeks a letter arrived from the hospital. It was a written letter about his progress and a drawing by her boy, showing the beautiful garden in front of the hospital. The mom couldn't believe that her own son had made this picture. It was ten times better than all the ones he had attempted to do before. She got very hopeful and started to sleep better.

Only two weeks later came another letter from the hospital. Her fingers were shaking. Full with joyful expectation, she opened it. There was no picture in it, just a letter from the hospital. It said, "With deep sadness we have to inform you that your son has died of a very bad pneumonia. His little body fought hard to overcome this horrible disease, and we were fighting with him, but to no avail! He died! We are very sorry! We will send you a container with his ashes pretty soon. Our condolences---"

Frau Hermann was frozen! Her face was white. She collapsed into the chair. "I should have never let him go with that nurse, never!"

The people near the hospital with all the children and other disabled people had to keep their windows closed because of the awful smell. It smelled like a slaughter house. It took a while, but the truth came out. The people in the hospital were killed by injection and their bodies burned.

The newspapers were full of the story and there was an uproar among the German people. Pastors voiced their disgust. Hitler had to say something about it and face the people. In a speech he called these actions a "killing out of mercy" for these poor individuals. He said that he actually wanted to help them by killing them, but if the people saw it differently, he would stop it right away. The German people were put at ease, but the killing of disabled people continued in secret. People in Germany felt darkness creeping into their land.

Sabine felt full of energy and was happy to start another day of school. She skipped, like always, down the road, looking for her friends whom she would normally meet along the way. "Oh, there is Sarah!" she thought. Coming closer she noticed that Sarah wasn't herself today. Her eyes were downcast. Sarah hardly looked into Sabines' eyes. Sabine got worried. "What is going on with you? Are you sick?"

Sarah shook her head. "No, somebody called me a very nasty name when I went shopping with my mom yesterday."

Sabine asked, "What was that for?"

Sarah's eyes filled with tears. "That person knew that we are Jews. The bad part is, she is in our class at school." Sabine felt uncomfortable about that. She had heard Hitler's propaganda against the Jews, that Jews were bad people and so on. It just didn't make any sense to Sabine. Sarah and her family were some of the most loving people she knew. Sarah was one of her best friends! She decided that Hitler was wrong! She put her arm around Sarah's shoulder and together they walked to school.

School hadn't started yet. Everybody was gathered in the compound and was talking. When Sarah and Sabine arrived, the talking stopped. The other good friends of Sabine looked in horror at Sabine having her arm over Sarah's shoulder. Sabine looked into the eyes of her friends with a question in her eyes. This was awkward! Finally the teacher came out ringing the bell. She told the students to enter the school in a calm manner. When Sabine and Sarah passed her, in a resolute fashion she pulled Sabine's arm away from Sarah's shoulder. Sabine was shocked! Sarah was hurt!

During dinner time after school, Sabine told her parents about the incident. Mom and Dad looked with sad eyes at Sabine. Father said, "I am sorry that you have to go through horrible situations like this. Hitler is evil, and this is one of his evil ideas. All the Jews we know are good people. Hitler has no reason to accuse them of being bad or dangerous." Dad was angry!

The whole family was glued to the radio in the kitchen. It was evening, and the news wasn't good! The SS, Hitler's special guard, were driving through the cities in trucks and stopping at the stores they knew were owned by Jews. They smashed the windows, ransacked the place and joked about their evil doing. The newspapers the next morning called it Kristallnacht, the 'Night of broken glass.' Some of the owners of those stores were loaded into trucks and taken away. People heard they were taken to labour camps.

From a distance, Sabine could see the damage to Sarah's parents' store. People gathered at the front of the store, standing in the midst of thousands of pieces of broken glass. Two people came out of the store, their arms full of items. Coming closer, Sabine saw the empty shelves. The store had been looted and destroyed. "Where is Sarah?" she wondered. Looking up to the family's windows, she shuddered. All the windows of their apartment were broken as well! Sara was nowhere to be seen.

School went on in a normal fashion, but without Sarah. Time went on and once a week, all the children that were 13 and 14 years of age had to go to the church in the afternoon, to study the Catechism. The pastor was a tender-hearted man who loved Jesus his saviour, and his Bible. He was eager to pass on his passion to the children in his care. Sabine always looked forward to those afternoons. She made good on her promise to get to know the God of the Bible.

Today the pastor said, "I am very sorry that my time with you is coming to an end. It was truly a pleasure to teach you the Bible and to bring Jesus closer to your heart. This Sunday is your big day! You will be invited to publicly confirm that you want to follow Jesus in your life. It is up to you if you mean it or not. But you have the chance! We have to follow the direction of the church, which means, you have to recite some of the Bible verses that you have learned and memorized."

One of the boys raised his hand. "What happens if we don't know the verse you ask us to say?"

The pastor smiled. "No worries! If I ask you to recite a verse, everybody will raise their hands. The ones who know it will put up their hands outstretched to the full length. If you don't remember that verse, you put your arm only halfway up. I will accept your choice, but I would be happy if each of you would know at least one verse."

The whole family went to church on Sunday for this occasion. It was called 'Confirmation'. Everybody was dressed in their Sunday best. Mom was in her black dress with the fitting hat, her little bun was sticking out at the back. Father wore his only suit, so did Emil. Emma was in a wonderful looking blue dress, with fitting shoes. She was a master in sewing and made her clothes all by herself. Sabine had one of the hand-me-downs from Emma. It was green and fit her well, and, it brought out her green eyes in a beautiful way. Sabine had two small sisters now. They had arrived in the past years, with a large age gap between them and the older three siblings.

All the students to be confirmed today had to sit in the first bench. Everybody could see if they put up their hands to say a verse and hear when they recited it. Now came the important part. The pastor asked one at a time to step up in front of the altar and to repeat his words, which gave them the chance to ask Jesus to forgive their sins and to follow him. It was Sabine's turn. She was standing in front of the altar, her knees shaking. She was very much aware of the stares from the congregation, but she also knew the seriousness of the confirmation. In her heart she had decided to ask for forgiveness and to follow Jesus. With tears in her eyes, she stepped back to the bench.

CHASING AFTER YOUR DREAMS

Thomas was standing in front of a huge structure. His eyes and mouth open as he stared at the many train engines, the many tables with parts on them, the wagons, and all those people that filled the hall, lots of people! He had heard that the factory had 150 students in their care, never mind the technicians, workers, engineers, supervisors and anyone else you could think of. This was a city in itself, bigger than his entire village at home! The hall he was standing in front of was not the only building. The area the company occupied, was huge! He was amazed!

Yesterday in class, he had passed his entrance test for the course to become a technician. Thomas was very proud of his achievement. A lot of the other boys came from schools in the city with so much better teaching than he had had, but he passed it anyway. He had moved right away into his rented room in a family home. Today was his first day in the factory. Before him was an amazing scene of all the trains in their different colours. A lot of locomotives were black, but a few were a shiny silver and one was even a deep burgundy. "That one must be for a king in another country," he thought. He looked at the many train tracks coming out of the halls. He was in awe!

"Are you one of the new students for this year?" a middle-aged, sporty-looking man asked Thomas.

"Yes! Yes! I am a bit early, but I wanted to look around before we start. I am sorry!"

"Ha-ha, nothing to be sorry about I like it if a boy gets up early and is keen on learning! My name is Herr Hollwert, and I am your instructor for the first year. Why don't you join me on my walk to the field? We are going to start with the flag ceremony."

The area around the flag pole filled up with students. Thomas had never been part of such a large group of boys as this. He was excited! All the boys had to do their "Heil Hitler" salute. They raised their right hands and sang the German anthem while the flag climbed up the pole. The new students were told that everyday would start like this. After the ceremony was over, the whole group had to jog to the next field. Here, Herr Hollwert started exercises with them; push ups first and then running around the field and other movements. It was pretty much the same type of exercise Thomas had at the Jung Volk. Herr Hollwert started to speak at the end. He welcomed everybody and explained how they would learn their trades. Sport would be a big part of their day. Apart from the morning routine, there would also be swimming, gymnastics, running long distances, and other conditioning activities. Herr Hollwert was eager to have his group of boys in top shape.

Thomas was happy about this. He was in a good shape anyway and loved sports. His favorite was long distance running. He had the endurance for it! He disliked the days they had inside the school, learning about theory and how to master their new skills. He noticed the boys from the city were much more prepared than boys like him from the country, but he would be fine, he promised himself. He would work hard. He knew how to use his hands. He knew how to use tools and how to handle them because he had helped Grandpa and Dad back home. That part would be fun!

Thomas was filing away on his iron block. Each side of the block was supposed to measure 10 cm, but Thomas' sides were wobbly and not exact. The boys were also charged with filing down the faces of the block so that they would be perfectly smooth and flat and the edges sharp. The hours went by and Thomas watched all the other boys as they were already done and talking to each other. Thomas' hair was hanging down over his forehead. Sweat droplets came running down his cheeks and his shirt showed the sweat marks from his hard effort. He was hot! It took some work, and more time, but Thomas' block became wonderfully smooth with even edges. Herr Hollwert was very pleased.

A couple of weeks later Thomas left the factory and started his first days of training at the 'Flieger HJ', a Hitler Youth training centre, for learning how to fly an aircraft. This group was supported by the company where Thomas was learning his trade. It was a group, created by the Hitler Government to teach young boys how to fly a glider. You could call it the 'Airforce for the Hitler Youth'. Thomas was in heaven! This group was actually one big reason why he had chosen this company to work for as an apprentice technician.

Thomas and two other boys received two weeks off from their apprenticeship to travel by train to the town of Duerrkunzendorf, which was located close to Glatz. The instructor, Herr Ellermann, greeted the boys in front of a huge warehouse. "Heil Hitler! I am Herr Ellermann, your instructor for the next two weeks. You will sleep in this warehouse and use the facilities in the barrack next door. We will have a good time together! Everybody, please go inside. Find your bed with your name on it, written on a piece of paper."

These young boys came from all over the country to learn how to fly. Thomas loved to be part of this group! Here, they also performed the flag ceremony in the morning, did exercise, and learned theory and skills. Her Ellermann, who's passion was flying, explained the different types of weather and what to look for before you go up in the air, including the different types of winds. Winds could be very dangerous for an airplane, even more so for a glider. The teacher tried to train his group in fast thinking and good decision making.

"72 minus 15…13 plus 98… 14 times 33…". He hammered them with one math question after the other. It was fast, and it was challenging. Thomas had to concentrate like never before in his life. He liked to think things over a bit, before making a decision. To decide on the right answer and focus hard to reach it, was a challenge to his brain. The teacher called them by name for the answer, Thomas never knew if it would be his turn, so he had to always be ready.

Herr Ellermann said, "Tomorrow is your big day! Your first flight, but from a modest height. So, you don't have to worry, it will be safe! I'll meet you at the normal time at the flag ceremony and we'll go from there!"

Everybody broke out in chatter when they left the classroom. Finally, their first flight would actually happen. Their big dream would come true! It was exciting!

The next morning the group went on a long hike up a hill, where they saw the glider waiting for them. It was sitting on an earth launching pad carved out of the side of the hill. There were several of these dirt platforms at different heights on the hill. The first platform was 30 meters high, and the others got consecutively higher.

The boys reached the first platform and looked at the glider. The instructor had told them beforehand that this would just be a training glider. Looking at it for the first time was disappointing! The glider looked naked! It had bones, but no skin! It was just a frame made out of light weight metal pipes with a seat, and wheels on the bottom. "At least the wings are solid!" thought Thomas.

Thomas' turn came to take the seat in the glider. The glider was sitting at the very back of the lowest platform, resting against the hill. At the pointy front of the glider was a strong built-in hook. A thick elastic cord hung loosely on this hook. The hook was holding the elastic at its mid-point. The stretchable cord ends fell to the ground, on each side. The boys split up into three groups, two of them held on to their ends of the elastic. The third group, was standing behind the glider, ready to hold on to it for dear life! Thomas' ears got red with excitement. His heart pounded in his ears! Herr Ellermann gave the command for the two front groups to move forward. The elastic was stretched out and pulled out more and more, towards the edge of the hill, where the drop could be seen. The boys holding the plane at the back were digging their heels into the ground. The front teams thought they couldn't go any further, but the instructor yelled, "Not yet! Work harder, a bit more!" The boys pulled a bit more.

Herr Ellermann shouted, "Let go! Now!" All at once, the boys holding on to the plane at the back let go. The front boys still holding the elastic, let themselves fall towards the side, out of the way of the glider which like a big rock from a sling shot, flung through the air, above the rope zone. The elastic fell out of the hook which was open towards the ground.

"Wind! Wind!" was all that Thomas could think of. The wind was a pillow, holding the glider up in the air. Thomas' stomach was lodged in his throat! He wasn't able to swallow. Time came to a halt! All too soon the glider hit the ground! It was a hard landing, but not too hard! Thomas, his legs shaking, placed his feet onto the ground and climbed out of the glider.

"How was it?" One of the boys at the bottom of the hill asked.

Thomas had to swallow before he was able to speak. "Wow! Good!" He had to gather himself, hoping that nobody would see his shaking legs.

Everybody else got their turn. The days went on with the boys catapulting the glider every time from a higher point. The end of the two weeks brought them to the 50-meter height. The two weeks went by so fast and each boy in the group was sad to go back to their workplace. Thomas had his "A-certificate" in his pocket. He was looking forward to the next year, when he would do the "B-certificate". It would be done at the same place, the same practise glider, but from a higher platform.

Back at the factory Thomas focused on learning his trade. Some days were hard work, when the company was in a time crunch. Herr Hollwert pushed the students hard and had them involved in real projects for the company. During school time, he almost failed a test, but managed to get a passing grad. Thomas was OK with his performance, but his real focus was on the next course, flying the glider.

During the second year Thomas earned his B certificate and started the C-challenge the following year. He had to travel a longer distance for the last course. This one would be more serious with a real glider, and a jeep pulling it up. The first step and task for training, was to produce the cable, made out of metal. It would be a couple of hundred meters long. The boys had to learn how to make it strong enough. The countryside they were in now was a flat area, without any hills, but with lots of fields. The glider was real. It had a skin over the metal frame. It looked beautiful in the eyes of Thomas!

Horst was the first boy to go up in the real glider. All the other boys watched with some envy and a bit of respect, as the glider was pulled up by the speeding jeep. "Release!" Herr Ellermann yelled. Horst of course wasn't able to hear him, but Herr Ellermann couldn't hold it back. Horst was on time to release the cable and was now supposed to start the landing maneuver right away. This was only supposed to be a take off and landing practise.

"Nose down!" Herr Ellermann commanded, again to nobody in particular. Horst did not show any attempt to prepare for the landing. The glider circled over the landing field one time and another time and another. "What is he thinking!" Herr Ellermann barked. "Let that brute come down. I will show what it means to disobey my orders."

Matthias, a boy of small stature, said in a quiet voice, "I wonder if he is scared of the landing? It is scary!"

Herr Ellermann looked at Matthias; "You could be right! Let's hope he will make up his mind!"

Horst, gripping the control stick of the glider with white knuckled hands, looked down onto the field. Cold sweat was running down his forehead all the way into the collar of his shirt. "I have to do it!" He told himself. After another circle around the field, he pushed the stick downwards to set the glider on course towards the ground.

"Ease up! Don't push it down too hard!" Herr Ellermann shouted. The boys looked at each other in horror. Horst must have heard Herr Ellermann's shout, it seemed like. He corrected the nose of the glider a bit upwards, but remained on course for landing.

Touch down! Horst was on the ground! It was a hard landing, but the glider was OK. When the glider came to a stop, everybody, Herr Ellermann up front, ran towards Horst and the glider. Horst was bent down in the pilot seat, his head in his hands.

"What happened up there?" Herr Ellermann bellowed at Horst. Horst looked up at Herr Ellermann, his face beat red and wet with tears.

"I got scared! I thought I would die! I didn't know if I would be able to land! I am so sorry!"

Herr Ellermann looked at him with some compassion in his eyes. "Do you want to quit, or do you want to go up right away again?"

Horst couldn't believe what he was hearing. "Right away up again? No, I quit! I am sorry! I don't have the nerves!" He climbed out of the glider and sat down on the grass.

"Thomas you're next!" Herr Ellermann barked. It was time. Thomas took his seat in the glider and waited for the jeep up front to start moving. He tried not to think about Horst. This was his chance! A sudden jolt got the glider moving along the grass until it finally lifted up into the air. The jeep drove fast and the plane got higher. The rule was that when the glider reached the 500-meter height, the pilot, being Thomas, had to release the cable.

Thomas was now at that point. He released the cable, which fell to the ground. Thomas hardly had time to enjoy the feeling of the air holding up his glider. His orders were to land right away. Demonstrating all he'd learned he made it to the ground. His legs were shaking, his heart was pounding almost out of his throat, but he was proud!

He was excited about his first flight in a real glider. When he got to his room, he found the other boys all talking to each other about being in the air. The whole group, wide awake now, asked Thomas! "Hey Thomas, are you going to join us? We're going to the train station. Somebody said, that girls would be there."

Thomas sat up in his bed. "Girls? Hm, why not? How do you get out of here without getting caught?"

Another boy explained, "No problem! We will escape over the roof! Nobody will see us, and anyway, all the boys before us did it and they never had any trouble! I think the instructor knows what is happening. They are OK with it, as long as we are back in good time to get enough sleep."

All the boys made their way over the roof, down the other side and quietly crept towards the train station. The girls were waiting! This was the promenade of the town!

Thomas had no problem connecting with a nice girl. He looked smashing with his shiny, black hair, a bit longer than anyone else's. His hair was his pride. He had managed to avoid the very short military style cut that every other boy got. Hitler wanted the boys to look military, even at a younger age. Sonja, a girl with a blond pony tail and good looking all the way, was attracted to him right away. She said a shy "Hi!" to him and Thomas answered with another shy "Hi". He was taken by her. Thomas asked her about her family and hobbies. She came from a farmer's family and horseback riding was her favourite pastime. Time passed quickly as they told each other what their life's were all about and then the boys had to head back to the barracks.

The days went by way too fast. Tomorrow would be their last day! Thomas was sitting in the glider. He didn't want to think about it, that it all had to come to an end. The wind underneath the wings sounded like a wonderful melody in his ears. He was now advanced and able to stay in the air for a long time. He pretended to dance with his glider to the rhythm of the wind. It was almost a lullaby!

Woosh, a gust packed into his right wing. Thomas knew what to do to avoid trouble. He instantly responded with the needed adjustment and put the nose of the glider down. Time to head down to the ground. The instructor greeted him at the field. "Good job, Thomas, your reaction was perfect! You are one of my best students!" He turned around to the rest of the group and announced, "This is the end for today. The wind has picked up! Everybody has to go home!" The boys made sad faces and started going back to their barracks.

When Thomas arrived at his bed, he had a note lying on his blanket. It was to inform him, that his Dad just arrived home from the war, and asking him to come home right away. "So, today was my last flight! Hm, that is sad!" Thomas thought.

He showed the note to his instructor who said, "This is not a problem Thomas! I am not sure how the winds will be by tomorrow anyway! I will write out your C-certificate right away and you will be able to head home tomorrow morning."

Thomas took a deep breath. The certificate was important! He got it!

Thomas met up with Sonja again. She was standing, leaning against the wall at the train station, waiting for him. A nice smile greeted him and both reached out their hands, to hold each other. But tonight, was the last time for the two and Sonja seemed to be very sad about it. She was happy for Thomas, that he would be able to see his dad again. Her dad was fighting in the war as well and she didn't know if she would ever see him again. She missed him very much! "What are your plans after you get back from your parents?" she asked.

Thomas replied, "I have to finish my technician papers. I am almost there! My three years in the company will be over. After that, I have to join up with the Hitler

Youth brigade. This is a must now. They want us to be prepared for war, just in case." Sonja looked down at the floor. A small tear went down her cheek. She had hoped that there would be a future for the two of them, but now it became clear to her, that this would never be. Thomas felt very awkward! He wasn't able to change his future plans, and to be honest, he wasn't sure if he wanted a future with Sonja. At the end of the evening, they kissed each other a shy 'Good Bye', and it was over.

August, Thomas' Dad, had spent most of the time he was away in France. He had changed a lot. He had slimmed down drastically, and his face looked older. On his head he wore a new hat, he had found in France. It was black and flat like a plate. He had it on sideways on his head. Thomas and the rest of the family thought that it looked funny, but Dad loved it and was proud of it.

He was full of stories to tell. Food was scarce, he said. The support trains got shot up by the enemy and never made it to the troops they were supposed to supply. The same thing happened with the munitions. They were always short! Since Dad was a genius in trading and organizing, his comrades didn't suffer hunger too much. Deserted houses had food in their basements or containers of food that the groups were able to find. Potatoes left in the ground could be pulled out and roasted over a fire. The troops were happy when they found a cellar filled with wine. This was the best for them! The wine stories were the funny ones.

"I have to tell you the story with the boar in the woods!" Dad said, "We were famished! Luckily there was some water from a creek nearby, but otherwise we had had nothing to eat for days! We were stuck in this wooden area, waiting for the enemy to attack. Nobody knew how close they were! It was a waiting game! Here comes this boar running towards us! We were not allowed to shoot, because that would give away our position to the enemy, but we had to kill him. We were hungry, desperate! Two of us hid behind a tree. The others formed a half circle around that wild pig and chased him towards the men standing behind the tree. The boar approached the tree, running fast. The first guy hit it with the end of his gun. He got the tail! Ha-ha. The one behind him was faster and hit the pig right on his head. It collapsed and we were able to kill it properly. We carved it up, took the intestines out, and cut the meat into small pieces. Everybody was able to roast his meat over the fire. This was the best meal I had ever tasted. It was so good!"

Thomas then asked his father. "Did you ever shoot anybody?"

Father's face got serious. "A soldier doesn't talk about something like that, and you should never ask a soldier this question!"

Thomas was embarrassed! He didn't understand why he shouldn't ask the question, but it seemed like the war had changed a lot of things. Dad changed the topic right away. He was still full of humour and told some of the jokes from his buddies.

Life in the city was a bit more difficult than it was in the country. People lived off food stamps. There were no pigs or chickens or cows in the neighbourhood. At the start of the war, the food stamps seemed to be enough, but over time, food became scarce. Germany had trouble to feed its citizens. Sabine's family had a little garden which came with the apartment that they had rented from the Braukman & Rahmede company that Dad worked for. This provided some help during the summer and harvest time. You had to be thankful for every potato and even for swiss chard, which Sabine hated so much. They only got a few points for clothes, so only essential clothing was purchased.

It was 1943 and school was over for Sabine. Her wish for the future was to learn a social job of any kind, but she wasn't sure yet what that should be. To get closer to her goal, she became a helper in a household with two young children, and also worked in the family's hardware store. The repair shop of that family was a 'men only' area. Sabine moved in with this family. She moved way down the hill, away from Luedenscheid where her parents lived, to this small town named Halver. Her duties were all over the place in the house, the store, cooking and so on. Erna, the housewife was a very skilled person, capable of passing on a lot of household tips to Sabine. Guenter, Erna's husband, was a compassionate man, with good knowledge of how to fix things and how to get along with people. The children, Helmut, five years old and Hans Werner eight years old were well behaved boys. Sabine had no trouble falling in love with her new family.

Erna looked into the kitchen. "Sabine, are the potatoes done?"

Sabine, standing at the stove, poked a potato with the knife. "Yes, they are, we can eat! I'll pour the water out."

Erna looked at her. "Please do that and put all the other dishes on the table. I'll get Guenter and everybody else." Sabine checked the eggs in the mustard sauce. It was all fine! One egg for each person. Erna had her own chickens. This was a great help. The spinach was from the garden. Sabine was worried if it would be enough for the eight people at the dinner table.

Dinner was always served at midday. The dinner party included Rudi, the apprentice. He was in his second year working in the shop. The other two men were Victor and Paul. Both men came from Russia and were taken prisoner by the Germans. Victor was a former medical student in the Ukraine, and Paul came from Kiev where his wife and two children remained behind. Prisoners of war were put into factories or other workplaces to help out due to the shortage of men. They stayed at a barracks nearby where they were held captive. Guenter was a very good boss to his helpers,they were very lucky to be in his shop and house.

Everybody took their place at the table. Sabine was last, serving her people. Little Helmut and Hans Werner were sitting beside each other, with Erna to their side. Guenter was at the head of the table, Rudi beside him. Across from Erna were Victor and Paul. Sabine sat at the other end of the table. She had to get up and serve during dinner. Guenter said a short prayer before the meal and everybody enjoyed their food. Guenter looked at Rudi. "You are awfully quiet today! What is troubling you?"

Rudi's face turned a bit red, he had to swallow at first, and said with a very quiet voice, "I became a father last night."

Erna fumbled with her long, blond hair, tied together with a comb in the back. Her face got a bit red as well, but before she was able to say anything, Guenter took charge of the situation. He padded Rudi on his shoulders and told him "We can talk about it later, just the two of us! Right now, congratulations from all of us."

Everybody looked down at their plates. Rudi was 15 years old and not married. Sabine and everybody else wondered how old the mother was. Sabine felt sorry for the mother and Rudi. She had great doubts that the two of them had planned to bring a child into this world at their age and during a war. This was not a situation you wished for! The table got quiet, nobody knew what to say at the moment.

A loud bang on the door came next. It sounded as if there was an emergency! Erna jumped up! How much more bad news would this dinner bring to her fine family she wondered? She excused herself and went to the door. You could hear a strong voice, that from a man and the nervous voice of Erna. The people around the table got worried.

Erna came into the kitchen with two German soldiers behind her. She looked worried!

"I don't believe I see right! Prisoners of war sitting with a German family around the dinner table? What is this?" The round-faced soldier shouted, getting beet red in his face. "Don't you know it is forbidden to give any food to a prisoner of war? They are the enemies of our 'Deutsches Reich'! They have all they need in the barracks from us! Good we came by and checked on you!"

Victor and Paul got up and went right away into the shop. Guenter got up from his chair in order to look straight into the faces of the soldiers. "I am sorry for not being a very good German citizen! I should have known! How stupid of me! We will never again have those two foreigners sitting at a good German table. Heil Hitler!" The two soldiers had nothing to say anymore and left the room with their "Heil Hitler".

Erna collapsed at the table after she closed the door behind the soldiers. "That was close! Good job Guenter! From now on Sabine, you'll have to bring dinner into the shop for Victor and Paul!"

Sabine's favorite time was in the store. She was very good at math. When products like nails, screws or household articles arrived it was Sabine's job to figure out the sale's price. She had to add a certain percentage to the price of what the store purchased it for. Germany had price control people, going from store to store, unannounced, to check the prices. They never found any incorrect price in the store where Sabine worked. She was very proud of it. The door opened, and her sister Emma came into the store. Sabine's eyes grew big. "What are you doing here?"

Emma replied, "Bad news, they drafted Emil. He has to go to France into the war. Could you come home to say goodbye to him?"

THE TRUMPETS of WAR

Emil was sitting in the train on his way to his camp to join the troops. Sabine had told him at her 'Fare Well', that she would pray for him. He thought that Sabine took this God-stuff really seriously. He was impressed! He wished that he could believe in God like she did. "How does she do it?" he wondered. He had to admit it made him feel safer knowing she was praying for him. From listening to the forbidden BBC news Emil heard about the fighting going on in France. They said that Germany had the west front in their pocket. The people living in France had to flee and suffered endlessly even after escaping. People had nothing to eat! This was one of the reasons why Emil's biggest enemy was Hitler himself. If he would have had a choice he would not be on this train, ever! But if one declined the order to join the war, the next tree would be one's end. Emil didn't have a choice!

Emil arrived at the train station near the base and was met by officers that guided him to the fields and to the barracks where the troops were gathered to receive their orders. So far, so good. He was having a good time with the other boys in his group. They were all his age, around 18 years old. Some of them had a lot of jokes to tell, others were awfully quiet. Emil empathized with the quieter ones. He knew what they must be thinking! Two beds down the row were a group of recruits gathering around a boy who loved to have an audience. Emil joined them and listened like the others.

The boy said, "This story is totally true; it shows you how strong the German army is! General Rommel was leading his troops further into France. At one point, his tank and another tank didn't notice that they were driving too fast and were getting way out in front of the rest of the German advance. No problem for General Rommel! The two tanks turned around and made their way back to meet up with their army. Rommel's tank drove beside the road, the other one was over in the fields. At one point on the road, there was a line of support vehicles that were supposed to supply the French troops with munitions and so on. Rommel in his tank, all by himself, drove right in front of the whole convoy of trucks and stopped them, pointing the cannon right into their faces.

General Rommel stepped out of the tank. He had no weapon in his hands. He told the drivers to get out of their trucks and disappear into the woods. All the drivers ran away as fast as they could! The boy's face beamed, "Ha-ha the French are scared of us. We are the winner! They fear us!" The men around the boy laughed. Emil hoped he was right.

The next day promised to be a wonderful warm day under a blue sky. The sun was the hottest it could get in May and the new recruits were burning in the sun as they stood in the field, in their new uniforms with their weapons and their gear on their backs. They had finished their exercises and had to stand still in order to listen to the commander.

The commander greeted them and explained, "You are Germany's hope! With you, we will keep our victory at the west front. The latest information we have from the front is that the Allies are gathered together to fight against our beloved 'Deutsches Reich'. They are determined to push us out of the west. Our beloved Fuehrer, Adolf Hitler, puts all his trust into your hands. We will have victory! Let's pledge allegiance to our Fuehrer, to the flag!"

Emil almost threw up! Hitler was not his beloved Fuehrer. He didn't want to pledge his life to a person who was pure evil. He just couldn't do it! The flag was being raised and the pledge would follow. A guy beside him fell hard onto the ground. The heat had gotten to him. He heard another one, farther away suffering the same fate. Emil had no choice! He let his knees buckle and fell hard onto the ground as well.

Red Cross people came running onto the field and gathered the collapsed recruits onto stretchers. Emil was brought into a nearby tent. He held his eyes closed. An orderly slapped him on his face a couple of times. Emil let him do it again and he opened his eyes slowly. The orderly smiled at him and told him that he had fainted. Emil smiled back. They took his jacket off and gave him water to drink. This felt good. Other recruits came into the shade of the tent and took off their gear and jackets. They showed a lot of care and compassion for Emil and the other men that had fainted. It made Emil feel really bad because it was a just a pretend faint, but he had escaped the pledge! "Thank you, God!" He said quietly to himself. That was close!

Sabine got a shout from Erna and Guenter in the evening to come into their bedroom. Hidden in the bedroom was a special radio, capable of receiving the BBC channel from England. Erna and Guenter knew about Emil, Sabine's brother, fighting in France. In the evenings the BBC would send special news from the front in the German language. A lot of Germans listened to this news feed. Here was the truth, not Hitler's propaganda, but you had to be careful, it was strictly forbidden!

The three were sitting around the radio and listening. Today's news told them, that the allies were planning to help the French get the Germans out of the West with the help of the Americans and Canadians. Sabine's face turned ashen. Looking into the eyes of Erna and Guenter, she knew that she had every reason to worry. Would Emil survive? "Thank you for letting me listen to it! This is serious!"

Guenter told her, "Sabine, you are not alone! We will always be with you!"

Turning around on her way out she said, "You are so good to me! Thank you! Good night!" She went to her bedroom, which she now shared with Helmut, the younger boy. The house of her employer was filled with people. Erna and Guenter had taken in a family that had gotten bombed-out in a nearby town. Everybody had to move in together. Helmut was still awake. "Miss. Sabine, would you please read a story to me? I have trouble falling asleep."

This was their daily routine in the evening. Sabine loved the little boy and loved to read a bedtime story to him. She took the book off the shelf and started reading. It didn't take long before he was asleep. Sabine put the book down with a smile on her face. "It must be great to be so small with no concern on your mind!" she thought. She went to her bed and knelt down beside it. Her prayers for her brother came from deep down in her heart!

Emil and his buddies were sitting and standing around in the trenches at Omaha beach. Some of the soldiers were having a smoke, while others that had run out of cigarettes looked on with envy. As it happened, like so often before, one of the German supply trains filled with munitions, food, cigarettes and other supplies, was bombed by the Allies just the other day. Emil had one slice of dry Kommisbrot this morning. This hardy bread, made out of dark rye flour had a long shelf life. It would have tasted really good with butter and cheese on it, but there was no such luck for Emil or the other guys in the trenches. Emil was just thankful that his stomach had something to work on.

So far, they hadn't spotted any of the enemy. The German trenches were way up, above the beaches. Emil had an amazing view of the ocean and was dreaming of better times. He dreamed of having his own family and spending a summer day on the beach with them. He imagined his wife and himself watching the kids play in the sand and running into the water to cool off once in a while. The waves rolled unendingly towards the shore. Today was a stormy day and they washed higher up onto the beach than usual. Emil enjoyed the sound they made, like a caressing melody playing over the sand, high-lighted by the call of the seagulls. The rhythmic sound of the waves soothingly washed over his mind, bringing on a calmness and a moment of peace.

His eyes followed the birds as they were gliding over the sand and ocean waves. "Hm, what is that?" he murmured to himself. Way out on the sea, the waves became dark, almost black. He looked from the left to the right. Was it all the same? Emil turned around and looked for a soldier with binoculars. "Friedrich, could you check out the dark waves on the horizon? I wonder what that is?"

Friedrich, who was sitting bored on the ground, got up and took his field glasses. He put them in front of his eyes and said, "I see that something, something is moving towards the shore. Where is the officer with the good binoculars?"

Emil pointed to a man farther away and both of them went to ask the officer to take a look at the horizon. Other men in the trenches grew concerned and pointed to the dark waves. The officer took his field glasses and spent a long time looking through them. He turned to the left and to the right, just looking. All the men around him were holding their breath. The officer lowered the binoculars. His face was white. "Those are boats, hundreds of boats. You can't count them!" He left the trench and approached another officer in the next one. In a short time, the officers of all the trenches had a meeting. Emil and the other soldiers waited with a bad feeling in the pits of their stomach.

The officer came back and gathered his soldiers around him. He said, "The Allies tricked us, I suppose! We had the intel that they would try a huge attack at Pas-de-Calais. It was the wrong information! A lot of our troops are stationed there, but have courage, we have the better position. When they arrive on shore, they can't shoot us in our trenches, but we will have easy game, shooting down on them from up here. Don't shoot right away! Let them come close, so you have a better aim at them. Heil Hitler!"

Everybody moved to their position, and the waiting started. Waiting was the hard part, because you paint horrible pictures in your mind which makes you scared to death. To be honest, Emil had to admit that he was scared to death. Emil was sure that he was not the only one. His buddy beside him, who was looking through his binoculars, had a face that was white as a wall. He stuttered. "Hundreds over hundreds! You can't count them, and they keep coming one after the other! We are doomed!" Emil felt that way too. He looked at the line of boats coming closer and closer to the shore. After the first line came a second one and another and another. Some were big boats, the kind where you just open the front like a gangway and the troops walk right out. There were plenty of those. Lots of allied troops were coming to the shore.

The first boats pushed up on the beach and let go of their cargo. The soldiers walked through the waves marching up onto the beach. "Let them come! Wait!" the German officer shouted. Emil and the others had their rifles leaning on the edge of the trench. They had their first target already in sight. Bang! The first of the Allies was shot. Bang-bang! More fell to the ground. The allied troops down on the beach started shooting up at the trenches.

"Ow!" A buddy at the end of the trenches got shot in his shoulder. Emil took cover. At first, it seemed to Emil that they would actually stand a decent chance, but the boats kept coming and coming and, oh no! He looked up in the sky.

Allied planes had let out hundreds of paratroopers who were now descending from the sky. Some ended up on the shore, others behind the German troops. Emil didn't know which direction to aim his rifle. It was clear that the German troops were outnumbered. Emil and his buddies were shooting in every direction. Emil looked at his officer hoping he would have an idea of how to save them. At that moment the officer was hit from behind right between his shoulders. Blood came out of his mouth, he went down. Oh no, ping---.

Emil was out! This time for real. A bullet hit his helmet and knocked him out. He was unconscious.

"Ow!" somebody kicked Emil. He had trouble opening his eyes. Slowly the faces of two soldiers came into focus. They were speaking in a language that he didn't understand. One of them poked him with his rifle, motioning for Emil to stand up. Mustering his strength, Emil made it up onto his feet but his knees were shaking with fear. A kick in the buttocks signaled Emil to walk forward. He stepped over the corpses of his fellow soldiers and climbed out of the trench. A long walk into the dark countryside followed. "I am a prisoner of war! I am alive! God, you let me live again! Thank you!"

It was nighttime when Guenter and Erna called Sabine into their bedroom again. The BBC gave their first estimates of the battle, which they called; "Operation Overlord". On the 6th of June 1944, 1,200 aircraft, 5,000 vessels, and nearly 160,000 troops crossed the English Channel to fight the Germans at different locations. The Allies met the German troops fiercely. The foot soldiers alone outnumbered the Germans three times over. The BBC concluded that with this attack, the German troops would be pushed back, and the West front would be free of their control, but the numbers of casualties were high on both sides. Early estimates guessed that the Allies had lost 4000 of their men and the German troops had lost 9000 men, many of which were young boys with a mother or father. Others had wives and children. Sabine and the others didn't know what to say.

Guenter found his voice first. "You never know Sabine, maybe Emil survived? They will send a note to your family either way. You have to be patient now!" Sabine excused herself and went back to her room. Helmut was already asleep. She was thankful for that. Kneeling at her bedside she said her prayers.

Thomas was now old enough to attend the camp for boys that were training to become soldiers. There was no choice! Every German boy had to attend the camp if they didn't want any trouble that interfered in their future plans. Thomas was put into the communications group to learn morse code. In a way he was happy about that. This group had some of the sharpest young men and morse code presented itself to Thomas as an interesting challenge. Compared to other soldiers his group had a good life. Rain or not, the foot soldier had to practise marching and shooting outside, while Thomas and his buddies were able to sit inside and practise their communication skills. Once in a while they had to join the foot soldiers in outside training as well, just in case they had to fight in the war.

One day, the trainer had a special outdoor challenge for all the boys, including Thomas. They were divided into small groups and given a compass. The trainer instructed the groups to use the compass to navigate to a location, where he himself would be waiting. The challenge was for the groups to reach the instructor, without being seen by him. If he spotted anyone from the group, the team lost.

Thomas's group huddled together around the map. "This is the direct way." One of the boys said. "He will see us right away if we go straight to him." Thomas had an idea.

"Why don't we walk a huge circle around him and approach him from behind?" Everybody agreed that this seemed to be the best plan. They followed the person with the compass and made their way in a big circle around the trainer. Coming from behind on all fours and hidden by the bushes, on command, they all jumped up and yelled, "Hurra!"

The trainer got startled! He managed a smile on his face and said, "Good job! I guess you will get a prize!" They had to wait until after the evening meal for the awards to be handed out. Thomas' group got third prize. It was a bowl of pudding for every boy. Better than nothing, they thought. The time at the camp came to an end.

Thomas was now back working for the company where he had learned how to be a technician. He had written his test. His passing grade wasn't the top of the class, but he was very satisfied with his result. He had reached his goal of becoming a technician.

Prisoners of war were also recruited to work for his company. Trains were needed in Germany and all over the world during the war. Never mind the ones that got blown to pieces by bombers, with the aim of cutting supply to the German troops. The company was busy! Thomas got two prisoners of war as his helpers. One was from the Ukraine and the other one from France. The three of them were a good team! Thomas enjoyed working with them. Every time Thomas visited home, his Mom gave him a care package with food, which he shared with his two helpers. They appreciated it very much! Everybody was hungry during these times.

Thomas had a good time at his workplace. He met a girl named Erika that also worked for the company. She was a very intelligent girl with common sense. The two had a lot of interesting talks together. Erika lived in a village in the area where Thomas grew up. Over the weekend the two met each other at their parents homes. His mother liked Erika a lot and the parents of Erika liked Thomas as well. Her dad especially took a liking to Thomas. In the evening her dad and Thomas had lengthy talks about a lot of interesting topics. The parents allowed Thomas to sleep in their spare bedroom overnight, so that he wouldn't have to walk alone through the forest and over the hills to his house.

Thomas loved the blue dress Erika wore. It made her look stunning in his eyes. The dress matched her blond hair and blue eyes perfectly. He looked at Erika and couldn't believe how lucky he was, to call her his girlfriend. Today was a wonderful morning, but Thomas had to go home in order to help his mother with a load of chores. "I'll go with you for a ways!" she said. The two were holding hands and set out towards his home.

Thomas asked Erika, "Did they ask you already to help in a hospital?"

"No," she said, not yet, but a letter might come any day now. Ute, a classmate of mine had to go already. I wouldn't mind to help with all the wounded soldiers! I love doing things like that! I might even try to become a nurse when times are better. The only problem is, that I'd have to go so far away from home and be in a city all by myself and I might not be able to see you again."

Thomas replied, "Yes, I would hate that too! I enjoy every minute we have together! It would be sad to not have that anymore." The two reached the point where they had to part. A long kiss and hard embrace made it feel even more cruel to separate in different directions, but Thomas pulled away from her. His mother would have been waiting for him for a while already. He set off towards home. They both waved to each other as long as they still could see the other.

PREPARING for WAR

In late July of 1944 two days after Thomas and Erika had said their goodbyes, the good times were over. Like so many young men, Thomas was ordered into a work camp for boys that were still too young to be soldiers. Thomas, together with two of his friends from work were sitting in the train, wondering what their near future would look like. The place for this work camp was called Hirlshagen near Sprotebruch. The camp was supposed to be a model for exemplifying good German discipline.

Thomas chatted away with his friends in the train and discovered that the man sitting beside them was one of the trainers for the camp. He was very nice to the boys. "What is your name, young man?" he asked Thomas

Thomas replied, "I am Thomas Wenzel from Riesengebirge."

The leader spoke again. "Do all people in the Riesengebirge have long hair like you do?"

"No, I don't think so," Thomas said, "I just don't like those short cuts! I like my hair, that's it! You can still see my ears. I always comb it to the back, and it stops at the neck. The same as every other boy!"

"No offense, but with that hair, you are going to have trouble in the camp. If I were you, I would cut it before getting there!"

Thomas got worried. "How can I do that? We're already on the train!"

The leader said, "We will have a one hour stop at a town very soon You could try to get it cut in a barber shop there. I would try it if I were you!"

"Thanks," Thomas replied. This was not a good start for this new part of his life. Thomas loved his hair! Erika loved his hair! His hair was a great asset for him. To cut it off would hurt!

The train soon stopped at the small town. Thomas had only one hour time. He got off and looked around the train station for a barber. He was in luck! He went in and told the barber his misfortune. "Ha-ha, those military guys, they wouldn't mind if every soldier would just be bald," the barber remarked. "I am with you, young man. I like hair as well, but I will give you a short cut. Let's hope this will ease their minds." Thomas' stomach was in knots as he saw his wonderful, strong, black hair laying on the ground. He paid the barber and looked for his friends. Walter and Uwe were waiting for him outside.

"Boy, he lowered your ears quite a bit!" Walter joked." Didn't even know you had those wonderful looking ears! I don't think the girls will like it! Ha-ha." Both boys laughed. Thomas didn't really think this was funny, but he laughed as well. They had to get onto the train again. This time they chose the last train car, hoping there would be no leader and nobody else to bug them.

The train finally arrived at their destination, Hirlshagen. Thomas and his friends left the train last and walked out into the city to get an idea of how to use up the rest of the day. It was the afternoon and still plenty of time until they had to be at the camp. They were too busy thinking about what to do with their free time to notice the commander of the camp welcoming all the new recruits, down at the front of the train. Thomas and his friends went into a bakery, to get something to eat and walked around the town. Later they showed up at the camp just in time for the evening meal.

The leader, the one they had met in the first train car, was not their friend anymore. Instead, he chewed them out saying, "What made you think that it would be alright to just take off without permission? I was waiting for you three at the train station, thinking that you might have missed the train when you got your hair cut. And what kind of a hair cut is that anyway? German boys have their hair as long as a matchstick. That is the standard and there is no exception! Thomas, after dinner you have to go to our barber and get your hair cut to the appropriate length." Thomas got another haircut that same day. He hated how he looked in the mirror. This was an abuse of his beautiful hair, he thought.

The camp was divided into four groups of boys, and of course, Thomas and his two friends were separated into different groups. They sadly waved to each other on the way to their designated barracks. The barracks were simple wooden structures with beds to sleep in. The washrooms were in a separate simple wooden building, with the toilets made out of a very long wooden sheet, with ten holes in it. Everything was done together in this camp! The camp had one entrance, which was guarded by two of the recruits. The boys had to take turns standing guard at the entrance and watching the "bad boys" in the little jail, right next to the entrance. You became a bad boy by not following the rules, like not obeying the curfew. The jail had its own toilet, where the guard with his rifle at hand stood next to the prisoner until he was done his business. Thomas hated it when it was his turn to stand guard.

The daily drills were challenging. Even though all the boys were in good shape, they were pushed to their limit, with more push-ups, more sit-ups, longer runs, and so on. Thomas loved it! He was good at sports and loved to be pushed to his limits.

After the first morning of exercise, the boys were led to a pile of rifles and shovels. "What are we going to do with the shovel?" the boy beside Thomas asked the group.

The trainer spoke, "Everybody take a rifle or a shovel, whatever you're able to grab! We are going to have our weapon's drill. Sorry that we are out of rifles, but they are badly needed at the front." Thomas and his buddy both had a shovel in their hands and couldn't hold back their smiles. It was funny! The shovels were as clean and shiny as if they were brand new from the factory. They handled the shovels like a real weapon. The trainer was serious about this. They held the shovels against their chest while they saluted upright, and aimed the shovels in pretend shooting. Thomas thought it was a lot of fun!

The marching drills, while singing the well known 'volkslieder' songs made it a good time for everybody. German boys had a great arsenal of songs in their repertoire. Schools and the Hitler Youth taught them the German 'folk songs' never mind the many songs from their child hood. During the marching drills, one boy would start a song and the whole group would join in, singing through verse by verse. This gave a wonderful feeling of belonging to the group and was also a reminder of home. The boys loved it. Some of the songs were just fun and had lyrics not meant for sensitive ears. One of the songs mentioned the gas one would release in more private places, like the toilet. This one became a favourite, but after awhile it was forbidden by the leadership. The word "vergasst", meaning gassed, was too close to what was being done in the concentration camps to the Jewish people. The boys had no idea about that, but the leadership already knew what was going on in those so-called 'work camps'.

"Everybody get up! Get out of your bed!" There was no mercy from the officer. It didn't matter how wonderful your dream was. Thomas was just flying his glider with a beautiful blond lady sitting behind him. She adored him, you could see that in her eyes! She just marveled at Thomas' skills as he flew over a wonderful, blooming meadow, piloting the glider with his strong hands.

Reality set in for Thomas. His bed was hard and the officer was still shouting. "Maybe one day my dream will come true," he thought. He jumped out of bed, got dressed and ready for breakfast. He had just swallowed his first bite in the mess hall, when an officer entered the room.

"Group number two," the officer announced, "you have to pack your backpacks right after breakfast. You will go by train to the river Oder. On the west side of the river, you'll have to dig trenches for our brave, strong, winning, German army. Eat your breakfast and get ready!" Thomas belonged to group number two. He was OK with going to dig trenches and helping out in that way, but he had doubts about this 'winning army the officer boasted about. Digging trenches at the west side of the Oder was a very serious matter. The river was on the east side of Germany, inside German territory. Having to defend Germany on the inside, was a sure sign that the war would be lost. It meant that the Russian troops must have pushed the Germans back out of Russia. This was losing, not winning! Of course, there was no BBC for the boys. They only heard what their commander told them. Thomas got ready and packed his belongings into his backpack. He thought about his Dad. Since the West front was lost, Dad was fighting in the East. Russia didn't have the vineyards that France had, and the climate was rougher in the East. Thomas worried that his Dad would be having a hard time right now.

The trainer cried out, "Everybody get on board! Climb into the wagons!" Thomas and his buddies were standing in front of a freight train. They would be shipped like animals, sitting side by side on the floor in a box car. Most of the boys thought that this was funny. One said, "Wouldn't it be great to have a lady sitting beside you instead of just us. I could travel like that for a long time if a girl would be beside me!" Thomas wondered why all the good trains in Germany had disappeared. The ride wasn't too bad though, and it only took two hours to reach their destination close to the river.

The place where the train came to a stop looked like a small town out of a fairy-tale book, with one big, beautiful house beside another. The streets were generously wide with lush trees framing them on each side. Thomas had never seen such a beautiful place. "This must be a town for the rich!" he thought.

The group moved into the dining area of an extraordinary finely furnished restaurant. The main floor, filled with heavy looking tables and chairs, had some cozy sofas along the walls. Lamps were placed beside the sofas, to give the guests a more private, living room like feeling. The restaurant had closed down for business and the whole place had been taken over by the German army. The boys pushed the tables and chairs to one end, and were to sleep on the hard floor but were not allowed to use the washroom of the restaurant. The officers slept on the sofas and got the washrooms for themselves.

Quickly the boys were given shovels for completing their first task of digging a huge hole in the backyard for them to do their private business. After the hole was deep and wide enough, they had to build a sitting bench around the hole. This was done with strong branches, placed at the convenient height. In order to get some privacy, they created a wall from smaller branches with leaves. They pushed these into the ground and were mighty proud of their achievement. After a couple of days, they noticed, that those leaves started to fall off. It was humorous, but it meant no privacy!

The next morning after arriving the boys walked to the river with their shiny shovels in their hands. There were a couple of boats, waiting for the boys. The trainer led them in groups into the boats and told them to follow him to the other side of the river. "We don't have paddles!" one boy piped up.

The trainer smiled and said, "What do you have in your hands? Use your shovel as a paddle It works beautifully!" Thomas was surprised at how good a shovel could work as a paddle. Dreaming took over while he was in the boat. He pretended to be sailing on the great Amazon river in South America. He had read that it was the second longest river in the world and pictured a lush jungle with all kinds of animals right beside the river. Of course, there was this beautiful blond lady sitting behind him again.

Reality again set in as they reached the other side of the river. Everybody exited the boats with their shovels in their hands. The officer spaced the boys 10 meters apart from each other along the shoreline. They were given the responsibility of digging a 10 meter long trench each day. This was not a joke! The days were hard labour! Some sections were more difficult to dig being grown over with bushes. Thomas was sweating like everybody else. The daily torture from the mosquitos and the sunburns on their backs became painful and made it hard to work. A normal workday was 12 hours long. Thomas had finished his 10 meters and noticed the other boys were getting ready to call it a day as well. The commander called them together at the shore.

"Everybody strip down to your birthsuit, we are taking a dip!" "YEAH!!!!!!" The boys took off their clothes and jumped into the river. This was great! The trainer joined them as well. The evenings that followed a day of trenching were good times, with the fire in the backyard of the restaurant and the singing of folk songs.

It was Sunday, the day off! The boys were allowed to sleep in and got a good breakfast and a better dinner than on normal days, but in order to avoid trouble, they were prohibited from wandering off the premises of the restaurant. The trainer entered the dining room after lunch with a list in his hands. "Everybody listens carefully! The boys whose names I read out loud, come forward!" He started saying one name after the other, including Thomas' name and then said, "All of you standing now, show me your comb and handkerchief. The ones with a dirty comb or handkerchief had to go back to their chairs and sit down. Thomas was still standing. The leader started again. "Everyone who is still standing gets an award for good workmanship. The clean comb and handkerchief prove to me your good personal hygiene. Please come forward and receive your condom. The ladies are waiting for you in the bar down the road!"

Thomas' ears got a bit red. "The ladies are waiting for you in the bar? Are you kidding!" He and the other lucky boys spruced up and got on their way. Thomas had a knot in his stomach. Was this another way to become a good German man? He wondered. He got a bit scared!

The group of boys were standing in front of the bar. They looked into each others faces. Everybody had red ears and felt awkward. One of them opened the door and -- yes, the ladies were waiting. The room was full of girls smiling at them as the boys made their way into the room. The ladies didn't act as shy as the boys, who were still standing together at the entrance. The evening proved to be a memorable experience for the boys.

The daily routine had them digging trenches again. Time went fast. Thomas' group had fulfilled their duty of digging trenches and was being shipped back on the train to their camp in Hirlshagen. After a couple of days, Thomas and his group had to pack their backpacks again. This time the boys received a rifle in their hands. Thomas was shocked! "Are they taking us to the front?" he wondered. The freight train was waiting again and the boys took their places on the floor in the wagons. It was a long ride, the hours got longer and longer. Nobody knew any jokes anymore. They all fell asleep. The stops in-between were just to eat and to use the washrooms. It was already dark outside when the train came to its final stop.

People welcomed them at the train station with a good number of bikes standing beside them. Each boy got a bike and the commander started riding in front. It was a long ride over fields in the dark. The boys had a hard time to keeping steady and also to not lose sight of the rider in front of them. Thomas was sweating like all the other boys.

At last, they reached their destination. It was a small Polish town in the middle of nowhere. The little town looked like a poor place. The houses and stables were very small and in a bad condition. The boys waited with their bikes in their hands until the commander had figured out a place for them to stay. It was a stable full of hay. Thomas was very happy. Sleeping in the hay was great, so much better than on a hard floor! The first night, the boys just slept wherever they found hay. The trainer explained to them, "Tomorrow will be the day to move in and get more organized."

After breakfast, the digging for the private place in the back yard started again. Everybody knew the drill by now. After that, they were told to prepare their own place in the stable. The trainer said, "This stay will be longer, so try to make your place as homey as you can. The yard has enough wooden sheets, nails and tools. Everybody can build their own shelf and create their personal place." The boys emptied their backpacks and placed their belongings in the shelves they made. Thomas liked his place! The daily wash was done outside the stable in a bowl of water.

"It is a good thing that we live in a stable!" Thomas said to another boy. "We will smell like cows in no time!"

Thomas' group wasn't the only one in the area. The German army had asked for a lot of youth to come and dig trenches for the German soldiers to fight off the Russian army that was coming closer to the West. Thomas was thankful to have an honest, generous leader to oversee their provision. His group always had lots to eat! Once in a while if they had too much of one kind of food, like sugar or potatoes they could trade it in for something special. One farmer gave them a couple of geese in exchange for some bags of sugar. The boys cleaned out the geese at night and roasted them over the fire. That night and the next day after, the boys were busy running to the toilet. Nobody knew why, but this was a minor problem. One day at the trenches a boy from another group told Thomas, "Our cook is a thief! He takes a lot of our good food away from us and goes into town to trade the food for stuff for himself. We get just enough food to survive!"

"How about going to your officer and reporting that guy?" Thomas said.

The other one replied, "We did, but as it turns out, at least we think so, they are both in on it. We believe there are some ladies in that town who are willing to give them a good time for good food."

Thomas had nothing to say about that. He just shook his head. The work was as hard as before. The boys had to dig their 10 meters of trench everyday. Everybody collapsed into the hay at night. It was getting colder. Fall was coming and the hay didn't keep the boys warm anymore. The solution for the boys was to get dressed for the night instead of undressed.

"This is brutal! Doesn't the great 'Deutsche Reich' have coats for their people?" The boy standing guard with Thomas was shivering. Thomas, in his thin jacket, was cold to the bones as well. He agreed with his buddy.

"I wonder if they give the guys fighting the Russian army warm clothing. Russia is colder than Germany! My Dad is fighting in the East."

The other boy felt warmer already. "They must be cold, lying in the dirt and fighting the Russians. Good that we are still too young to join the war! At least we have a bit of hay when our shift is over, to warm our butt." Thomas not only thought about his Dad, he wondered about Erika as well. Was she waiting for him? Had she met someone else already?

The next morning, after Thomas had a few short hours of sleep, the commander called him over. "Thomas, we need you to drive with Rudi to bring supplies to the other trenches. This will be a bit dangerous, but you will remain in German territory. Rudi's truck is fuelled with wood. Your job is to fuel the oven with wood during the trip." Thomas was happy to have a change in his routine. No digging or standing guard for a couple of days. That sounded great!

It didn't take long before Rudi came around the corner in his truck. "Hey buddy, are you the guy helping me with the wood burner?" he asked Thomas. Thomas told him that he, indeed, was his guy. He told Rudi his name and gave him a hand unloading the supplies for his group, and the two got on their way. Rudi seemed to have a problem with keeping names. Buddy it was from then on. Thomas had seen a truck fueled with wood before, but got a closer look now. Beside the door, towards the front, was a wood burning chamber. Thomas had to feed the wood into the oven every time the truck was low on power. This was an easy task.

Rudi started singing after they were on their way. "Vor der Kaserne, vor dem grossen Tor, stand eine Laterne… (In front of the barracks, before the large gate, stood a lantern….)". Rudi was a big fan of Marlene Dietrich, the well-known actor and singer of the time. This 'Lilli Marleen' song, a sad love story, was heard all over Germany, including where soldiers were stationed. The longing for a normal relationship was deep. Thomas had heard it many times before and felt the same as Rudi. The countryside was great, and on top of that, Rudi was a man of many stories and jokes.

"Hey buddy, do you know this one already? Fritzchen entered the classroom in the morning. He put up his hand and the teacher gave him permission to speak. Fritzchen said, 'Do you get punished even though you didn't do anything?' The teacher answered, 'Of course not! That would be unfair!' Fritzchen was relieved and told the teacher, 'Oh good! I didn't do my homework!'" Ha-ha, Thomas had a good time! Rudi reminded Thomas of his Father. Wherever they stopped, Rudi made contact right away, and won the hearts of the people. Since the army had given him new tools, he traded his old ones for pieces of bacon or eggs from the farmers. Just a good word or a compliment to a woman got them a cup of coffee, and with some luck, a piece of cake as well! It was too bad when the good times were over and Rudi drove the truck back to the familiar area where Thomas' group was housed. "To bad our time is over! You were a good Buddy!" Rudi said. Thomas stepped out of the truck and said his farewell, as the commander approached him.

"Thomas, I have another special job for you! Two kilometers to the South is a village where some of our German high-ranking officers are staying. You and some other boys have the honour to support them, by doing anything they need. You will find out for yourself what you have to do. Just grab your stuff and walk over there. The place is easy to find! The house that the officers are staying in is the biggest in the village."

Thomas got ready and walked towards the South. He wondered what his new job would be like. He had never met a real high ranking German army officer. The commander in the boy's group had no real say for making decisions in the real war. This was kindergarten compared to the real soldiers. He reached the village and looked for the biggest house. It was right in the middle of the village. "What a wonderful house!" thought Thomas. It had two stories with a lot of windows everywhere, a nice garden area and a stable. Thomas went to the stable first. A boy was sitting in front of the stable chewing on a piece of straw. "Is this the house with all the officers?" Thomas asked.

The boy answered, "Yes, are you Thomas?" After Thomas told him that it was him, the boy showed Thomas his place to sleep in the stable and told him about his new job. "The food and the girls come from I don't know where. We have to take care of anything else they need and want and make sure that they don't make trouble."

"What? What do you mean by not making trouble?" Thomas asked.

"I'd rather let you find that out for yourself." The boy said. "Why don't you help me prepare the kitchen for dinner?"

The two of them cleaned the floor, which was very dirty, and emptied the garbage. The chairs from the kitchen table were all over the place. Thomas wondered what had happened here. A farmer's lady came in with a huge basket in her hand. She was very friendly and told them to keep the pots warm for the officers. She took the empty ones from the last day and went on her way. Thomas heard some voices. The door opened and he met his first important officers. There were five of them, all in undershirts, suspenders over their shoulders, and hair uncombed. Thomas swallowed. "Heil Hitler" he said, lifting his right arm.

One of them said, "A new boy! Hi!" and all of them gathered around the table. Thomas and the other boy put the plates with the dinner right in front of them, while they were talking, totally ignoring the two. The day went on with household chores, nothing heavy or difficult for Thomas. He was very happy that it was this easy!

Evening came around, and Thomas thought that he could go to the stable and his day would be done. The other boy laughed, "You have no idea! Our real job starts now!" He had just finished saying that when a big car drove into the driveway and stopped. The doors opened and five young ladies dressed to the ninth exited the car. Their faces had heavy makeup on, with bright red lipstick, deep black eyelashes, and dark rouge on their cheeks. Laughing and talking they made their way to the house. One of the officers opened the door, he himself dressed in his uniform, looking smashing! Thomas and the other boy had drawn the curtains after the sun had set. This place was too close to the front, and you didn't want to see any light. Thomas heard the sound of music. They must have started a gramophone with a waltz on it. Thomas thought, "OK they're having some fun, just let them have it!" After an hour or so, the laughter got louder and the music as well. The other boy said, "Our job starts now, you'll see!" Thomas didn't know what he meant at first, but then he noticed a bright light from one of the windows.

"Let's go in!" the boy said and Thomas followed him. As fast as they could, they made their way through the dancing couples, to reach the window and pull the curtain back into place. Both went outside again. They agreed to post themselves on different sides of the house in order to spot any light coming out of the windows. It didn't take long, and then there was the next spot of light. Thomas went in and discovered that the uniform jackets had come off in the meantime and the alcohol level of officer's blood had gotten higher. The atmosphere got heated, the couples were clinging to each other. It went on for a long time! The faces of the ladies got heated, the make-up smeared. Thomas was not impressed with the behaviour of these important officers.

It got really late when the boys knew that all the officers had their lady in their bed and the curtains wouldn't be moved anymore. Finally, Thomas was able to go to sleep! He was very disappointed in the officers! His picture of an officer that was so important to the war was very different. He was shocked, to say the least.

The days went on in a similar fashion. It was disgusting! Thomas and the other boy were cleaning up the dinner table, when the highest-ranking officer came through the door. He pointed to Thomas saying, "Hey you, clean my room really good today. I am expecting a very important visitor tonight!" Thomas heard the other officers laughing. Thomas had a good idea who this important visitor would be, but he decided to do a good job! He had cleaned a lot of rooms for the summer guests at home! He knew how to do it right!

He entered the room and almost fell back. The smell, the dust, the mess, was horrible. He opened the window and started the cleaning job by rearranging the furniture in the right order and putting on clean bedsheets. It was a big job! He was sweating, but was finally almost done, with just the floor left to do. He got on his knees and with the broom in his hands he bent down to look underneath the bed. His face turned white, his hand covered his mouth, he had to run outside. Reaching the garden, his dinner came back up. "Uh, no! Disgusting! That was it! He had it!" he thought. Grabbing the garden shovel, he went upstairs again. With the shovel he reached underneath the bed and pulled out a huge pile of used condoms. He had to go twice in order to pick them all up. He threw the mess in a hole in the backyard and covered it with dirt, finishing the job.

As he put all his cleaning supplies away, one of the officers told him to bring a message to the commander of Thomas' group of boys. Thomas went into the stable, got his backpack, and walked to the place where his old group was. The commander greeted him warmly as he liked Thomas very much. "Hi Thomas, what's up? Why do you have your backpack on?"

Thomas replied, "Here is a letter for you from one of the officers. I have a problem working for the officers. They have parties almost every night with a bunch of girls and are getting drunk pretty much every day! I don't want to be part of it! Please, please send somebody else, somebody who doesn't mind all that stuff. I am sorry to disappoint you, but I have a hard time watching all of that."

The commander got worried. "Hm, this is Ok Thomas! I didn't know that it was that bad! I will send another boy! Just go into the stable and put your stuff back in your place. Tomorrow you'll go back into the trenches again!"

"Trenches are wonderful!" Thomas thought. At least the trenches had real dirt! He could cope with that!"

Thomas went into the stable to put his stuff away into his homey, little corner. Everything looked fine. His things were neatly folded on the shelf. He reached underneath the shelf to get his tobacco. The tobacco was gone! He looked everywhere; his smokes were nowhere to be found. Stealing from a comrade was punished severely. Thomas was getting really depressed by now with all the things going on during the last few days, and now this! But he didn't tell the commander about his tobacco. It wasn't worth it! He rarely smoked anyway!

The evening was a much better time for Thomas. The boys had a good fire going and sang one folk song after another. Those songs made everybody, Thomas included, homesick. Once in a while a tear made its way down the cheek of a boy and was hastily wiped away. Thomas liked this so much better than taking care of those officers.

At the meeting in the morning, a higher-ranking commander from the Nazi Party put himself in front of the boys spouting his propaganda. He talked about the winning German troops fighting on the East Front and the strength and pride of the German people. He told the boys to become just as faithful as German soldiers, fighting for the fatherland.

Thomas and the boys had heard it many times before. After what Thomas had just witnessed with those officers, he had his doubts about the proud, German army.

The boys worked hard at digging trenches that day. All of a sudden, trucks with German soldiers from the front stopped where they were working. The soldiers jumped off the trucks to inspect the trenches. Thomas looked into their faces. There was no pride, no strength. Their faces looked fallen in, the soldiers were all skin and bones and their eyes had a red rim around them, like sore eyes. They were certainly malnourished. Their summer uniforms were ripped and tattered. "Those men must be cold and hungry!" Thomas thought. "It is all a lie! We are not winning the war! We are losing! They can't even supply the soldiers with warm clothing and winter is right on the doorstep. He had his lunch sandwich still in his pocket. He gave it to the one soldier standing right beside him. Thomas thought he caught a flicker of joy and thankfulness in the soldier's sad eyes. Thomas turned around in shame. "I want to go home!" He was sure about that.

The month of workcamp was over. The commander approached Thomas the evening before everybody would be able to go home. "Thomas, we need a man like you! We would love to have you stay with us and be a leader for the next group of boys. You would be able to teach them a lot. You have it in you!"

Thomas smiled at his commander. "Thank you so much for saying that, but I have to go home, my family needs me."

He was more than happy to step onto the train the next morning together with the other boys. While on the train, the boys heard rumours that the Russian troops were coming closer to Germany, their homeland. As he was sitting in the train, it became clear to Thomas, that the war was lost. He would need to stay with his family and help them through this.

Thomas stood in front of his home. He teared up. He couldn't believe his eyes. It was all the same as before, so beautiful and normal. Now he understood why he got scared during all those camps; he was scared that it would all be gone. His little sisters spotted him first. "Thomas is home! Thomas is here!" they shouted. Mother, grandfather, and grandmother, came running out of the house. Everybody hugged each other. It was good to be home!

At the dinner table, they all listened to Thomas' stories. The Wenzel family didn't have a radio with the BBC channel. It was good to hear the truth from Thomas. The mother had done a great job running the guesthouse in the meantime. She had made a good profit every summer. The Wenzel family became one of the wealthier families in town. Dad would have been proud of her!

Thomas started the job for his mom, that he had done before, getting the most out of the stamps used for buying groceries. His grandfather was thankful to have his help with chopping wood. The winter was almost here, the days and nights were getting colder.

Trudi, Thomas' mother, told him that Erika was taking care of wounded German soldiers in a faraway town. "To bad!" he thought.

Nevertheless, Thomas had spent three weeks with his family, having a good time, when he met a good, old friend, Edward. Edward was at home with his family, because of his poor eyesight. He couldn't join the war. He was already older than Thomas, and he knew how talented Thomas was in shopping. "Thomas, did you hear about the amazing deal they have in Hirschberg? There are selling out the old warehouse with cookware and other stuff you need around the house. I am planning to go there tomorrow. Would you like to join me?"

Thomas replied, "Why not, let me talk to my mother, I am sure she would love to have some good deals!"

The next morning, he and Edward took off by train to the nearby town of Hirschberg. They jumped out of the train in Hirschberg and looked around. Edward spotted a friend of his and told Thomas, "Oh, there is Karl, an old friend of mine. Please come with me, I would like to introduce you to him." Standing in front of Karl, Edward said, "Hi Karl, this is Thomas a good friend of mine!" Thomas got a bad feeling when he looked into the eyes of this Karl, and the smiles Edward and Karl had on their faces.

Karl opened his mouth, "Hi Thomas, I am a leader of the Hitler Youth and work at the homefront in the drafting department. As I heard from your friend Edward, you are already 17 years old. We are now drafting the 17-year-old men, to help our winning troops on the East Front. You are drafted! Please go with me to the office!"

Thomas had no choice! Edward had tricked him! The people in the office made him fill out the papers and told him to be at the train station in Hirschberg in three days. To refuse would mean to be a deserter, punished by hanging.

Thomas went by himself back home to his family.

It was a sad goodbye!

THE FRONT ADVANCES

The BBC was broadcasting the news in German. Sabine and the couple she worked for surrounded the radio, listening eagerly to the latest news. Today, the BBC talked about the many assassination attempts on Hitler. They said that in April of 1943 Dietrich Bonhoeffer and his friends, who had made several attempts on Hitler's life, were hold captive in a prison. Hitler survived all the attacks. "Dietrich is such a good man! He founded the Confessing Church! They will kill him!" Guenter's face turned serious in concern as he walked around the bedroom grieving.

"Who knows if he isn't already dead! It's 1945! Who knows?" Erna exclaimed.

Sabine remarked, "How many lives does Hitler have? As far as we know, there were already a couple of assassination attempts, and all failed. It is like somebody tells him to leave the room just in the nick of time, before a bomb goes off."

Erna said, "I am so sorry for the people now being tortured and shot. These are good people risking their lives for us, to free us from this monster. They might have families that have to suffer now. It will be horrible for them! Germany is becoming a state of horror and evil! When will it end!" Sabine got to her feet and wished the couple a good night. Her heart was heavy as well. What will happen to Germany? The West Front was lost and they were losing on the East Front as well. She was thankful that her brother was alive. Her parents had received a message from the army, that he was a prisoner of war. After she read a bedtime story to little Helmut, she said her prayers and went to bed.

The next morning, Sabine had to go by bus to a school that she attended once a week. Everybody who wanted to work in a social job had to attend this school. When she arrived, the other girls were standing outside in front of the school, talking to each other. "No school today, they didn't say why!" one of the girls announced.

"We have the day off! Yeah!" Another girl said, "Why don't we go home to Luedenscheid and visit our families? We haven't seen them for a while!" Everybody agreed.

Sabine and a couple of her friends walked up the steep hill towards Luedenscheid. They reached the street of Sabine's home first. They walked around the corner by the pub and got a look at the house Sabine's family lived in. Everybody stopped in their tracks. "Oh no!" Sabine exclaimed. It was all she could say. Her face went ashen and her knees buckled. The other girls held her up. Sabine's home was surrounded with broken glass. All the windows of this two-story apartment building were shattered and glass had showered onto the street. The blood flooded back into Sabines veins. She and her friends started running towards the house. They ran to the back where the entrance of the house was. "No!" was all the girls managed to say. The yard in the back of the house was filled with a huge crater where a bomb had landed. Luckily it didn't explode, but the impact was still devastating.

Sabine and the girls ran inside the house and up the stairs to her family's apartment. Nobody was there! It was eerie! Images of her mother bleeding and her little sisters harmed, flooded Sabine's mind. "Where are my parents?" The whole house was empty, all the neighbours were gone as well. The girls stepped outside and spotted a neighbour from another building. Sabine ran over and asked him, "Do you know where my parents are?"

"They are at your grandmother and aunt's place. I think they are OK."

Sabine said, "Thank you!" She said goodbye to the other girls and went running down the street to her Grandmother's house.

She knocked on the door of her Grandma's place. When her Mom came to the door, she was shocked to see Sabine standing there. "What are you doing here? Don't you have to be in school?" Sabine took a moment to gather her thoughts.

"School? Oh yes! We didn't have school today! So, we thought we'd come home instead. I came to the house. All the windows are gone! Are you alright?" Mother let her into the living room, where the whole family was sitting and looking at Sabine, wondering why she was there. Sabine's two little sisters came running up to her right away and started crying and telling her about the glass and loud boom from last night. She comforted them and listened through their sobs. Mother continued the story.

"We woke up from a loud bang. Glass shattering was next. Heini and I got out of bed right away, putting our house shoes on first, because the floor was covered with shards of glass. We went right away to the children. Walli was sitting up in her bed, crying, clutching her doll close to her chest.

Our little Gerdi was still lying flat in bed, but crying. She was covered in a blanket of shards of glass, but not one of the pieces cut her." Sabine got scared picturing her little sister covered with glass. She knew that God had protected that little one!

"Did you get any warning about the attack?" she asked her mom.

"Not at all! It was a total surprise! We believe that it was an accident from a bomber flying over Luedenscheid, luckily it didn't explode. The house owner is going to put the windows back in. We will be back in our home in no time, don't you worry!" Sabine was relieved. God had protected her family. "Thank you, God!" she thought.

A week later, Sabine was back in her classroom. The school was open like normal, although the sirens were screaming throughout Germany more frequently. Suddenly, a loud siren went off announcing the attack of bombers in the area. Sabine felt like a cold hand had gripped her heart. The sound was horrible! "Everybody into the basement!" the teacher announced. Her face was white as a bedsheet and her hands were shaking. Reaching the basement, the girls had to sit together with the teachers on the floor in the hallway. Everybody was thinking the same thing, "Will the bomb hit us? Will the bomb hit my family's home? Will I be able to go home after school?" When the attack was over, nobody, including the teacher, had the nerve to keep going as if nothing had happened. So the teacher sent the girls home.

Sabine and her friends decided to go back to Halver, the town were Sabine lived and worked. At the train station they were told that no train was going to Halver today so the girls walked beside the train tracks following its route home. On their way they came across a train on the tracks, totally destroyed. Emergency vehicles were parked beside the train and people were looking for survivors under the pieces of metal and glass. It looked horrible! The girls couldn't find out if the train had any passengers or if it was targeted because it was loaded with munitions. The war was now in their neighbourhood. This was scary!

Even though the war was now here too, life had to go on. The stores were open and families had to be fed. Sabine was as busy as in normal times. She was organizing and dusting the shelves in the store. Dusting was a favourite chore for her. She loved to sing one folk song after another, while she worked happily away.

The door opened and Guenter, her boss, came into the store barking. "Drop everything you are doing! We have to go away from here to the other side of the village! The 'Jabos' are coming! They are going to bomb a train at the station carrying munitions in it. Go, go!"

Sabine understood! 'Jabos' was a nickname used by Germans for these particular American war planes. They were small airplanes designed to drop bombs.

Sabine left the store and rushed to meet up with Erna, the wife of her boss, who was holding her two boys in her hands. Erna's face looked shocked. Her hair was loose around her head, something you would normally never see on her. "Sabine please go to Mathilde, she is all alone today. Tell her to join us. She has nobody else to help her, but please, be fast!"

Sabine ran to the neighbour's house, where Mathilde lived with her husband Otto. They were a nice, older couple. Sabine rang the bell, no answer! She rang the bell again and knocked on the door loudly. Time was running out! Finally, she heard some heavy footsteps. The door opened. "Oh Sabine, what brings you to our house today?" Mathilde greeted her.

Sabine was shaking. "Please hurry! The Jabos are going to bomb a train at the station! We have to get out of here very fast! We are too close to the station! The explosion will hit us too! Please come with me to the other side of town. We will be safe there!"

Mathilde, holding her hand in front of her mouth said, "Oh no! And today of all days my husband had to go to Luedenscheid. Let me just get my bag with the papers from the bedroom." She shuffled with her heavy body along the hallway to her bedroom. Sabine got very scared and impatient!

"OH, no, uhhh." Sabine heard Mathilde moaning. She went up into the bedroom where Mathilde was lying in pain on her bed. Mathilde, holding her middle, moaned, "My gallbladder, it's my gallbladder! Why does it have to hit me now? I am so sorry! Please give me a minute?" Sabine's face was white, her hands shaking.

"Where are you?" Erna came running into the house.

Sabine yelled from the bedroom, "We are in the bedroom. Mathilde has a gallbladder attack! I don't know what to do?"

Erna came into the bedroom and assessed the situation. "Mathilde you have to get out of here. Sabine and

I will help you up and together we will walk to the other side of town. You have to be strong!" And so, they did! While groaning and sweating profusely, Mathilde, supported by Erna and Sabine, walked in the direction of the other side of town. They had only made it a short distance when Mathilde plopped down on a bench and announced

"This is it! I can't walk anymore! You two just go ahead! I will stay here!"

Erna and Sabine looked at each other. "This will do!" Erna decided, "We will have some protection here! Let's sit together! We can see the station really good from here." All three sat down and looked down towards the train station. The Station had a tunnel on the far side. That would be a great place for the train to find shelter, Sabine mused. It didn't take long and the three women heard the incoming train. Sabine got a better look at the tunnel. "Ohhh no! There is already a train in the tunnel!"

Erna noticed it at the same time. "Too bad, now the train has to stop in front of it. The train is doomed!" The incoming train made a loud, grinding, braking noise. It took a long time for the conductor to stop the train. As soon as the train came to a stop, the door of the locomotive flew open. A man in blue overalls, jumped out of the train. Right after him was another man in work clothes, and a third man came jumping off the train. All of them ran into the tunnel. They had just made it!

Sabine and the others heard the sound of the Jabos overhead. With a deafening, horrible howl, they approached the train from various directions. Two from the North started their descent first. When they were low enough, right over the train, they released their deadly cargo. The bombs dropped 'pop, pop, pop' onto the train. Bam! A loud explosion! The three on the bench covered their heads with their arms. Looking up they witnessed fireworks display like they had never seen in their lives before. Now the two Jabos from the West were getting ready for their attack. Descending like the other two planes. The same pop, bang and fireworks explosion erupted. Then silence. It all came to a stop. Sabine only heard the plane propellers in the distance. If it wouldn't have been so horrible, the fireworks would have been a beautiful sight.

Erna broke the silence, "The train must have had only small munitions, otherwise the explosions would have been much more severe!"

Mathilde chimed in, "Good for us! Otherwise, we would have been hurt! I am sorry about my gallbladder!"

Sabine asked her "Are you feeling better now?"

"Yes, much better! The pain is almost gone!"

Guenter came running with his two boys and the other helpers from the shop "What happened to you? We were worried! Why didn't you join us on the other side of the village?" Erna told him the whole story and concluded that they were able to see the attack because of Mathilde's gallbladder. Guenter was relieved that the explosions weren't so big, and that his whole family was safe, and that the house was not damaged.

Sabine walked Mathilde back home and the others followed. On their way, they had to cross the area beside the train station. The ground was covered with empty shells. The two little ones, Helmut and Hans Werner got excited. "Oh, real shells!" They started picking them up.

Guenter, who walked right behind them, said loudly, "Stop in your tracks, you two! This is dangerous stuff! There might be some live ones! You better go home with your Mom." Guenter and all the men from the shop started to clean up the area around the station.

Mathilde started having breathing problems on the way home. Sabine began to cough a lot as well. The train was still burning and the fire filled the area with a huge cloud of black smoke.

In Luedenscheid, Heini, Sabine's Dad, stood in front of the house. A huge black cloud came up from Halver, the town where Sabine was living in. Heini was surrounded by some of his neighbours, who had watched the attack as well. A neighbour believed that half of the city of Halver was gone. Heini got a shock. "Sabine!" he thought. He went inside the house and told his wife, "Otti, there was an attack in Halver. I have to go and check on Sabine. Don't wait with dinner for me, I don't know what time I'll will be back."

Now Otti got worried too. "What do you mean, attack? Who was attacked? Did the Americans bomb Halver?"

Heini tried to calm her down. "Not really Halver, just a train in Halver. I'm sure Sabine will be fine. I am just going to check on her." He went off, walking and running down the long hill towards Halver. Coming closer to the town the smoke got much thicker. Flames were still tenaciously burning and flaring up. He spotted the house where Sabine lived and saw that it was still standing and fine.

Sabine was busy in the kitchen, preparing dinner. The store and the shop were closed today. Every man available was involved with the cleanup around the station. A knock on the door made her wonder if it was a customer in urgent need of some nails or what not. She opened the door and looked into the worried, blue eyes of her Father. He took her into his arms. "We were so worried that something happened to you! We heard about the bombing and saw the smoke!" Sabine felt good in her Father's arms. It had been a hard day! That somebody was worried about her felt good.

Sabine said, "Thank you for coming! Please stay for dinner, we have lots!" Her father agreed. Dinner was filled with chatter. The fireworks from the train were the main topic, especially for Helmut and Hans Werner, who in their young lives had never seen fireworks before, and couldn't stop talking about it. Heini was more than happy to hear all their stories and relieved about the better outcome of the bombing, much better than he feared. He excused himself right after the meal. Otti was waiting anxiously back at home to hear from him about Halver and Sabine.

Sabine's Father was just out of the door, when the phone rang. The city of Bochum was bombed and the people needed support. Guenter had his truck with supplies ready for this scenario. He was part of a group of people who were prepared to help. Bochum was a half an hour drive away from Halver. Erna called all her friends and together the women worked hard to produce piles of sandwiches for the poor people who got bombed out of their homes. Sabine was glad when she was finally able to go to bed and rest. Hours later she heard Guenter coming back in the middle of the night. She heard new voices talking quietly downstairs. When she got up the next morning, she found a whole family, spread around sleeping in the living room. Erna was already up and told Sabine that this was one of the bombed-out families and that they would stay with them for now. Everybody had to move together.

Just a couple of days later, Sabine witnessed some new action in the neighbourhood. The German army was putting a trailer onto the large grass area near the house. Next, she noticed trucks driving up with soldiers and four huge pipe barrels. She went into the shop to ask her boss what it was all about. He took a look and came back into the store with worry lines on his forehead. "Those things are canons to shoot airplanes down. They are going to try to shoot the Jabos down from the meadow close to our house. This is very dangerous! I wonder if the Americans won't spot them first and shoot our soldiers down instead. They are sure putting themselves on display!"

It didn't take long and the neighbourhood heard the loud, horrible, howl of the sirens turned on by the administration of the village. Everybody ran into their basements. The people from Guenter and Erna's family, together with everybody else, gathered in the basement. Little Helmut and Hans Werner noticed that two basement windows looked directly towards the meadow on which the cannons were. "I can see the cannons and the soldiers in front of them!" little Helmut shouted to his Dad. Everybody now gathered in front of those windows. It didn't take long and they heard the sounds of the approaching Jabos. The soldiers in front of those canons noticed them as well. The Jabos came closer and closer. The group in the basement stopped breathing. At the same moment all the soldiers ran for their lives in all directions. The Jabos came again from all four cardinal points, two at a time, flying very low, dropping their bombs that shattered the cannons to pieces. The scrap metal flew like projectiles into the air in every direction. It was an amazing show for those little boys, but the adults new that the end of the story wouldn't be so good.

The Jabos had completed their mission! Sabine could hear them getting farther away. "One is coming out of the bush!" Hans Werner told everybody. The group watched one soldier coming slowly out of his hiding place, looking carefully to the sky in all directions, making sure the attack was over. He must have said something to the rest of the soldiers, because a second one appeared. Both of them looked up at the sky and down onto the meadow and the bushes.

"There, there is one on the grass!" Guenter exclaimed. Everybody saw it now; a soldier was lying on the grass. The two other soldiers went to the one on the grass, talking to him and trying to help him up, but he stayed on the ground. "He must be wounded!" Erna said in a sad voice. They watched one soldier talking into a walkie-talkie. "He will call for help!" Erna said again. The soldiers walked around more and started to help up another soldier. Erna took the boys away from the window. This soldier was missing his left arm.

"This is awful!" Sabine thoug This wasn't the last injured soldier that was found. Another one was lying on the ground, close to the bushes. The two soldiers helped him onto his feet and he stood up. Turning around, he faced the windows where the group was watching the scene.

Everybody in the group gasped. His face, his arm, and part of his chest, were caked with metal splinters from the canons and shell casings. That poor soldier took a lot of those pieces in his body. He was in great pain and bleeding hard. Finally, the Red Cross arrived. The meadow close to the house turned into a hospital. One soldier was carried into the ambulance right away and driven with loud sirens to the hospital in Luedenscheid. The one with the missing arm got into the next ambulance. The rest of the wounded were taken care of on the field.

A couple of days later, Guenter heard that the first soldier taken by the ambulance didn't make it to the hospital. He had died on the way. Everybody agreed, even the little boys, that this was a bad story!

Sabine had her day off and was sitting in the train going to Luedenscheid. She was planning to spend the day with her parents and play with her little sisters. She was very attached to her little sisters, who thought of her as their second mother. Sabine looked forward to being at home. After all the excitement, home would be a good place to be.

The train was on time, climbing up the hill with a loud puff, puff. The hill up to Luedenscheid was very steep, the engine had to work hard. Sabine was sitting right beside the window and was able to see the "Sichter" tunnel coming up. "Good news!" she thought. Her hometown was coming closer and closer.

A loud howl pulled Sabine and the other passengers out of their happy thoughts. "Jabos" Sabine said out loud, and all the other passengers agreed. Her word struck their hearts! Their faces went white. Everybody was looking around as if there would be a place to hide in the train.

No such luck! The conductor in the engine had heard the terrible sound as well. His face was just as white, but he had to man up. "Put more coal on!" he yelled to his helper. The engine made louder puffs, climbing up the hill. All the passengers were now standing at the windows, watching the sky. "Faster, faster!" they screamed, "Please go faster!" The conductor was now sweating, trying every trick in the book he knew to get the train to go as fast as possible, to hide in the "Sichter" tunnel.

It got dark. They had entered the tunnel.

"That was close!" Sabine thought. She was shaking. One of the train employees came into the wagon and announced, "Please stay seated, we will keep going to Luedenscheid as soon as we are sure that the Jabos are gone. Please remain calm!"

"Not with me!" Sabine thought. This was too close for comfort! She made her way to the exit door, opened it, and looked at the walls of the tunnel. It was dark in the tunnel, but the end of it was clearly in sight and gave her enough light to see her footing. She jumped out of the train and ran towards the light at the end of the tunnel. The people in the train followed her with their eyes, but nobody joined her. They trusted the man telling them to stay calm. Sabine reached the end of the tunnel and peeked out to scan the sky for airplanes. All clear!

Sabine stepped out and looked around for the trail to reach her hometown. She knew this trail very well from her past hikes with her father and all the other times she had to walk home instead of taking the train. It was a steep climb up to the city. After a while she heard the train coming from below. She had a good view from where she was walking and looked at it. With horror she heard the awful howl of the Jabos again. There was no hiding place for the train now! It was in plain sight!

The train was an easy target! The Jabos dropped their deadly cargo again and again. Sabine watched in agony. Her stomach was in knots. She walked slowly up the hill towards Luedenscheid. "Did the Americans believe there were munitions on the train? How many people just died?" She thought.

The next day, the newspapers talked about the wounded and dead. "On the 16th of February 1945 we lost 24 people to an air attack by the Americans-----" Sabine fell on her knees and thanked God for his great protective hand on her life. She also brought the wounded and the families of the deceased before the Lord.

Going to war! Thomas' heart was filled with excitement and fear. "Is it possible to have both feelings in your heart?" he wondered. His train arrived at the train station in Hirschberg. The station was full of young men his age. When Thomas jumped off the train, he was engulfed in an atmosphere that was filled with excitement and laughter. Some boys were boasting to each other about their experience with the ladies or with stories from the work camps. Thomas listened to all the chatter around him.

Just behind him stood another boy who was watching the whole scene just like Thomas. His hair was blond, his eyes bright blue, a true German look. He reached his hand out to Thomas. "My name is Harri."

Thomas took his hand, shaking it, and said, "I am Thomas. I am supposed to go to Glatz to join the 55th tank brigade." Harri's eyes lit up.

"Me too, let's go together!" They entered the train to Glatz together and were on their way to war. The train rolled through a lot of familiar places for Thomas. The first stop was in Duerrkunzendorf, the town where Thomas did his training to fly a glider. All the good memories came up and Harri was a good listener to all the glider-stories. It took a long time until the train arrived in Glatz.

The commander, waiting at the station, ordered the men to assemble and march to their first camp. Harri and Thomas were happy to hear that this camp had had no action. It was still a training camp, until the troops would be needed. That could be any day from now. The accommodation was of course a stable again, filled with hay, the old story!

Everybody assembled in front of officer Bernhard. "What are your qualifications? He asked the men. "Is there anybody here who knows morse code?" Thomas put his hand up and was asked to come to the front. Officer Bernard led him to a barrack, filled with tables and chairs where soldiers were working. There was a constant beep, beep, beep, all over the place. "Let's see what you are able to do!" officer Bernhard said. Thomas didn't feel so sure about his abilities anymore. He hoped he wouldn't disappoint the army. Thomas had to take his place in front of one telegraph station where a soldier told him the message he had to send. A second message followed, then a third, until the soldier gave his approval, and Thomas became a telegraph operator.

Thomas was relieved! To sit in the barracks and do the telegraphing was so much better than all the other exercises the rest of the troops had to do. But the messages out of this barracks were not for training, they were for real. Thomas was already part of the war! The Russians were coming closer, so communication would be key. Thomas worked hard and did a great job. He worked his way up to 120 letters a minute and was proud of it. On some days he had to join Harri and the rest of the troop in their field training, in order to be ready to fight the enemy, if he had to. It was winter, not the best weather to be outside marching through snow. The winter months passed without incident, and Thomas was glad he had spent most of the time inside.

The door of the barrack flew open and officer Bernhard came charging into the room. "Everybody get up, pack your gear and get into the trucks! We have to join the army to fight the Russians!" It was April, and time now for Thomas and his fellow soldiers to actively fight in the war. He and the others had to fasten the telegraphs and other equipment onto the trucks, but most of the telegraphs were fastened onto backpacks. Thomas concluded that his unit would be infantry instead of part of a tank group. The trucks were filled with equipment. The soldiers had to squeeze in to find a place. Harri and Thomas were sitting together right at the back of the truck bed. They had a great view of the landscape while they were driving.

"Oh no!" Thomas got a shock. "We are driving to my home town! Are the Russians already so close?" Luckily, they just passed by and kept driving. People were already working in the fields. Thomas would have loved to jump off the truck and just run home. He was sure that Harri felt the same way. Any hard work in the fields would be better now than to join the war!

Thomas' town fell back into the distance, and it became clear that their goal would be a place close to Berlin, or the German capital itself. Thomas and Harri wondered, "If the Russians were in the capital, that would mean the war was over… Germany had lost the war!"

THE FRONT

The convoy of trucks that Thomas was in came to a stop. Officer Bernhard commanded, "Everybody, get off!" The boxes with the munitions have to be taken off the truck. Get going!" He looked at Harri, Thomas, and the young officer Gerd. "Harri, Thomas, and Officer Gerd, you stay with the crates and wait for the truck that will pick them up. After that, you will be under the command of officer Schlagmeier! Heil Hitler!" Those were the last words Thomas heard from officer Bernhard. Harri and Thomas were sad to leave his troop. Officer Bernhard was a good man.

The wooden crates, filled with munitions were standing on the ground right in front of the trio as the rest of the troops left in the trucks. Officer Gerd, a very young man, not much older than Thomas and Harri, said, "Lets put the machine gun up onto the tripod! That will be our defence against the Russians!" All three worked to connect the machine gun to the top of the tripod. This was the most accurate sure-fire way to take out a small airplane in the sky. The Russian army had a light airplane, that the Germans called "Sergeant at work". It was filled with very tiny bombs and flew regularly over the German positions every evening, to spy on them. You could set your clock to it! After they were finished with the tripod, Officer Gerd said, "It could take a while until the truck arrives. Why don't we all take a break and try to get some sleep! You never know when you will be able to get a break!"

Harri and Thomas decided that this officer Gerd was a very wise guy. Sleep was always good, even in the middle of the day. Officer Gerd built himself a small cave, made out of wooden crates and put himself down onto the ground for a restful nap. Harri and Thomas put their tarps onto the ground and followed the officer's advice. It didn't take long before everybody was snoring peacefully.

"What is this supposed to be?" The loud, angry voice of officer Schlagmeier rang in their ears and woke them up. Harri and Thomas had a hard time focusing their eyes on this angry man. The sun was shining right into their eyes and it was hard for them to open them up.

Officer Gerd came from behind. "I am sorry, but we were told to wait here for the truck to pick up the boxes and join up with you, officer Schlagmeier, Heil Hitler!"

Officer Schlagmeier, who was a small man with a mighty middle section, opened his mouth again. "Heil Hitler to you too, but your order is wrong. You have to put the crates up on the hill by the forest, close to the train tracks. The boxes will be picked up there!"

Officer Gerd waved to Thomas and Harri. "Lets carry the boxes up the bank, over the road, to the edge of the forest."

Officer Schlagmeier said, "You'd better be fast! The boxes were supposed to be there already a while ago!" He was standing and watching with his feet apart, his hands holding on to the buckle of his belt which encircled his enormous belly. His loud, barking voice made up for his short stature.

Officer Gerd, Harri, and Thomas, worked hard to lift and carry all the crates up the bank and across the road to the forest. Officer Schlagmeier watched as they sweated. Thomas and Harri were just about to lift the last two boxes when they heard a brum, brum, brum! Officer Gerd said, "I wonder if that is the truck?" Around the corner came a truck with a familiar face sitting at the wheel. Rudi, the Austrian who Thomas had driven with before, was the driver.

Rudi brought his truck to a stop and jumped out of the vehicle. "Hey buddies, where are all the crates I am supposed to pick up? Are there only two?" Thomas noticed the ears of officer Schlagmeier getting red.

Officer Gerd said, "The boxes are up there by the forest, but we will bring them down here for you!" Thomas, Harry and officer Gerd had to start their labour again, with officer Schlagmeier watching them like before, still having red ears. Thomas thought "At least he feels a little bit sorry." The crates found their rightful place on the back of Rudi's truck. Officer Schlagmeier was the lucky one to sit up front with Rudi. Thomas and the others joined the crates at the back. The truck started and they were on their way. It was time for another nap, Thomas thought, you just never know!

It was a long ride until they arrived at Lausitz in the Brandenburg area. Lausitz was a 'prairie-like' county that was very flat, with lots of fields. The sun had gone down by the time they arrived. The truck stopped at a barn, where their beds would be in the hay. Thomas had gotten used to it and wondered if this might be his last night in the hay.

Lausitz was very close to the front. Because of the danger, Thomas and Harri had to stand guard for the first half of the night, Officer Gerd would do the rest of the night. Thomas and Harri stood outside the barn looking up into the night sky. The sky was clear and the air crisp. Thomas was able to make out the stars and explained them to Harri. Thomas knew the names of them and in which direction they stood. He was able to find his way without a compass. "See?" he said, "That is the Northern Star!" Whoosh---- a huge shadow passed over the two. Thomas and Harri fell flat on their belly and forgot to breathe for a moment. Thomas looked at Harri.

"That was a plane!"

"I didn't hear a motor!" Harri said, "That is odd! Let's wake up the officers!" Thomas and Harri went into the barn.

"An airplane without motor noise, just flew over us and landed in the field not far from us!" Thomas loudly announced.

Officer Schlagmeier managed to sit up remarkably quickly, despite his full figure, and then he barked, "We'll split up into two teams, and the team that finds the plane first, will tell the others. Be careful! Have your rifle ready and stay low so they don't see you." Harri and Thomas went first and searched the field for the plane. It didn't take long before they stood in front of a small German airplane, the JU52. Thomas knew this kind of plane. They ran and found the officers to report back their findings. "There wasn't any pilot around." Thomas told them.

Officer Schlagmeier said, "Spread out and look for the pilot, he must be somewhere nearby. Thomas and Harri walked around until they found a small village. Right in front of them was the pilot with his co-pilot. They were just trying to break into a farmer's house.

"Hey," Harri yelled, "we are friendly, wait up!" The pilots turned around and looked at them in relief.

"Happy to see you!" one said, "We were spying out the Russian position when we ran out of fuel. I turned back towards our line, right away, but I wasn't sure that we had made it far enough. I am so glad we made it!" Officer Schlagmeier and officer Gerd must have heard them speaking because shortly thereafter, they showed up. The officers took over the conversation and officer Schlagmeier, whose troops were stationed nearby knew of a tank division in the area that was able to help out with fuel. The pilots gave their thanks' and everybody went their way.

Officer Schlagmeier released Rudi and the truck with the munitions after the sun rose in the morning and marched together with Thomas, Harri, and Officer Gerd, to his waiting troops. This troop was made up of a small group of young men that could have not been older than Harri and Thomas. All of them had to climb onto a truck that would bring them closer to the enemy line. It was a long drive over lots of fields and rugged terrain. The night ended in another barn. Thomas was thankful for that!

Boom, boom, boom! Everybody woke up. Harri yelled "cannons!" Everybody agreed. The Russians were very close. Thomas' stomach felt as if there was a solid rock in it. "This is serious!" he thought, "The Russians are close! We will see action!"

Breakfast tasted like cardboard. Nobody was really hungry. It didn't matter to officer Schlagmeier if the enemy was near or not, he gathered his troops for the daily roll-call. He placed himself right in front of the soldiers, who were standing in a straight line, facing him. He barked "Breast out, belly in, shoulders back! After, everybody was standing to the officer's satisfaction. Officer Schlagmeier walked slowly along the line of soldiers. He inspected them from top to bottom. A German soldier's hair had to be short, he had to be shaven, the uniform had to be clean and the boots shiny. The German soldier had to be the best-looking one of the whole war. They were Adolf Hitler's pride. Hitler fought in the First World War himself and was a good soldier. Hitler took pride in that fact.

The sound of the cannons was close by and Officer Schlagmeier determined the bellowing sounds were coming from the North East. Thomas, together with officer Gerd were ordered to take a seat in a Volkswagen, driven by another soldier. Officer Gerd had his binoculars and sat in the front seat next to the driver. Thomas' job was to feed the car's little burner with wood. The Volkswagen was Hitler's invention. It was the 'Car of the People'. Most of them had a gas burner, but this one was fuelled with wood. Thomas knew what to do!

The car ripped through a forest and over fields, while officer Gerd looked through his binoculars to spot the enemy line. The officer told the driver to drive up a steep bank so he would be able to get a better view. The driver took aim at the little but steep hill, trying to get enough speed, but couldn't make it up the hill, so he quickly threw down the hand brake. A Volkswagen fueled with a wood burner had its limits. The officer and Thomas helped push the car up to the crest. A wonderful meadow with the first spring flowers in bloom lay before them. Thomas was sweating from his efforts to push the car, but drank in the beautiful soul soothing view. Thomas wasn't sure if officer Gerd had spotted any Russians, but the officer told the driver to return to the troop. When they got back, he talked to officer Schlagmeier who called the troops together; "Get ready, pack your things, we are going to leave first thing in the morning!"

Every soldier had two things to pack. One was their backpack with their personal belongings, maybe fresh underwear, a book, a photo of loved ones, or even a Bible. The other item was a leather strap in a 'Y' shape. The single strap went down the back, the other Y-lines went over the breast. It held the holster that was filled with the bullets for their rifles. Grenades were placed on the lower part of the strap. A tarp to sleep on was rolled over the shoulder and a bag with emergency food and a water bottle hung off the backside of the strap. The 98K rifle was slung over the other shoulder. The German army was proud of their 'Made in Germany' Karabiner 98K. This weapon was produced by the German company 'Mauser' who made 14 million of them. It was a 57mm bolt action rifle, reputedly capable of killing a person 500 meters away. All of the troop's equipment was loaded onto a truck for the next morning.

The group had another peaceful night with the far away sounds of the cannons as their lullaby. The morning started again with the normal drill, with officer Schlagmeier inspecting his troops. After that, it was time to climb up onto the truck bed and head off to the front. Thomas was deep in his thoughts. He wondered how much a soldier would be worth in the eyes of Hitler. He concluded that he was just a number, but would he be a number with a plus sign in front, or a number with a minus sign in front after the war was over? Did Adolf Hitler ever think about the pain a mother was going through, when her son died in the war?

Thomas looked at Harri and the rest of the group. All of them were also deep in thought. Some of them were looking at a photo of their girl-friend and having a quiet talk with her. Thomas had a photo of Erika, but he didn't take it out of his pocket. "She wasn't that close to his heart!" he thought. He surprised himself with that. Erika was very nice, but that was it. He wondered about his Dad, who was fighting on the front right now. "Was he still alive?"

The sounds of the cannons got louder every kilometer the truck drove. In fact, they were really loud now. The truck came to a stop right beside a wooded area. Officer Schlagmeier barked, "Get out and run as fast as you can into the forest!" One after the other, the boys ran into the woods. The trees would provide shelter, like a safety canopy.

The Russian troops spotted the new German contingent right away and sent them a hail storm of grenades. Everybody dove down into the dirt. The procedure in a case like this was to stay glued to the ground until you knew that the enemy had moved on. Thomas pressed himself to the ground with his face sideways. He didn't move at all, thinking of the moment when his little brother Ludwig, stood with an axe in front of him. Not everybody had the nerves to remain still. Some of the soldiers, jumped up and down like rabbits. The grenades exploded on impact at the tree tops, but the shrapnel shot to the ground. The moving soldiers made themselves too much of a target and were hit everywhere on their body. Thomas was left unharmed on the ground when the attack came to an end.

Officer Schlagmeier got up from his spot. "Everybody get up on your hands and knees, we move deeper into the woods!" Thomas looked around for Harri. He was alright! The troops crawled deeper into the forest. A boy beside Thomas had been hit with shells in his face. He was one of the jumpers. His face was bleeding, he was in shock, and was hardly able to move. Thomas grabbed him by the arm and pulled him deeper into the trees. One piece of metal shrapnel was still imbedded in the boy's upper lip. He couldn't speak.

"I hope there will be a medic in the woods that can help you." Thomas said, "You will be fine! But next time, no jumping around! Just stay on the ground!" The wounded soldier started to cry. Thomas guessed that he probably just wanted to go home. He couldn't blame him.

Deeper in the woods officer Schlagmeier got up to stand in front of his troop. "This was your baptismal with the enemy fire! I am proud of some of you. I am angry at others. Who told you to jump up and expose yourself to the fire? Next time you better stay on the ground!" Two men in the group had training as medics and took care of the wounded. There would be a lot of scars on faces, arms and legs.

Officer Gerd came to Thomas, who was lying on the ground, drinking from his water bottle. "Thomas, you have to go back to the edge of the forest to the spot where we entered at the start. Lay down there so the Russians won't see you, and watch what is going on. If you see the Russians starting an attack on us, come back right away and give your report."

Thomas acknowledged the order and went on his way, scrambling, bending down at the edge of the woods. He was approximately 200 meters away from his unit. He made himself comfortable on his belly under some bushes beside a tree and waited for things to happen. One hour passed and nothing happened. Thomas made his first move. He carefully reached with his left hand towards his water bottle and started drinking.

"Oh" he heard a noise. He listened carefully and concluded that this was the sound of a tank. He slowly closed his bottle and put it back to his side. Lying motionless, he waited. The tank came closer. He was able to see it! The tank had a German emblem on it. Was it German, filled with German soldiers? "Stop!" he thought. "The tank could have been taken away from the Germans by Russian soldiers, and now they were searching the area for the enemy. "Stay down!" he told himself. The opening at the top of the tank popped up and a soldier with binoculars looked out into his direction. He was Russian! Thomas didn't move a muscle. The soldier disappeared into the tank again and the top closed down. "Should I report this?" he wondered, "But this isn't an attack, so I'd better stay put."

Another noise came from above and was getting louder. It sounded like a coffee mill, when the handle is turned to grind the coffee beans. Thomas knew the grinding noise well. It was the UVD, the small Russian airplane used to find the position of the enemy and bomb them. The plane came right towards Thomas in a funny way! It was swerving from left to the right, leaning sideways. "Oh, this guy had too much vodka," Thomas thought. The airplane opened up its underbelly, and the small bombs came crashing down, exploding as they hit the ground. Thomas squeezed himself tight to the trunk of the tree and remained still, motionless. All the bombs fell at least thirty meters away from Thomas, onto the field. After the plane had dropped its cargo, the UVD turned around and flew back in the direction where it had come from. Thomas took a deep breath! "That soldier in the tank must have seen me! Was my helmet shining? What gave me away? Lucky me that the pilot had had his vodka!"

Thomas thought, "Should I report this? No, it wasn't a real attack on our troops, I'd better wait. He had just finished the thought when out of nowhere a group of German soldiers entered his part of the woods. Nobody detected Thomas, but he decided to report to the commander of this group. He got up and explained to the young officer, "Heil Hitler! I am Thomas from officer Schlagmeier's troop. We came under fire and went into hiding deeper in the woods. They sent me to the edge of the woods in order to watch if we were going to be attacked! So far I didn't see any approaching enemy troops." The commander understood and was going to say something, but… crack, crack, bumm, bumm, the grenades came flying again. Everybody was on their belly. The grenade shrapnel came hailing down on them like bullets, as sharp as broken glass. Thomas lay motionless again. He didn't move a muscle.

The scene around him was just as bad as it was the first time with his original group. A chorus of moaning told him a lot of soldiers had been hit. "Why can't they keep their cool and stay put?" he thought. Everyone lay still for a long while. The attack was over, the enemy seemed to have moved on. The soldiers around him gathered themselves, taking a drink from their water bottles. Thomas spoke to one of them who was also just 17 years old, the same as Thomas. He was going to ask more questions when they spotted a Russian group of soldiers marching in their direction.

Thomas jumped to his feet, but kept his upper body bent down as low as he could. "Now is the time to make my report!" he decided. "My group is under attack!" He made his way, as fast as he could towards the place where his group was waiting. He reached the spot in a very short time and stopped in his tracks. His company was gone! Fear gripped his heart. If a German would see him all alone running through the forest, he would believe that he was a deserter. The punishment was death. On the other hand, if a Russian soldier would detect him, he would be shot just as well. He was in a bad situation.

Thomas kept running, looking around. He had to find his troops! He found them not too far away from where he left them before. Officer Schlagmeier was shocked to see him. "Thomas, we thought you would be dead by now! I didn't think that you would come back to us! We heard the bombs and the grenades. We thought for sure you were one of the victims! Good to see you!" Thomas didn't expect a good word from Officer Schlagmeier. He was very proud of it. He gave his report and settled down with the others. The Russian troops had passed them, and were now further away.

"Good to see you!" Harri said, "We thought you were a goner! Good to see you man!" Everybody reached for their food ration of the day and settled down for the night. The tarp was partly the bed sheet and the other half the blanket. The trees protected them from the cold air of the night. All the boys reflected on their first day of battle. Thomas could see a bit of the sky. "God are you there? Are you really there? Are you watching us?"

It was a funny thing, but the night was peaceful, no shooting, no attack. "This doesn't feel right!" Thomas thought, "It seems like they know where we are, knowing that we are in their hands. Are we in their hands? Are we surrounded? I would love to have the view from an airplane to see the area?" He fell asleep.

Once again, Guenter, Erna, and Sabine, were sitting around the radio, listening to the BBC. The newscaster said "One can only imagine. Adolf Hitler has sent his young German boys, just 17 years old into possibly the last battle of the war. It looks very grim for those young boys! Close to Berlin in the wooded area of Spremberg, the German army is surrounded by the Russian troops, to finish off those young soldiers. The German army is stuck in this inferno of grenades, machine guns and bombs. Will anyone survive?" Guenter and Erna had two boys themselves. They felt the same worry that all parents had for their sons, so their hearts were also hurting for those families. Sabine was just one year under the age of all those young soldiers. She was shocked to hear that such young boys were getting killed in the war. A war which seemed to be pointless now! A war which was lost!

The sun was still up and Erna asked Sabine to run to the next farm and get milk for breakfast for the next day. "No problem! I will be fast!" Sabine replied. She got the pitcher with the lid and was on her way. The air was still warm and she even spotted a butterfly. She took her time to enjoy the walk. The farmer filled up the pitcher with milk. On her way back she was deep in her thoughts, praying for those young soldiers in the woods by Spremberg. Sabine walked home slowly. She looked up and was surprised that the sun had gone down and darkness was already spreading over the countryside.

The bushes, framing in the path, looked like dark monsters. "I'd better speed up!" She thought, and picked up her pace. "What is that? That can't be!" Sabine heard the sound of clopping hooves of horses, but not only the horses, she heard voices of men as well. They got louder. She heard the men speaking in English. It was an American troop, riding horseback through her area. Holding her milk pitcher steady, she bent down in the bushes beside the trail. She knelt down, holding her breath. "What would a group of American soldiers do to a young girl walking around at night?" She didn't want to find out!

The voices got louder, the horses came closer. One of the horses looked down at Sabine as it passed by. Sabine's heart was beating right into her throat. The American troops passed Sabine. "Wow! That was close!" Sabine took a deep breath. After the soldiers had gone a good distance away from her, she walked home as fast as she could.

"Sabine, we were worried! What took you so long?" Erna was standing at the doorway her face ashen. Sabine told her what happened. She was so happy to have made it. Erna told her, "We just heard that the Americans made it over the Rhein, into our area. Some are on horseback and will stay with us from now on! We have to be careful now! I'll make a warm cup of milk for everybody so we'll have a better night's rest!" Sabine was thankful for the warm milk. She was still shaken up. Her prayers were serious that night. She couldn't get those young German soldiers at Spremberg out of her mind.

The next day Sabine was singing her folksongs while organizing things in the store. She was wondering how things would be in the future with the Americans around. The door opened and her sister Emma came into the store. "What are you doing here? Did something happen at home? Did you walk all the way here?" Sabine asked.

Emma, taking a deep breath, replied, "Hi, yes I walked all the way from Luedenscheid. After your experience with that blown up train, I will not enter a train anymore, even though I am totally exhausted from the walk. Nothing happened at home, but the Americans are in our area now! Mom and Dad are getting worried, and so am I. We all want you to come home! Dad says the whole family should be together at a time like this."

"Hm, I'll have to tell my boss and pack my things. Come with me!"

Erna got very sad when she heard that Sabine had to go back to her parents. "You are such a great help for our whole family and the store, we are very sad to see you go, But I am a mother myself! I fully understand your parents. Let's have dinner together and after you've packed your things, the two of you can go home." Helmut was especially sad to see Sabine go. He had gotten used to the bedtime stories Sabine read to him every night. From now on he would be sleeping all alone in his room. Too bad! It was a sad meal that the whole family had together and a tearful farewell at the doorway when Sabine and Emma left.

Sabine didn't have too much to carry. Everything she owned fit into a bag as big as a pillow case. She slung it over her shoulder and the two walked up the hill towards Luedenscheid. They decided against the shortcut through the forest. Lately the forest was full of prisoners of war, who had escaped and were trying to stay alive by stealing from German people. Emma and Sabine followed the road home. "Come on Emma! How can you walk so slow?"

Emma replied, "How can you walk so fast? You carry all your stuff! I am exhausted!" Saying this, Emma sat down on a tree stump. "My heel on my left foot hurts!" Sabine came close to Emma to take a look at her heel.

"You got a mighty blister on your heel! How can we fix that?"

Emma looked very dismayed. "I don't have any bandages with me. I don't know what to do?"

"Do you have your handkerchief?" Sabine asked.

Emma looked at Sabine with big eyes, "This is my heel, not my nose. What can you do with my handkerchief?"

"Tear a small piece of it off and put it under your stockings onto the blister. Your stockings and shoe will keep the piece of fabric from moving, and with that you'll have your bandage!" Emma did as Sabine told her and was able to keep walking. The two girls made it up the hill all the way to Luedenscheid.

"Sabine!" both little girls exclaimed at the moment Sabine and Emma entered the apartment. Sabine embraced both girls at the same time. Little Gerdi ran as fast as she could into their bedroom to retrieve her injured doll. "Arm broken!" she said with a sad voice to Sabine.

"I will give her a real bandage tomorrow!" Sabine promised the little one. It was good to be home again! Otti and Heini were very glad to see their older daughters. The family was together, except for Emil. He was still in France, being kept as a prisoner of war.

SURROUNDED

Officer Schlagmeier repeatedly insisted, "We have to get through, we have to reach the main battle line!" But no matter where they went, there never was a battle line. The Russians waited right at the edge of the woods, watching whether any German would be foolish enough to stick his head out. "They were surrounded!" This was clear to Thomas and the whole group. How large the Russian encirclement was, nobody knew. The Russians had positioned their tanks and infantry around the area and pummeled the German soldiers with their bombs and grenades, together with the machine gun fire from their airplanes. It was hell with no end.

Officer Schlagmeier was standing up, holding on to his belt with both hands. Lately he was needing to fasten his belt tighter. "Everybody get ready, we are getting out of here!" The mood of the troops went up a notch. They gathered their backpacks and rifles and under the cover of darkness, they started their escape. Heads down, they came out of the woods, running to a small nearby village. Thomas got scared when some of the equipment made noises, but the whole group reached a farmer's house without any enemy fire. Harri said to Thomas, "We did it! They didn't see us!"

"I am not so sure about that!" Thomas replied, "It could be a miracle, or the Russians don't care because they have us in their hands anyway."

Officer Schlagmeier decided that this village was a safe place and told them to get a good night's rest in a barn.

"Do not light a match for your cigarettes! That would give us away!" he told them. The barn was pitch black. The soldiers had to feel their way around the barn to find a place to sleep. Thomas and Harri stayed close together and found a stall, which might have been used for a horse. The two put down their tarps and laid down for the night. After a lot of bumping into each other or standing on each others feet, finally, everybody settled down and a peaceful, restful night fell on the troops.

The next morning, with the morning sun shining through the cracks, the soldiers were well rested and much happier than in the last few days. Laughter filled the place when soldier Karl stood up and discovered to his dismay that his backside had been lying in cow dung all night. He didn't bother to put down his tarp because it was a wooden floor. He had to laugh as well. "This is war!" he told the other boys. Officer Schlagmeier called for his daily inspection, but he was in a good mood.

"Everybody, go into the farmer's house and look for anything you can find to drink or eat. The house is yours! Just be quiet!" He announced. This was great news. The soldiers crept down over the yard into the empty farmer's house. The boys looked all over the house, the kitchen, the cellar, everywhere, but couldn't find anything! It was clear to them that they were not the first group to look for food in this house.

Thomas was standing in the kitchen, his stomach growling, looking around when he got an idea. "Give me a stool, please!" he said to Harri, who was standing beside the kitchen table. Thomas put the stool right in front of the kitchen cupboards. He climbed on top of the stool, to get a good view of the top of the cupboards. He spotted what he was hoping for. Right at the back of the cupboards, pushed against the wall, was a pottery vessel. Would he be lucky? He wondered. He pulled the vessel towards him and opened it up. His eyes filled with tears. The lady of the house was hiding her Christmas baking, the same way that Thomas' mother did every year. It was supposed to be out of reach of the little ones. The pot was filled with the good German Spekulatius cookies.

His hands were shaking in excitement! Thomas got the cookies down and put them on the table. He took two cookies out of the pot and told his buddies to share the rest. Thomas walked right up to officer Schlagmeier and gave him one of his cookies. The eyes of officer Schlagmeier filled with tears. "I sure appreciate this!" he said. Other soldiers found some water in the well outside and everybody filled up their water bottles. Thomas enjoyed this wonderful breakfast of a real Spekulatius cookie and fresh water. The cookie tasted just like the one from his mom.

Everybody got scared when they heard the sound of a motorbike. A German messenger on a motorbike arrived out of nowhere. Officer Schlagmeier had a talk with the messenger and walked up to Thomas. "Thomas, I have a special mission for you! You have to ride with this driver to deliver my message to the other troops. Be careful, keep your head down! Heil Hitler!" He handed Thomas a piece of paper.

Thomas took his place behind the driver on the bike. "Hold on tight!" the driver told him. Thomas put his arms around the middle of the driver and did just that. The bike was flying over the fields. The bumpy uneven terrain caused the two to repeatedly fly up from their seats. Both men made themselves as flat as they could on the bike. It was a wild ride! After a long time, they reached the other group of German soldiers.

Looking at this troop, Thomas got a shock. These soldiers looked just as young as he was, and the officers leading them didn't look much older. "How much experience do these officers have?" he wondered. He retrieved the piece of paper out of his breast pocket and gave it to one of the officers. Not long after, he received a message back to him to give to Officer Schlagmeier. The ride back was just as wild, but they arrived safely. He handed the new message to Officer Schlagmeier, who was eagerly waiting, and read it right away.

Putting himself in front of the troops, Officer Schlagmeier barked, "We are going back into the forest! Be fast and stay low!" The soldiers looked at each other. What else was new, they wondered. The whole troop made it safely back into the woods and settled down. The day was quiet, except for a visit by a German supply truck. The back of the truck was full with pots of soup. They were driving around to feed the German army.

Officer Schlagmeier stood beside the truck and said, "I had serious concerns you wouldn't be able to call me "little fat guy" anymore after the last meager days. You'd better fill your stomachs, you never know when the next supply will reach us." The soup smelled wonderful! It was pea soup. Everybody ate as much as they could. It wasn't the same as his Mom would have made it, but to Thomas, it tasted like heaven. The only problem was the water supply. The bottles of the soldiers were now empty, and there was no creek or any other water to be found in the woods. The supply truck didn't provide any water either. The only drink they had for the German soldiers was a small bottle of schnapps they gave to each soldier. After the supply truck left, the group settled down for the night. A lot of soldiers took to their schnapps during the night. Thomas allowed himself only one drop at a time when his tongue was very dry, so that his tongue wouldn't stick to the top of his mouth. The battle sounds not far away kept Thomas up for most of the night.

The next morning greeted a sorry bunch of soldiers with splitting headaches and no water whatsoever to help them, but officer Schlagmeier had his orders. "We have to break through the Russian lines! We are pinned down in these woods. We have to get out of here! Spremberg is still a free city. We have to march to Spremberg! Be hopeful we will make it!"

Thomas had heard about the city of Spremberg from the troops he had delivered the message to. He said to Harri, "Spremberg is under fire! We are marching right into enemy fire!" Harri's eyes looked worried. But the troops marched on!

It was amazing! They reached Spremberg unharmed. At the first house, they stopped and looked for water. Yeah! The well in the yard was full of water. Wow! The whole group gathered around the well, filled up their bottles, and had their drink. One said, "Hopefully this will ease the headache. No more schnapps for a while!" In the shade of the house, they had a short break to fill up and recover.

Spremberg was under attack. The grenades came flying from all directions as the troop move on. Officer Schlagmeier said, "Don't shoot! We don't want to announce ourselves to the enemy. Just keep close to the walls of the houses. We have to go right through Spremberg in order to reach our troops on the other side. One after the other, Thomas and his buddies hugged the walls of the houses as they made their way through Spremberg. Keeping close together, the group reached the other side of town where the German trenches were.

"Down into the trenches!" came the command from Officer Schlagmeier. The whole group made it safely into the trenches, sitting on dirt, but safe for now. Here they hunkered down, awaiting the end of the day, when they would be safe under the darkness of the night. Like every evening before, the Russians sent their light airplane to spy out the area. That was OK! Everybody put their heads down, so the pilot wouldn't spot them. The plane was flying right over them, turned around and flew right over them again. This was too much for some of the boys. They lost their nerves and without any command shot at the plane. The gun fire from the ground was no problem for the plane, but now they had told the pilot, "We are here!" Thomas couldn't believe it!

Officer Schlagmeier angrily barked out, "Thank you very much! Out of the trenches, we have to march! The group marched through most of the night until they reached another village. It became obvious that the area the Russians had them encircled in was much larger than they first thought. They hadn't broken out of it at all. The Russians were still all around them. They walked up to a house and the men got permission from the officer to look for food and water. They got lucky. One of them found potatoes and another one found a pot of lard. This was gold! They were allowed to make a small fire and roasted the potatoes right over the fire. The lard was the topping. It was delicious! The well was full of water. Everybody had a full stomach and was ready to hit the sack. But not this time!

"We have to keep going, tired or not! We will be discovered in this village in daylight. We have to find a better place!" Officer Schlagmeier told the group. Thomas and the rest of the exhausted soldiers walked through the night until Officer Schlagmeier was comfortable with one line of trenches they could hide in.

The rest of the night was quiet, but at dawn, the sunlight gave away their position to the Russians, who approached from the bottom of the hill. The Russians started their attack, firing the first shots. The Germans had an advantage, though, because the trenches were located on the ridge of the hill. The Russian troops were exposed to them as they came up. A German officer, belonging to another group that was also in the trenches, walked back and forth on top of the ridge, overseeing the whole battle. "Why doesn't he get shot?" Thomas wondered. The German soldiers had easy game shooting down the poor Russian soldiers who were walking right into their fire. As long as the Germans kept their heads down, they were safe. Thomas didn't see any German soldier being hit, but the advantage they had ended when Russian planes came flying right towards them. The German officer on top of the ridge yelled, "Everybody out of the trenches, run, run into the woods!" All the Germans quickly crawled out of the trenches and dived into the woods behind them.

Thomas reached the forest at the same moment the rain of grenade shells started. The Russians were right behind them as well, throwing grenades into the woods. "Ow!" Thomas was hit! Shrapnel had hit his right shoulder and the bottom of his foot. "I need more cover!" he thought. Thomas crouched down and looked around. He spotted a hole in the ground, long enough for a person to hide in. He crawled on all fours towards it and let himself fall into it. He felt something. "Oh, sorry!" He discovered he was not the only one in this hole. He looked at the person beside him. It was an officer. Looking closer, Thomas discovered that it rather used to be an officer! The man had his coat on and his machine gun over his shoulder, but right in the middle of his forehead was a bullet hole. The face was ashen. His rank colours had been pulled off. Because the rank colours were pulled off, and the bullet hole was right in the centre of his forehead, Thomas was certain that this was an execution by the German army. "Maybe he had had enough and wanted to surrender to the Russians," Thomas guessed. The officer's eyes looked into the sky, not moving. Thomas felt sorry for him. With one hand, he closed the eyes of the officer forever, and tried to stay away from him. Thomas was sheltered from the grenade shells.

After lying still beside the corps for a while, Thomas heard a sound. It sounded like tanks. "I hope those are

German tanks!" he thought. He stuck his head out of the hole, just to take a peek, and felt relieved. The tanks were German, picking up German soldiers in the area. Thomas climbed out of the hole in order to show himself to the approaching tank. The tank stopped right beside the hole and Thomas said, "I have a shot officer here in the hole. It would be good if he could get a decent burial."

The soldier in the tank said, "No problem soldier, he is not the only dead one today. We had a lot of dead already. Just lift him up, so I can put him onto the tank." Thomas did what the soldier told him and then climbed on top of the tank himself, holding the dead officer so he wouldn't fall off. The tank brought Thomas and the dead officer to the 'red cross' area, where the rest of his troops were.

Thomas finally had time to examine himself. He looked at the places where he got hit by the shrapnel. His shoulder had a red spot, but it didn't even cut into the skin. He checked out his right foot. The shrapnel was still sticking in the bottom of his boot, but it didn't go through into the foot. "Not even a scratch!" Thomas said to himself, "Was there a God who put the hands of an angel right between the shrapnel and his body? Hm!" Thomas was very thankful!

Officer Schlagmeier called his troops to the side. "Heil Hitler! We have lost one soldier and another is wounded. I am very proud of you guys! You proved yourselves worthy of being German soldiers in a difficult situation. You are the Hope of Germany! You are the Pride of the German nation! You are the Intelligence Germany will talk about in the future! Keep a clear head in all situations! Don't let the enemy take your life! Germany needs you!" Thomas and the rest of the group felt very important after that speech. After getting food and water, they marched into another wooded area. Later on, they heard that just after they had left the previous location, it was taken over by the Russians.

The group found a good spot in the woods and everybody took care of themselves. The weapons had to be cleaned, beards had to be shaven, the boots had to be shined up, and so on. Thomas sat beside Harri, happy to have his friend by his side. Harri had gotten a piece of shrapnel in his left upper thigh. He had to be treated by the red cross and was OK. "Nature calls!" Thomas said to Harri. He took his rifle and made his way to the nearby bushes. To get some privacy, he pushed himself a bit more into the bushes, bending down the branches in front of him.

As he was doing this, he exposed a set of eyes now staring at him in shock and disbelief. Thomas stared back with the same emotions. The set of eyes belonged to a Russian soldier, who was now caught in the act of spying on the Germans. Both men turned pale. Thomas lifted his hand in front of his belly and waved to the soldier to run away. The Russian turned on the spot and ran as fast as he could away from Thomas and his group. Thomas was shocked! "What did I do?" He thought to himself, "I should have shot him! If Officer Schlagmeier hears about this, he will kill me! But I just couldn't shoot him!" Thomas did his business and walked back to his group. He tried to look normal and sat down beside Harri again.

"Guess what I found?" announced another boy from the group as he came back from the bushes. Thomas' ears got red. He expected the worst. This was it! The boy said,

"There is a German wagon on the tracks beside these woods and it is filled with tobacco." Thomas let out some air. He was relieved! This was OK!

The whole group got excited about the prospect of getting a lot of smokes. They were assembling a team to make a run for this train car. "Stay put!" officer Schlagmeier yelled, "This is looting! A German soldier does not loot! And we don't know if it is a trap by the Russians. They might be in the bushes waiting for us!"

"Good officer!" Thomas thought. He had the same idea, but the rest of the troop didn't see it that way and were very much upset at Officer Schlagmeier. They complained that the Russians would now get all the good tobacco from the German army. It didn't seem fair.

Thomas was concerned about the Russian spy. "Will he tell his troops where we are?" But the whole day and night was quiet. "The spy has character!" Thomas determined. He returned a favour with another favour! Good on him!"

After the morning inspection, the group had to move on again. Officer Schlagmeier told them, "We have to go to another area of trenches to break out of here! In order to make it harder for the Russians to detect us, we will march in one line, one soldier after the other, but each of us will be 10 meters apart from the other. This will make it hard for them to see us! Stay low and keep your eye on the man in front of you!" Officer Schlagmeier was first, Officer Gerd was second, and the rest followed. Thomas was ordered to be last. Harri walked right in front of him, and Thomas kept Harri always in his view.

The woods were dense in some areas, and Thomas had a hard time keeping up with Harri and not losing him. The march went on for a long time. Harri stopped, and apologeticly said, "I lost my man in front of me! I guess I must have lost him already a while ago! I always thought I would catch up with him, but I didn't, sorry!" Thomas got scared! If another troop would find them walking all alone, they might conclude that Thomas and Harri were deserters on their way to surrender to the Russians. That would be the end of their lives.

Thomas said, "We'd better be fast and walk in the same direction! We have to catch up with them Harri!" Thomas and Harri walked fast through the woods. It didn't take long and they met another German group of soldiers on tanks. This troop must have just started out their engagement in the war. Their uniforms looked clean, everything was proper and shiny, it might have been their first day. Thomas went up to the officer, who was another very young man. "Heil Hitler! We lost our troop in the woods! We had to march 10 meters apart from each other, and lost the man in front of us in the dense woods. Would it be alright if we join up with you?"

"Of course, no problem!" the young officer replied. Thomas and Harri got hopeful, climbed up onto one of the tanks and traveled with them. They came to a very large open area, where munitions were exploding like crazy. A German train wagon filled with munitions had been hit by the Russians! The explosions were huge! "Less ammo for the German army!" Thomas thought. The tanks drove fast past the fireworks and stopped at the next trenches. The young officer yelled, "Everybody, into the trenches!"

Thomas and Harri jumped into the trenches and couldn't believe their eyes. Officer Schlagmeier and the troop were sitting in the dirt and looking back at them in disbelief. Thomas was happy to see his old group and said, "Finally, we thought we had lost you for good! We lost the last man in front of Harri and couldn't find you anymore!"

The guys all smirked, and one replied, "Lost you? Lost you? You must be kidding! Your escape wasn't successful! That's what you mean! You never wanted to find us! Ha-ha!" The men standing around looked at Thomas and Harri with the same accusing stare.

Thomas' stomach felt like a rock, his face got white, he couldn't speak! Harri stepped in, "It's all my fault!" he exclaimed. "I lost my man in front of me and that made the two of us lose the whole group!" With pleading eyes, he looked at his old buddies and the officers. The whole group turned their backs toward them and started talking to each other, completely ignoring Thomas and Harri.

Thomas shrugged his shoulder, as a gesture for Harri to stop talking. He felt that the group had made up their minds against them. They assumed that Thomas and Harry were deserters. He couldn't believe it! It was sad! "How can we win the war if we can't trust each other!" he thought.

Officer Schlagmeier had an idea. "Thomas and Harri, you can make good on your commitment to the German troops. All of our water bottles are empty again! Do you see that farmhouse at the far end of the field? There might be a well with water and the whole troop needs water. You two take all the water bottles from us around your necks and run as fast as you can over the field. Fill up the bottles at the well and come back as fast as you can!"

Everybody gave their water bottles to them, without looking into Thomas' and Harri's eyes. Thomas and Harri put the bottles with the straps over their shoulders. The farmhouse was a long distance away; approximately 500 meters, Thomas guessed. They looked around for the enemy and then started running as fast as they could over the open field, with their heads tucked in. The hearts of the two were beating right into their throats. Any second could be the end of their lives. At last, they made it to the farmhouse. Out of breath, they looked around for a well.

Harri saw it. "There it is, behind the house! Let's get the bottles filled fast and run back as long as it is safe!" Both looked into the well and let the bucket down to bring the water up. No water, the well was dry! Thomas and Harri looked at each other. This was bad news! All for nothing, and the guys would not be happy with them! Thomas said, "We'd better run back! Maybe the Russians are still gone!" The run back to the trenches was just as dangerous as their first run. Thomas and Harri made it safely back to the trenches.

Everybody looked at them with one question on their mind. "Do you have water?"

"No water! The well was totally dry, sorry about that!" The boys took their bottles back, still avoiding eye contact. Thomas and Harri knew they didn't have friends here! Officer Schlagmeier told Thomas and Harri to climb into the next trenches in order to be their defence from the right side.

Thomas was glad to be away from people who had negative feelings towards him. This small hole in the ground was a good place to be, for now! Harri and Thomas sat down and took a rest from all the running and excitement. Both still had a bit of water in their bottles and enjoyed the drink. Harri looked downwards and was very quiet. After a long time, he looked up, his eyes red, full of tears. "I am very sorry Thomas that I put you into this situation, but I have to tell you, I am not surprised. I was waiting for something like this to happen!"

Thomas looked at Harri with astonishment. "What do you mean by waiting for something like this to happen?"

Harri started talking again. "I am sorry, but I never told you that I am a Christian. I believe in the Bible, I believe that Jesus is the son of God, God Himself. I believe in the Holy Spirit, and God the Father. I should have told you that a long time ago, especially since we could die any moment, and you might not know where you will spend eternity."

Thomas interrupted, "What does that have to do with the troops turning their backs to us?"

Harri explained, "There is the story about Joseph in the Bible. The youngest of twelve sons. His father loved him to pieces and spoiled him rotten, right in the face of the other eleven brothers. One day their jealousy got the better of them. They were going to kill Joseph, but ended up selling him to a caravan out of a foreign country. Jealousy can be very dangerous! Officer Schlagmeier always put you first! You were the one driving with the messenger on that bike, you were asked to go to the edge of the wood to look out for us and so on. He put a lot more trust in you than in the others.

They got jealous! I believe the officer had a hard time to punish you, but he had to take care of the others. Maybe he thought that getting the water would even things out between you and the rest of the group."

Thomas had to think about that for a while. "I can believe all that stuff with the jealousy, but what you said about being a Christian, do you really believe that you go to heaven after you die?"

"I know that I will go to heaven after I die," Harri answered, "because Jesus died for me on the cross, to take my sins. After he died, he rose from the dead. He died for me and for you on the cross, so we can go to heaven after we die. I believe him! I'll tell you a story, which makes it clearer. There was a father going home with his two little girls after the funeral of his young wife. One girl asked him, 'Daddy, what happens when you die?' At that moment a big truck drove past them, letting its shadow fall over them. The father said to his daughters, 'Did you see the truck driving past us? It was a bit scary! But we only got the shadow of the truck. In Psalm 23, verse 4, it says, 'Even though I walk through the valley of the shadow of death—' We will only get the shadow of death, like the shadow of the truck. But Jesus went under the truck! He died for us! He rose from the dead and defeated death for us.'"

Thomas was quiet for a while and then said, "I wish I would be able to believe like you!"

Both heard tanks coming their way. Thomas and Harri decided to ask Officer Schlagmeier what to do if those were Russian tanks. They climbed out of their place and entered the trenches of the troops.

No troops! The trenches were empty! They had left without them! "Out of here!" Harri said. They ran across a huge area interspersed with large piles of dirt. The place looked like a former coal mine. The huge piles of dirt provided the protection they needed from the gun shots and grenades that the Russian troops were now sending their way. 'Zing' a bullet almost got the ear of Thomas. The two had to jump from one dirt pile to another to stay alive. Always bending down and moving fast, the two were able to avoid being hit. After 10 minutes or so the Russians gave up and drove on.

"That was close!" Thomas said. Harri and Thomas sat down on the dirt to rest. They didn't have water anymore, but they were still alive.

"Look at that! That is our group!" Harri pointed to the edge of the woods. They watched as the group entered the forest.

"Not again, Harri! I don't want to join up with them anymore. Let them go!" Harri agreed. "Let's follow the road, it looks safe to me!" The two walked on the road for a long time and were surprised to find a huge area filled with all kinds of vehicles. Thomas looked at all the tanks, the jeeps and trucks. They were all German, with troops standing around talking. One wounded soldier was sitting in a jeep. "What happened to you?" Harri asked. His sad, broken eyes looked up to Thomas and Harri. His face was ashen and with his shaking hand he pointed towards his abdomen. He had gotten a shot there, a young man in their age. The empty stomachs of Thomas and Harri churned inside of them. The sight of this young fellow made them nauseated. Thomas and Harri spent some time with him, trying to encourage him.

A group of officers came towards Thomas and Harri. "Heil Hitler! Which troop are you from? How come you are all by yourselves?" Thomas tried to explain their situation, hoping they wouldn't get into more trouble. The officer's face brightened and said, "Good for us that you lost your group. We need you! You can help with our backup! We are trying to break out of the Russians' grip! With all the vehicles here on this site, we are going to drive through the forest, break through the Russian line, and into freedom on the other side. It will be hard, but this is our only chance. You have to wait with the rest of the backup and come after us."

Thomas and Harri said their "OK" and went to the rest of the backup troops, who greeted them friendly. There were ten soldiers, fewer than Thomas' old troop. The officer gave the command and the first tanks led the line of vehicles entering the forest. Thomas heard the fire from the Russians right away. One vehicle after the other was swallowed up by the woods. Thomas and the rest of their group had to stay back for the whole night. The battle fire went on and on. They could only imagine how fierce the engagement was. Did they break through the Russian line? When daylight broke, a German truck came out of the forest to pick them up.

They were glad the troop cared enough to pick them up. Thomas and the rest of the backup had to sit in the back of the truck. The ride through the forest started. The truck was flying through the fire of the Russians. The terrain was filled with holes and uneven areas. The soldiers on the truck were holding on desperately for dear life! At one point the truck couldn't make it anymore because the forest was too dense, so everyone had to get out and go on foot. With their heads tucked in, bullets were flying overhead. The group went as fast as they could towards the edge of the woods. The shooting eased up, and they made it without losing any men.

Thomas and his new group started to relax. They had gotten water and something to eat the night before at the place in front of the woods. Now they sat down and enjoyed the rest of their water. The officer came running towards them. "Get up, the Russians are coming! We have to go to the next forest, over the field."

Thomas and Harri looked at the field beside the woods and then at each other in disbelief. Harri said, "He must be kidding! We will never make it to the other side! That field is huge! We will be easy prey for them!"

Thomas was very pale, but he got an idea. "Here do this!" He took out his small shovel from his backpack and dug a small hole in the ground to sleep in at night. He turned the shovel with the grip side down and fastened it so the metal blade was right in front of his heart. Harri followed his advice. This was a good idea!

The officer commanded everybody to come to the edge of the wood and stay hidden in the bushes. Thomas and the others gathered around the officer, looking onto the field. The field was longer than the one to the farmhouse where they had to fill up the water bottles. Right in the middle of the field four German cannons were stationed with the appropriate soldiers to fire them. The officer commanded, "When the cannons start shooting, we will shout a loud "Hurrah" and make a run for it! Heil Hitler!"

Thomas and Harri looked into each others' eyes, into each others soul. Both didn't know what to say, even what to think. Was this the last time they would see each other? Both of their hearts were crying, trepid, and pumping hard in their chests.

The cannons started shooting! "Hurrah" they shouted. The troops started running. Thomas looked straight ahead. He used to be the winner of every long-distance race. "Would he be fast enough for this race he wondered? He focused on the edge of the wood ahead of him. So far, so good. There was no shooting from the Russians, but he could hear the loud noise of the tanks.

The first shots came from the back and a moment later from the sides. The Russians had caught up with them! "Ahh!" Thomas heard one of the others cry out. Thomas didn't look, he kept running, hoping that Harri would be right by his side, running fast enough. Bum! Splash! A grenade tore a German soldier to pieces and the blood and pieces of flesh splattered all over Thomas. "Run, run!" Thomas told himself. The edge of the wood came closer. Almost there…

He made it! He made it! Thomas was on the other side of the woods, gasping for air. Exhausted, he collapsed on the ground. Harri! Where is Harri? Thomas looked around for him. Another soldier, who made it as well, came up to Thomas, and throwing himself down beside him blurted out, "I am sorry about your buddy!"

Thomas said, "What do you mean?"

The other one started talking again, hardly able to get a breath, "I was just behind the two of you. Your friend got hit by a grenade! You have his blood all over you!"

Thomas looked at him. "Harri? Dead!" He looked at his arm full of blood and pieces of flesh. "Harri?"

Tears came running down his face.

DOWN

Thomas was exhausted. He was sitting on the ground, out of breath, trying to get through his emotions. "Harri is dead! I am alone!" Thomas inhaled deeply. With shaking hands, he took some leaves from a bush and tried to wipe off the little pieces of flesh and blood, which belonged to Harri. 'Where is Harri now? Is he in heaven? He said he would be in heaven after he died? He would be in a much better place!' Thomas looked around and discovered that the area was full of German soldiers, all the lucky ones who had escaped the Russians. Some were getting themselves cleaned up, just like Thomas. Others were drinking from their bottles if they still had water. A lot of soldiers were laying on the ground moaning in pain. Medics were walking around to help the wounded. Most of the wounded ended up on the flatbed of one of the trucks driving around. Those trucks were filled to the max. "Where are they going to put all those wounded soldiers?" Thomas wondered.

"Do you have a bandage pack for me?" A soldier softly asked Thomas. Thomas looked at a face, streaked with tears, a young boy's face. He had a wound on his right leg, which was not too deep. A bandage would be all that he needed. Every German soldier had a very small pocket in their jacket. It was designed to hold two emergency packs of bandages.

Thomas still had both of his and pulled one out for the injured soldier. "How old are you?" he asked the boy.

"17 years old," the young soldier replied, "just like everybody else. They drafted me right after my Birthday!" Thomas was very sorry for him and hoped that the boy would be alive for his 18th. He turned around and gasped at the sight of officer Gerd walking around all by himself in the woods. His face was downward in deep thought. Thomas looked around for the rest of his old troop. He saw nobody he knew. He searched the whole area for a familiar face from the group he used to belong to. "Nobody is left anymore, just officer Gerd. They must have been in an awful fight! Good we left them! God you are good!"

The German troops were safe for now in this part of the woods. Lack of water and food was now the biggest enemy. The wounded soldiers were especially desperate for water, their life depended on it. Every time Thomas got close to a wounded man, he would ask for water. Thomas was out of water like almost everyone else. He would have liked to have a little sip of water as well. The Russians didn't come close to them in the forest, but they kept throwing grenades from the outside. So far, the troops were managing to keep away from the grenades.

Thomas noticed a group of soldiers standing together in a fierce discussion. He walked over to them, wondering what they were talking about. He heard "At least we will stay alive if we surrender!" Thomas turned around right away. If an officer would hear these words, he would hang the man who said them on the next tree. Thomas walked off in the opposite direction, as far away as he was able to. He remembered Officer Schlagmeier. An officer like him would rather die than surrender to the enemy. Hitler's goal was to win at all costs, until the last German soldier died. The word 'surrender' was not part of Hitler's vocabulary.

As Thomas walked on, a jeep passed him. He wanted to escape the situation and asked the driver, "Could I get a ride with you?" even though he noticed that the jeep was already full with officers.

The driver looked at the other men in his jeep and then at Thomas. "We are totally full, but if you want to, you can stand on the running board and hold on to the window frame. Just give us your rifle, we will hold it for you!" Thomas thought, "What a nice guy!" and handed his rifle over to the officer sitting beside the driver. He stepped onto the running board, holding on with both hands to the window frame. He had to hold on for dear life while the jeep jumped over the rough terrain. The officer looked at him a couple of times, worried whether Thomas would still be there.

The jeep was approaching the edge of the woods when Thomas caught a glimpse of an open field far ahead. "Almost there!" he thought. 'Bang!' The jeep got too close to a tree on the same side Thomas was standing. Thomas hit the tree, lost his grip and fell at the foot of the tree. Blackness took over! The jeep kept going!

After a long time, Thomas woke up with an agonizing headache! "What is going on?" he thought. He looked around the woods and toward the field. He was all alone! He looked down at himself, noticing all those dark spots on his uniform. "Harri! Harri is dead!" It came back to him. He remembered the ride on the outside of the jeep. He must have been knocked unconscious by the tree. "My rifle! They have my weapon! I don't have a weapon!" he thought. He moved his arms and legs. Everything was fine. But his head felt like somebody had hit it with a hammer. "Ow!" He tried to get up, but it was difficult to stand up straight and get things into focus. It took Thomas a couple of moments to steady himself until he was sure he wouldn't fall over if he let go of the tree.

Letting go of the tree and looking ahead at the horizon he noted that the day was still young. He must not have been out for too long. He looked ahead to the edge of the forest. It was close! He would have almost made it with the jeep. "Where is everybody?" he wondered. He needed to find the rest of the German army. Most importantly, he needed to find a new rifle.

Slowly, Thomas made his way towards the field at the end of the woods. Sitting in the middle of the field was a wonderful farmer's house with a massive shed. The big shed, much bigger than the house, was right in front of him. "I'll look their first," Thomas thought and walked slowly towards the huge building. He heard some voices and the sound of people in pain. A very big, double door was at the side of the shed. Thomas made his way to the door and carefully opened it a crack. He was scared there might be Russian troops inside. The sound of the creaking hinges cut painfully through Thomas' drooping head. Nose first, he bravely managed to steal a look into the dark shed.

He couldn't believe his eyes! Thomas opened the door wider to cast more light into the building. The large floor of the shed was crowded with injured German soldiers. One beside the other, they were laying on the floor. Nobody said a word when Thomas opened the door. They feared that Thomas was a Russian soldier. After it was clear to them that

Thomas was German, everybody breathed easier. The one closest to the door asked Thomas, "What are you doing here? You can still walk! Run, run! This is not a good place to be."

"What will happen to all of you?"

The wounded soldier replied, "The Russians will take us as prisoners of war. At least that is what we were told."

Thomas felt bad to leave the wounded. "Do you have your rifle?" he asked the one in front of him. I lost mine! Could I get yours?"

The soldier smiled. "Of course! What do you think I can do with mine! Take it and leave! Better be fast and get out of here."

Thomas grabbed the rifle from beside the soldier and went out the door. The creaking hinges hurt his head but this was nothing compared to what other wounded men had to endure. He felt bad leaving these men and hoped they would get help from the Russians soon.

With a heavy heart, Thomas walked on. He had to find more German troops. Where were they? Around the corner of the next wooded area a road came into sight. He didn't hear any shooting. "It must be safe!" Thomas decided, so he walked down the road.

His head was aching, his tongue was sticking to his dry mouth. "Water would be great!" he thought. "What is that?" Thomas spotted something off to the side of the road. The closer he got the longer the lineup of all those things grew. Now he was able to make out what it was. It was one vehicle after the other. German trucks, jeeps, all burnt out! The sight was out of a horror movie! It was a long line of burned German vehicles. It was eery! He recalled all those military vehicles driving through the forest when the officer asked him and Harri to join the backup. All those vehicles now had a bluish and grey 'other worldly' colour and appearance. "I hope some of the men were able to rescue themselves in the forest!" He thought. "I wonder if the jeep I was riding in was part of this as well?" The acrid smell was sickening, he felt like throwing up. "I am still alive! God thank you!"

Thomas turned off the road to walk in the woods again. After a while he heard some voices. He met a small German group of soldiers. One officer was with them. The young officer had a kind face and greeted Thomas. "Heil Hitler! You are in good shape! Where do you come from?"

"I got thrown from a driving jeep," Thomas replied, "and ended up at a shed full of wounded German soldiers. After that I came across all these burned-out vehicles on the road. I thought it would be best to go back into the forest!"

The officer replied, "Good you are still alive and healthy. I heard the wounded will be taken care of by the Russians. They will be prisoners of war! I don't want to be captured! I have a plan to escape the Russian grip on us!" The other soldiers looked at Thomas with an uninviting demeaner. Thomas got worried! He was dead tired, thirsty and hungry and his guess was that all the rest of the group felt just the same.

The officer commanded, "Lets get going!" The whole group started marching behind this young officer with a plan to escape the Russians. They came to another edge of the woods and stopped. In front of them was a small field, which was closed off on the other side by an embankment. Behind this wall of dirt was a train station.

The officer said, "This is our chance! Behind the embankment are a couple of Russian soldiers, only a few. We will run towards them and shoot them down, and behind that is freedom! This is the safest way out of here! We start with 'Hurrah' and make a run for it. Get your weapons ready." Thomas thought that this officer was insane and the faces of the other soldiers told him that they thought so too, but an order was an order!

Everybody got their weapons ready. Thomas had his shovel blade in front of his heart again, but he knew he was not in good shape to run fast. His head was still hurting badly. The moment of truth came.

"Hurrah!" The officer shouted the loudest of them all and ran through the field like crazy. Thomas and the rest ran right after him. "Run! Run!" the officer screamed. Just a couple of seconds in, the shooting from the Russians started. It came from the right side, not from ahead, where the embankment was. "We will be safe after the embankment!" the officer yelled. Thomas got a surge of courage! "Oww!" A hard thing hit his right leg! It felt like somebody hit him with a metal pole. Thomas fell down. He looked up and watched all the other guys jumping over the embankment. They made it! He pushed himself up in order to follow them, but his right leg didn't cooperate, it didn't support him, he fell down again. Sweat was pouring off his forehead. He had to get out of here!

Thomas was on the ground! "Stay still!" He told himself. Let them think he was dead! He didn't move for a long time. The pain in his leg was worsening. After a few more moments, Thomas thought it would be safe to sit up and take a look at his leg. Pulling out the shovel from under his jacket, he carefully sat up. Nothing happened. No Russians came! "They might have followed the rest of my group!" he thought. Thomas looked at his leg and saw a wound on his right shin bone. The bullet had ripped the trousers open so he was able to see it. He remembered his leftover bandage package and pulled it out of the pocket of his jacket. The bleeding of the wound was not as severe as he had thought. He hoped that one pack would be enough. Pulling up his trouser leg, he took care of his wound the best way he could. "What will happen now?" He thought. "Will the Russians give me a shot in the neck when they find out I am alive? Will they take me as a prisoner of war?" His head was pounding. He needed something for his body. He looked into his bag for the emergency supply and found a tube of cream cheese still half full. "Yeah! This is food! Real food!" He opened his mouth and squeezed the remaining cream cheese into his mouth. This was good!

When he looked up, he saw three German officers walking towards him. Hope sprung up in his heart! Three strong German men! Getting a closer look at the officers he noticed their coats and boots were clean, like new, they were never in the trenches! Thomas determined that they had just entered the war. The officers came closer to Thomas and stopped right in front of him. "What happened here? Where are the others of your group?" Thomas told them about the brave attempt from his previous officer and hoped they would have compassion on him. The new officer said,

"Sorry, but we have to leave you here! We have to get going," and off they went.

Thomas' heart took a plunge! The officers let him down! He laid down on the dirt, tears running down his cheeks. Time came to a stand still. He thought about his Mom. If she would know...? But she didn't! His Dad! Was he still alive? Harri! He was in heaven! The area around Thomas was quiet. The birds made their chirping sounds. It was peaceful and Thomas fell into a restful sleep.

Thomas was startled awake by a loud voice talking to him in Russian. A Russian soldier stood in front of him with his rifle pointed right at him. Thomas got scared! He put up his hands, away from his rifle. In broken German the Russian asked him if he was injured. Thomas said, "Yes, I got shot in the leg. If you would be able to give me a stick from the forest, I might be able to walk." The Russian didn't like the idea and told him to wait until he got help. He left him alone and went away. Thomas lay back down and fell asleep again.

A blunt pain in his side woke Thomas up. Two Russian soldiers stood before him. One of them had Thomas' rifle in his hands. The ability of these soldiers to speak German was worse than that of the first one, and they were not as friendly. Thomas got scared again! After Thomas tried to explain his situation to them, both soldiers bent down, and searched his pockets for something they liked. The watch Thomas' Dad had given him was the first thing they took. This was painful! But when they found the photo of Erika, Thomas' former girlfriend, everything changed.

"Ho, ho!" they laughed. Both of them liked the photo. They pulled out their own photos of their girlfriends and showed them proudly to Thomas. All of a sudden, the atmosphere became friendly. They started bragging about the beauty and great shape of their girlfriends. Thomas became hopeful! The two Russians smiled at him and assured him that they would get help. Both of them left Thomas alone and left to get some help. They kept their word! In a short time, they were back with two German soldiers, prisoners of war.

The German said, "Hi buddy, what's wrong?"

Thomas smiled up to them. "I got shot in my shin bone. I can't walk. My leg won't carry me anymore!"

The other German said, "Don't you worry, we'll carry you!" The Russians gave the two Germans orders to take Thomas to a little village. The first one spoke up again. "We better get going so we will be able to make it before nightfall!" Both soldiers helped Thomas up onto his good leg and told him to put his arms on top of their shoulders. They connected their arms underneath Thomas' buttocks and started walking.

"This is awkward!" Thomas thought. This was almost the worst experience of the whole war for him. He had always been in good shape, never in a position of needing help, but instead always being the one who gave it. He looked around. The two Russian soldiers had left them. "Why don't the Russians go with us? We could just take off?" he said.

"Ha-ha! You don't know? Nobody gets out of here without meeting a Russian. The Russian army is everywhere around these woods. There is no escape! That's a fantasy of us Germans! The Russians have us securely in their grip.

Surrender would have been the only wise choice. The Russians are very kind to us, you will see. We have food and water, we are OK." The three talked a lot about their dreams and what they would do after the war. They were sure it wouldn't be long anymore until the war was over. The walk was a long one. The village was seven kilometers away.

Finally, they made it! The sun was almost over the horizon, when they reached the village. The two Germans carrying Thomas went to the Russian officer in charge, and reported to him. The officer looked at Thomas with empathy and pointed them in the direction of a house. The three stood in front of the house and knocked loudly on the door. A middle-aged woman opened the door. Her blonde long hair was tied in a knot at the back of her head. Her slim figure was dressed in a typical German farmer's woman's dress, with an apron overtop. She greeted them with a warm heart. "Oh boy, you poor guy, what happened to you?"

Thomas' eyes filled with tears. "I got shot in my leg!" He was overwhelmed with the compassion in her eyes and her kind voice.

The women turned towards the two German POW. "Please bring him to the second bedroom on the second floor. Take his clothes off before you put him in bed. I will be up in a short time." The two had a hard time carrying Thomas up the stairs. Thomas was sorry to be such a burden. One opened the door of the bedroom and whistled, "Man, you won't believe it! Welcome home!" Thomas looked at two real beds, with real bedsheets on them. There was a big bowl of water, a piece of soap in a dish, and a towel. The two helped Thomas to undress and wash himself. The farmer's wife gave them night clothes from her husband and Thomas was in bed feeling like a newborn baby.

"Have a good night! Not everybody gets a wonderful bed like you! You must feel like a king!" The two German soldiers opened the door and left. Thomas didn't know how to thank them for all their trouble. Thomas had just put his head down onto the real pillow to go to sleep, when the door opened again.

"Hi! How are you?" The farmers wife came through the door with a bowl of soup in her hands and a jug of water. "I warmed up some chicken soup. That will make you feel better! Here is a jug with water for you to drink. Your uniform was very dirty! I washed it right away and hung it outside to dry. You will be able to put it back on tomorrow."

Thomas smelled the aroma of the soup ."Thank you so much for everything! I feel really good, laying in a real bed. This is wonderful. How come the Russians didn't push you out of your house and are so friendly to you?"

The farmer's wife got a big smile on her face. "Ha-ha! In every soldier lives a boy! When the Russians came into our area, all of our neighbours fled in fear. We stayed! I baked a lot of cookies, we put a white flag on our door and then we met the first Russians with a friendly smile and a plate of cookies in our hands. They loved the cookies and let us stay in our house. They use us to feed the officers or to provide beds for someone like you. We have to help them, which is better than leaving our house. We worked hard for this house. It means a lot to us! How old are you?"

Thomas had to answer with a question. "What is the date today?"

"Today is the 21th of April 1945" she answered.

Thomas spoke again. "I turned 18 six days ago on the 15th of April. I knew that I was 18 years old during the last days, but I can't remember what happened on my Birthday. There was too much going on with grenades, and explosions, and so on."

The farmer's wife walked towards the door. "Happy belated Birthday! What is your name?"

"Thomas."

"Happy belated Birthday, Thomas! I hope you like the soup and sleep well!" Thomas took the bowl with the spoon and savoured one spoonful after the other. "This is like heaven!" he thought. "She is very nice! My Mom would have done the same! They are smart people!" After the bowl was empty a deep sleep came over Thomas.

LUEDENSCHEID UNDER ATTACK

Sabine was now home with her family in Luedenscheid. The room she shared with Emma was filled with Emma's things. The Singer Sewing machine with a table beside it, was surrounded with all kinds of notion's, piles of fabric, and rolls of yarn in an assortment of colours. Emma loved sewing and spent most of her day doing just that. It was good to be home again, but Sabine truly had enjoyed the evenings with little Helmut when she would read a bedtime story to him. She missed the whole family in Halver. They were good to her and to everybody else.

Today Emma and Sabine had some time to themselves and enjoyed going up and down the Wilhelmstrasse. The Wilhelmstrasse was in the centre of the city where all the stores were lined up, one beside the other. Butcher Ellermann right across from the 'Erloeser Kirche' (Saviours Church) had his famous 'Mettwurst' in the window display. Sabine could just taste it together with the 'gruenkohl' and fried potatoes, but not today. Today was a day for window shopping only. The stores, however, were not attractive anymore. They were mostly empty! Still, people walked up and down just to meet a new friend or run into somebody they knew.

Coming down towards the end of the Wilhelmstrasse, where it opened up to the "Adolf Hitler Platz" the two sisters noticed a lot of excited people standing together and talking to each other. One woman put up her arms. "This is unbelievable! What a crime in our small city of Luedenscheid!"

A man listening to her replied, "Things like this have never, ever, happened in our town! It makes me feel sick and makes me very ashamed of our city! This cries to heaven!"

Sabine and Emma got pulled in by their curiosity. Emma said to the lady who spoke first. "What happened?"

The lady pointed to the middle of the Adolf Hitler Platz and said, "See for yourselves, it is too hard to describe!" A crowd of people were standing around something at the centre of the large flagstone covered plaza. Emma and Isolde approached the crowd who made space for the two, so they would be able to get a better look. People left the area, looking downwards, some with tears in their eyes. Right in front of Emma and Sabine were three dead German soldiers on the ground, shot by the German authorities, accused of being deserters. A sign beside the dead soldiers told the story. Flies were attacking the corpses already and the faint smell of death could be detected. One of the soldiers looked like a boy. He must have been just 17 years of age. Emma's face turned white and with a shaking hand she took hold of Sabine's hand. Sabine pulled her away from the scene and both ran home, their hearts pounding in their chests. Both were still shaking after they arrived at home.

Dad, just coming home from work wondered, "What is going on with the two of you? Your faces are white like a bedsheet?"

Sabine found her voice first. "We came down the Wilhelmstrasse and walked onto the Adolf Hitler Platz."

"I know!" her father interrupted, "Too bad I couldn't warn you about those shot soldiers. My colleagues at work talked about it. This is not something I would have liked my daughters to see! Only evil can come up with ideas like this! I am very sorry that you had to see that! This is our city Luedenscheid! Nothing like that ever happened before in our town! This cries to heaven! You better help Mom with dinner and get those pictures out of your head!" Heini looked at Otti who understood. She gave both girls something to focus on and dinner time had a different topic. Little Gerdi had found some lady bugs in the yard and collected them in the little pocket of her jacket. For some reason those bugs decided to make their appearance right at dinner time, flying over the table and landing on heads, arms, and the dinner plates. Normally Mom and Dad would have been upset, but today the lady bugs were a welcomed distraction. Later on, at bed time, Sabine prayed for the families of those poor soldiers, especially of the younger one.

Days later, Otti, who was giving breakfast to her little daughters, said to Sabine, "The Americans are at our doorstep, and we don't hear a thing! I wonder what they are up to?"

Sabine wondered out loud, "They might have moved on! Maybe Luedenscheid is not important for them?"

Otti replied, "Wouldn't that be the best! But I have a bad feeling about the whole thing! Your grandmother and Aunt Irma, with the two little boys, live at the Talstrasse, where any army, if it would march into town, would come up. I was thinking about this scenario all morning. I just can't shake it!"

Sabine shrugged her shoulders and suggested, "If it makes you feel better, I could walk down and check on them."

Otti took her time to think about what Sabine had said. "Hm, it would be good to check on them! But it would make me feel better if you would go together with Emma."

"Yes," Sabine agreed, "that's a good idea! I will ask her right away."

Sabine walked into the room she shared with Emma. It was the same picture every day! Emma in front of the sewing machine. Sabine spoke to her. "Mom is concerned about Grandma and Aunt Irmgard. She wants us to go down there and check on them. Are you able to go with me?"

Emma looked up from her sewing, her face in a frown. "Do I have to? I am just sewing the collar for my new blouse. This is very difficult!"

Sabine answered, "Emma, your blouse will be here after we come back, but we don't know if Grandma and the rest will be alive at the end of the day. They are more important than a blouse!"

Emma gave in, "Alright! I am just going to change into my green skirt, and we can go."

Sabine got impatient. "Why do you have to change your skirt? You look just fine to me!"

Emma replied, "My green skirt fits better to the blouse I am wearing. The colours are a better match! If you go out of the house, you never know whom you are going to meet. You should always look your best!"

Sabine rolled her eyes. "You have so many skirts and blouses! I just have two sets, enough to wash one and wear the other. Why would anyone want to have more? And anyway, how did you get all that fabric for the clothes?"

"Dad gave me the fabric. He bought it on the black market." Emma changed into the green skirt. "I am done, let's go!"

Emma looked smashing with her curly, fine, blond hair and her daunting green eyes. Her outfit was just the right match for her features! The two said goodbye to their Mom and walked out of the house, down the Koellnerstrasse, all the way to the bottom of the hill where the Koellnerstrasse opened up to the Talstrasse in a "T". The girls turned left past the water treatment plant towards the house where Grandma lived. They walked along the edge of the forest when they heard a loud noise like hundreds of electrical cables hitting each other and exploding. Emma and Sabine looked at each other. "Grenades! Into the forest!" Sabine yelled. Both ran into the forest and hid behind a tree. Sabine had to catch her breath. "I know that sound from the attack in Halver. Those are grenades!"

Emma's face turned white; she was shaking like a leaf in the wind. "I'm scared! Are we going to die?"

Sabine felt scared as well, but she knew that one of them had to stay strong. "Stay hidden behind the trees!" She assured her, "We will be fine as long as they don't see us! I am more worried about Grandma and Aunt Irmgard with the children. The army is going in their direction! We have to reach them before the Americans do! Let's run from tree to tree! We are almost at their house!"

Emma was holding onto her tree. "I can't run that fast! Sabine I can't!"

Sabine reached her hand out to her sister and said, "Hold my hand! We will make it!" Emma's shaking, cold hand fastened itself with a tight grip around Sabine's. It almost hurt Sabine. She started pulling her sister with her, running from one tree to the other towards Grandma's house. They made it! Going into the apartment house through the back entrance, they ran to their suite. Sabine and Emma stood in front of the door, catching their breath, knocking loudly on the door. There was no answer! They looked at each other in disbelief. Sabine opened the door and both girls looked around in the apartment. Nobody was home! They must have left! "The bunker!" Sabine thought out loud. "They must be hiding in the bunker!"

Emma replied, "Of course! They must have heard the loud grenades as well! Do we have to go there Sabine?"

Sabine said, "We have to, for our own protection! The bunkers are there for moments like this! Let's go! Take my hand!" The two girls made their way back into the woods and again ran from tree to tree the short distance to the bunker.

Sabine opened the door to the bunker and both girls stepped into the stairway that led down to the basement. They closed the door behind them and descended the stairs. Bad air rose up into their noses, they heard the muffled sound of voices. They reached the big room where people were sitting on blanket covered mattresses. Mainly women and children were here, because the men had to fight in the war. Kids were playing with the toys they were able to grab in the moments before they had to leave home. Everything was immersed in a dim light. It was hard for Emma and Sabine to find their family.

Sabine said to Emma, "There they are! To the left! Can you see them?" Emma turned to the left and spotted Grandma sitting on the mattress, leaning against the wall and knitting a sock. Aunt Irmgard was right beside her talking to one of her little boys.

The boys saw the two girls first and shouted, "Emma and Sabine are here!" They came up to the sisters and gave them a tight hug! Sabine thought they must have been scared as well and so happy to see somebody familiar.

Sabine asked them, "What are you playing?" and sat down beside her Grandma.

The children showed their toys to Emma and Sabine, and Grandma said, "Why did you come all the way to us, did your Mom send you?" The girls gave the greetings they were supposed to from their Mom and told their Grandma what had happened. "I am sorry you had to go through all this trouble just to check on us," Grandma said, "but I am touched by the concern of my daughter. Please tell her that when you go back home. What will happen now that the Americans are here?" Emma sat down next to Grandma. The children started to play again, and Sabine was able to look around the room.

She knew all the neighbours of her Grandma, and said "Hi" to them. Every family had a little place for themselves on a mattress. In the corner, hidden by the stairway was a group of German soldiers. Sabine and Emma hadn't noticed them when they made their way down the stairs. The four soldiers smoked and with their weapons in front of them talked to each other while staring at Emma and Sabine. Sabine noticed that Emma took her comb out of her little bag trying to arrange her hair. The men liked what they saw! Emma liked to be noticed and smiled at them. Sabine's face turned red in anger. How could her sister be so dumb to make nice with the soldiers? She gave Emma a hard push with her elbow into her side. "Ouch! What was that for?" Emma said.

Sabine told her, "Don't look at them! Don't you know what they want from you?"

Emma frowned, "What do you mean? Nobody is doing anything! They are really nice guys!" Sabine let her head fall down in disbelief. "Emma is naïve and dumb at the same time!" She thought. Grandma had a smile on her face and Aunt Irmgard did as well. This was too funny!

The door opened at the top of the stairs and loud steps from heavy boots could be heard. The German soldiers stopped smiling, put their cigarettes out on the floor and tried to hide more behind the stairway. The first thing Sabine was able to see, was the front end of a rifle. One American soldier came into sight and after him another and another. The Americans pointed their weapons into the room, looking slowly, carefully around. The first one turned his rifle right away through the open spaces of the stairway into the faces of the German soldiers. The Germans let their weapons fall to the ground, and moved out of their hiding spot with their hands up in the air. There was no need to put all the civilians into a gun fight, they would rather surrender.

The whole room was quiet. Even the children knew that this was a serious moment and hung tightly onto their mothers. One of the Americans collected the weapons from the German soldiers and another one commanded the Germans to go up the stairway. With the rifle of the Americans in their backs, the German soldiers made their way up the stairs. They would now be prisoners of war of the American army. Emma looked down onto the ground, her trembling cold hand holding on to Sabine's. Emma was shocked! She had never seen a soldier in action!

When the door closed after the last American soldier went out, Sabine said, "You wonder what their future will be like? This is a bad sight when you see your soldiers being taken by the enemy. I wonder how Emil, our brother, is doing in France?"

Grandma nodded her head, "Me too! Your Mom is probably very worried about him!"

An older neighbour got up from his mattress, took a deep breath, and said out loud, "I guess we're able to get out of here now! We've been taken by the Americans! That is it!"

The children turned to their Mom, "Can we go home now?"

Aunt Irmgard replied, "Let's go home! If there still is a home!" Everybody gathered their belongings and made their way up the stairs. Outside, they looked at the house they lived in and were relieved to see it was intact and well. Grandma and the rest of the family went into the house. "Sabine and Emma, I'll make you a sandwich before you go back home."

"That would be great!" Sabine replied, "But we will eat it out here on the bench! I would like to see the next move of the Americans. I don't think it is safe for us to go home right now."

Grandma replied, "Alright be careful!" An older neighbour came to join Emma and Sabine on the bench. His head was bent down, he was a picture of despair! He turned to Sabine and Emma.

"Guess what Karl my brother-in-law just told me?" The neighbour took a deep breath. "Karl went to the barber at the "Braeuckenkreuz" this morning. The barber, Hermann Massalsky, was ranting on and on about the fact that the time of the Hitler Regime would be over pretty soon. He didn't notice that there was an officer sitting in the back of his shop, waiting for a haircut. This officer left the barber shop, got another like-minded official and the two arrested Hermann Massalsky on the spot. He got shot a short time later in the forest." The neighbour shook his head in disbelief, tears in his eyes.

Emma replied, "This evil has no end! When is this going to end?" The three on the bench looked on as the American soldiers were now securing the city of Luedenscheid. Not too far from where they were sitting, they heard some shooting, but couldn't see what was happening. The shots came from the Koellnerstrasse up the hill. The shooting stopped and all was quiet. After a short time, a Red Cross car drove towards the Koellnerstrasse. In the direction of the car came two wounded German soldiers, walking in front of the rifles of American soldiers who were right behind them. One of the captured men needed help from the American soldier. He had been shot in his upper leg and was having trouble walking. The group stopped at the Red Cross vehicle and the Germans were helped into it. One American soldier remained with the Germans for a short talk, reached into his right breast pocket and pulled out a pack of cigarettes. He gave the whole pack to the two Germans in the car. Sabine was impressed, "That was nice! What a nice guy!" she thought. The Red Cross car started and drove up to the hospital in the Phillipstrasse.

Off to the side of the three spectators, higher up the hill, was the Luedenscheider open air sports centre, 'Nattenberg'. The American army was marching up the hill to the Nattenberg. This was the highest point of Luedenscheid with a good view over the whole east side of the city. The heavy tanks propelled themselves up, accompanied by huge guns and the infantry. Every soldier that was marching up had his left arm full of grenades. The weather was beautiful; it was a very sunny April day! The grenades looked like gold with the sun shining on them. Sabine thought, "How beautiful they look! How can something that looks so beautiful be so awful?"

The old neighbour said, "The city will come under siege! Our mayor is one of my relatives! He loves our Luedenscheid!" tears ran down his cheeks. It didn't take long for the first rounds of grenades to fly towards the city.

Emma shouted, "That is in the direction of our house Sabine! They are shooting at our house!" Sabine got scared as well. The next round of grenades was aimed at one side of the hospitals.

Sabine got angry. "They can't shoot a hospital. The Red Cross is painted on it!"

The neighbour said, "You are right, and I don't think that they would normally do that, but I heard reports that the hospital is filled with German soldiers hiding in there, and my guess is that the Americans know it too. Don't be too concerned. The patients will all be in the basement by now." Sabine hoped that he was right.

Emma couldn't watch anymore! Her nerves were weak. She went inside to join Grandma and the rest of the family, but Sabine was determined to watch the whole attack on her hometown. This was a very important day in her life and her city. "What is the date today?" she asked the neighbour.

"Today is the 13th of April 1945! This is a history day for the city of Luedenscheid!" the neighbour told her. Sabine couldn't agree more.

"Look there! The white flag!" the neighbour shouted and stood up from the bench. Sabine got on her feet as well. She saw a black Mercedes with its roof rolled down coming slowly down the Koellnersrasse. In the car was the delegation of the city of Luedenscheid, all dressed in black suits. The mayor himself was waving the huge white flag, which was fastened on a long pole.

"That looks like a bedsheet!" Sabine said.

With Tears running down his cheeks the neighbour replied, "Doesn't matter, as long as it works!"

A delegation of the American army met the mayor and his officials on the Talstrasse and the talks of surrendering the City of Luedenscheid into the hands of the American army started right in front of their eyes. Sabine watched for a little bit, and after she was certain that the surrender had been accepted, she ran inside to bring the good news to the rest of her family. Grandma and Aunt Irmgard reacted with joy and great relief. "We have a good mayor!" Grandma said, "Why would you risk the lives of all the soldiers, the houses, and the lives of your citizens, for a fight which was doomed right from the start. What a good guy! Sabine and Emma, you better go home right away and check on your parents and little sisters. I hope they didn't get hit by the grenades." Sabine and Emma gave everybody a hug and walked very fast up the Koellnerstrasse to their home, with the great news of the surrender barely held down within them, waiting to burst forth.

On their way, they spotted some homes that were damaged in the attack. The worst was the 'Streppel' bar. They had to go around the corner of the bar in order to reach their home. The entrance of the bar was in ruins. The window beside the entrance was gone. The foosball table, which was close to the entrance, stuck out into the open. "No beer for a while!" Sabine said. She didn't like the smell of beer anyway.

Emma said, "Come on Sabine, we have to check on our home!" She was right. Both girls walked around the corner and their own home came into view "Ahhh." Both took a deep breath of relief. The building was undamaged. Both girls started to run. They opened the door, ran up the stairs, and opened the door to their apartment suit.

"Ohh You are safe!" Mother shouted. She was standing in her apron in front of the stove, stirring in a pot. Father came out of the bedroom with a huge smile on his face. Everybody embraced each other. Mother started crying. "I am so sorry I made you go and check on Grandma. Please forgive me! I was so scared for you two!"

Sabine had tears in her eyes. "Don't worry, I was very happy to watch this very important event in our city! I am so thankful that I was able to be there! We surrendered! The mayor came with a delegation of the city down the Koellnerstrasse and waved the white flag. You should have seen it. We surrendered! We have peace now! The war is over for us!" Tears came to Heini's eyes.

Heini said, "This is good news! We are now in the hands of the Americans, but those hands are so much better than the grip of Hitler and his SS men!"

New joy birthed in their hearts, relief settled over their minds and souls, and tears began to wash away the fear, the tension, and the angst of years of war.

After a few minutes of wordless embrace,

Otti shouted, "Let's all eat! You must be starved!"

PRISONER of WAR

The next morning Thomas woke up in a wonderful, clean, bed. Was this really true? He was wounded and sleeping in a real bed! As he was pushing himself into a sitting position, he felt a sharp pain going through his injured right leg. "Better be careful!" he told himself and slowed his efforts down. Sitting up, he looked around the bedroom and noticed a man in the other bed. "They must have put him here last night after I fell asleep!" he thought. The man in the other bed was fast asleep, still in his uniform. Thomas looked at him and noticed that the SS emblem, the scull, had been sown on his collar. SS men were the special guard of Hitler. Thomas rolled his eyes and looked up at the ceiling. He didn't like being in the same room as an SS man.

The door opened and the smell of coffee came to Thomas. The farmer's wife, holding a tray with two jam sandwiches and two cups of coffee in her hand appeared in the doorway. She had a smile on her nice, friendly face. Her apron was wrapped around her mature figure. Thomas felt as if his Mom would have just walked through the door. She said, "Good morning, Thomas, how did you sleep? Do you have pain in your leg?"

Thomas replied, "My leg hurts just a bit, especially when I move it. But I had a great night's sleep. Thank you so much! You are like a mother to me!" She put the plate and cup for Thomas right beside his bed and turned to the other man.

"Hello! Time to wake up! You have to eat breakfast!" The SS man opened his eyes and had a moment of confusion.

After he had his situation figured out, he smiled and said, "Good morning! Thank you for the good bed!"

"How is your injured arm?" She asked. "Are you able to eat by yourself?"

The man replied, "I will be fine! My left arm is injured. I am right-handed anyway! Thank you so much for your care!" The farmer's wife put his breakfast down beside his bed and excused herself.

Thomas started eating his sandwich, relishing every bite. He turned to his roommate. "Hi, my name is Thomas! I got shot in my right leg, what happened to you?"

The SS man answered, "Lukas is my name. I got shot in my left arm, the lower arm. I wonder if these Russian pigs will ever send a doctor to see us. I don't think they will care too much about my arm or your leg!" The door opened and two Russian soldiers came into the room. Both had smiles on their faces and came to offer some tobacco to smoke. Thomas smiled back at them and took the tobacco they gave. He knew the Russian tobacco. It was made out of leftovers of the tobacco leaf, the stem and such. The Russians loved it very much. Thomas offered them his cigarette paper in return. He knew they always used old newspaper to roll their cigarettes in, but both Russians declined. They loved their newspaper cigarettes. When they approached the bed of the SS man, they both got a shock. In very broken German, they explained to the man that it would be better for him if he got rid of the scull on his collar, as he would be treated badly by Russians if they saw it.

The SS man said to them, "Thank you for your concern, but I can't just take it off. I've sworn my life to Hitler! I just can't! You don't understand!" The Russians looked at each other, shrugged their shoulders, and left. Thomas felt sorry for the man. 'To swear your life to the Nazi cause was like giving your life into the hands of Satan!' he thought.

After the two Russians left, another pair of Russian soldiers came into the room. One of them had Thomas' clean uniform over his arm. "Time to get out of here!" he said and gave the uniform to Thomas. With the help of the soldiers, Thomas got dressed and ready to go.

Thomas and the SS man were helped down the stairs and out of the building, where they were able to use the outhouse. A truck was waiting for them in front of the farmer's house. The SS man refused the help of the Russian soldier, but Thomas was very thankful for being helped up onto the flatbed of the truck. The drive was a short one and ended up in front of a huge hall. Once Thomas was helped inside, he looked at the sight of an unbelievable number of wounded German soldiers lying on the floor, one beside the other. Red Cross nurses went back and forth, tending to the wounded. It looked like a warehouse for injured soldiers.

One of the German nurses came right up to Thomas and the SS man, "Welcome to our field hospital! You two have to go right away to the doctor to get your first treatment." Thomas was put on a stretcher and the SS man walked in front of them. They both followed the nurse. Behind a curtain was the doctor, busy operating on a patient.

The nurse told Thomas and the SS man to wait for their turn, and then left.

Thomas had a good view of the patient the doctor was operating on. The man was asleep and the doctor was cutting above his hand. Thomas looked at the SS man whose face turned white. The nurse assisting the doctor said, "Sorry guys! But we are too crowded. You have to wait here!" Thomas told himself to look away, but curiosity got the best of him. His breakfast came up his throat, but the nurse put a small bowl beneath him right on time. "Hold on to the bowl! You better look away!" Thomas made an effort to look away.

After the operating table was clear, the SS man was asked to lie down on it. His shirt was taken off and he was asked to stretch out his injured arm, so that the doctor could have a better look at his wound. Thomas spotted a tattoo underneath his armpit, maybe 20 cm up from his elbow. It was a small letter not even one centimeter long. The doctor spotted it at the same time as Thomas and said, "Hm, you are SS! Your blood type is written on your skin! Hm!" I am sorry, but I won't be able to save your lower left arm. We have to amputate it as soon as possible. The nurse will take care of the details!" The SS man was dismissed.

Thomas was next! They lifted him onto the operating table and the doctor looked at his leg. "Are you an SS man as well?" he asked.

Thomas said, "No, I am not!" The doctor smiled at him. He looked at his right leg and spoke.

"Hm, this is a fracture of the tibia with debris in it. If we are lucky, it will heal by itself, but you have to stay off your right leg. Let's wait and hope that you will be able to keep your leg." To the nurse he said, "Please put a new bandage on!" The nurse gave Thomas her attention and Thomas had a new bandage on his leg in no time. He was brought into the huge room and put beside another soldier onto a bit of hay.

The other man beside him didn't lie down but was kneeling and hanging with his upper body out of the window. Thomas wondered what was going on. A young soldier on his other side explained, "He got a shot into his lung! He is gasping for air! Poor fellow!" Thomas felt blessed to just have a small injury with not too much pain and complication. Compared to the men around him, he was in good shape! The night in the hay was not like the night in the farmer's house. The wounded were moaning because of their pain and his neighbour by the window hardly slept at all.

Morning came, and with it, another change. The doctor and a nurse inspected all the wounded soldiers and split them into two groups. The group where Thomas and the SS man belonged to was driven to a house where the rooms were filled with wounded soldiers, lying on the floor on hay. Young girls from the neighbourhood walked around, looking after the needs of the wounded men. Thomas found a place in one of the rooms and had better nights from then on, with more rest. The girls worked 12 hours shifts every day. Thomas and the rest of the wounded were impressed. "Those are good German girls!" he thought, but because they had no medical training nobody looked at the wound on

Thomas' right leg. He noticed that the pain was getting worse. Thomas got concerned!

One morning one of the girls asked the men in Thomas' room, "Do you want to know the latest news? OK, here it comes; the fight around Spremberg is over. Every German soldier who fought there is either dead, wounded, or a prisoner of war. The Russians are marching into Berlin as we speak!"

The man beside Thomas said, "That's it! The war will be over in a couple of days! I wonder where Adolf Hitler is and what he will do? I wouldn't want to be in his shoes right now!"

Thomas replied, "This is good news! When the war is over, we might be released us well."

The SS man who had had his lower left arm amputated by now, spoke from his place in the corner by the window. "Not so fast Thomas! We are Russian prisoners of war. The Russians don't have a reputation of being very kind and merciful. You better be prepared to be a prisoner for a long time! That's the way I see it!" Thomas knew that the man truly hated the Russians and hoped he was wrong.

The days went on and one midmorning one of the girls came into the room shouting, "Everybody has to come outside. Today is the great wash day!" Another girl joined her and together they helped the wounded like Thomas to go outside. The prisoners had to sit on the lawn in the backyard of the house around a huge pot of hot water. Some bowls filled with cold water were standing around the lawn as well.

The girls who told them to go outside spoke again. "Today is your lucky day to get rid of all your lice, if you have some. Everybody has to totally undress himself. Your clothes will be washed in this pot with soap and very hot water, and a girl will help you to wash yourself, your hair and, everything. You will be clean and free of lice after you are washed, and then you can put your clean uniform back on." The girls carried the bowls of water to the men and helped some of them bathe themselves. Thomas didn't have any lice yet, but knew from some of the others, that it was a very bad, annoying plague to have those little creatures crawling all over you day and night. He was happy to comply! To pull his clean, wet uniform over his head at the end wasn't that much fun. "But better clean and wet than dirty and filled with lice." he thought. They were allowed to sit in the sun for a while to dry off, but couldn't enjoy the sun too long, because a truck drove into the yard, and Thomas' group was loaded onto the flatbed to bring them to another place.

  The rooms in the building were filled with cots and mattresses in this new house. A rumour was going around that the Russians had signed a Geneva agreement with the allies. It dictated that every prisoner of war had to be placed at least 30 centimetres above the ground, so mice and rats would not be able to reach them. Unfortunately, lice were able to climb up to any bed. The mattresses were full of them. Especially at nighttime, when Thomas was tired and ready to sleep, they seemed to come to life. The top end of his blanket, near his neck, was like lice city every night. Everybody sat up in their beds and started popping the little creatures. When Thomas couldn't find more lice, he laid down, hoping to fall asleep right away. If it took him a long time to fall asleep, the crawling and biting started again and he would have to pop the creatures again.

Thomas, however, had other concerns. His wounded leg hurt more and more every day. This house had doctors and orderlies to care for the wounded. The orderlies cleaned his wound and changed his bandage, but after a couple of days, the wound was infected again, Thomas got a fever and the orderly took care of it again, cleaned the wound, and put a new bandage on. Thomas was good for a couple of days, but the wound kept getting re-infected. This rollercoaster went on and on.

"The War is over! Germany lost the War!" A Russian guard burst in, proclaiming the news to all the prisoners. Thomas hoped that this was good news and that the time of his captivity would be over pretty soon, but his first concern was his wound. His leg hurt a lot. Would he ever be able to see a doctor? Rumour had it that one of the doctors was actually a dentist and would do limb amputations here in the house. This was a scary thought for Thomas. He feared that his leg would be gone after so many infections. Finally, after one month, it was Thomas' turn to see the doctor in the operating room.

An orderly put him onto the stretcher and pushed him into the room where the doctor was waiting. Thomas was very scared! "Will I lose my leg now!" he thought. The doctor took the bandage off the wound and examined the hole where the bullet had hit Thomas' tibia. He said a lot of "Hm, Hm". Thomas's not-so-full stomach felt like a rock. With his scared brown eyes, he tried to read the doctor's thoughts.

Finally, the doctor said, "Thomas, we will try to keep your leg! I will do a real good cleaning to get all the small pieces out, and we will hope that it heals! Nurse, please give Thomas the cloth between his teeth and put your weight on his leg, so he can't move it. I need him to lie still. The nurse put her upper body onto Thomas' leg and the doctor started to work. The pain felt like hot lightening bolts firing through his leg and his whole body. Thomas saw stars! He had never experienced pain like this in all his life. The doctor gave him short breaks to breathe and then started working again. As Thomas was about to pass out, the doctor was done. He told the nurse to put a good bandage onto the clean wound and left to give the next patient his attention. Thomas breathed and gradually the tightness of fear and tension began to release.

The nurse smiled at Thomas, "You are a trooper! Others would have screamed through the whole house! Be proud of yourself! I will put a nice, clean bandage onto your wound and a brace on each side of your lower leg. That will ease the pain until the wound is healed." Thomas was very thankful and hopeful. "She said until my leg is healed. This sounds great!" he thought. With a new bandage, the braces and a lot of hope, Thomas returned to his room.

One of his roommates was sitting on a chair in agony. He had gotten shot in his sciatica nerve so his pain was constant and sleep out of exhaustion was the only break for him. Russian guards walked inside and outside the house all day and night. One just passed their room and Herman, the man with the damaged sciatica nerve, waved him into the room. "Would you be so nice and give me a piece of paper and a piece or two of charcoal? The Russian soldier was a nice guy who knew about poor Herman's suffering. "I will see what I can do." he told him and went to get the things Herman had asked for. It didn't take too long and he returned with a couple of sheets of paper and sticks of charcoal. Herman had a real smile on his face. Something nobody in the house had ever seen before.

He said to the Russian, "Please sit down! I am going to make a drawing of you."

The Russian was a good-natured guy and said, "Hoho, good!" He sat down on a chair in front of Herman, who started drawing on the sheet of paper. Herman's face relaxed! He was totally absorbed in his work. The room filled with more prisoners as well as Russian guards. Everybody was wondering if the subject of the drawing would react happily or not. The Germans looked at each other with concern in their eyes. If the Russian was not happy with the outcome, they might all be treated with disdain in the future. Some were holding their fingers crossed. People like Thomas said a silent prayer. Herman worked hard in his well-worn uniform, with his shiny black hair and his pronounced nose. A cigarette, the Russian had given him, hung from his smiling mouth. He was a picture of the consummate artist. Everybody in the room thought, "I hope he has a good reason to smile."

Herman was done! Just in the nick of time, as the guard's patience had come to an end. Herman had a smile on his face. The suspense in the room had reached its apex. Herman slowly turned the paper towards the Russian... The eyebrows of the guard went up! The cigarette in his mouth fell to the ground. With his big eyes and open mouth, he stared at the picture. He got up from his chair, took the drawing from the hands of Herman, and embraced him with his long, strong arms.

The pressure in the room released. Everybody expelled air and relaxed! The guard showed his portrait around in the room. It was perfect! Hermann nailed all the features of the Russian so well, and with a little bit of tweaking, the portrait was more beautiful than the Russian was in reality! The Russian model had tears of joy in his eyes. He left the room with his treasure in his hand, holding it up like it was a piece of gold.

The other Russian guards lined up in front of Herman asking him to draw them as well. Herman had his work cut out for himself from then on. He earned himself a huge stash of cigarettes, and a better provision of bread and soup which he shared with his fellow prisoners. It was the first time since their captivity that the Germans had a full stomach. Herman was a hero!

Some time later, Herman asked a guard, "Would you be able to bring me a big piece of cardboard, or a piece of a wall, as big as a door?" The guard smiled, "Hoho, what are you up to? I will see what I can do!" The Russian left and came back with a real door in his hands. Hermann had a huge smile on his face. He put himself into a corner of the room, with the door leaning against the bed in front of him. Nobody in the room was able to see what he was working on. It was a secret! For two days he sat in front of the door, his cigarette hanging out of his mouth, his face relaxed and happy. Everybody was waiting for the great unveiling.

Showtime! A prisoner called all the guards for the presentation. Thomas and the rest of the men were crowding around the room in front of the door. Herman had a big smile on his face. He was sure the guards would like his painting. When the room was crowded to the max, he slowly turned the door around so that everybody would be able to see the painting. There was a moment of astonishment and stunned silence and then "Ohhh, Ahhh", it went on and on! The guards couldn't hold back their amazement. All of them started talking at once in delight. Herman had painted their beloved Stalin in living size. Thomas had seen a picture of Stalin before and was impressed by what he saw. "Herman is good!" he thought. The guards treated the painting like the greatest treasure of their life. The door with Stalin on it became the hallway fixture. Everybody who entered the house was greeted by Stalin. Needless to say, the prisoners had lots to eat the following days.

Thomas was very happy about the way his leg felt. It wasn't getting infected anymore, and the pain was a lot less. A Russian came into the room. "Thomas, Lukas, you two have to move on to another house! The truck is waiting for you!" Other prisoners were already sitting on the truck. Thomas and Lukas were helped onto the flatbed and the truck drove away.

Lukas, the SS man, drew a frown and said, "I wonder where these pigs will bring us now? It will probably be another one of their swine holes!"

Thomas looked at Lukas, who was almost 40 years old and had deep blue eyes and blond hair. Thomas said, "We lost the war! So far, I am okay with how they have treated us! We are the losers. They could have killed us! Hitler lost the war! You better break your alliance with Hitler!"

Lukas said, "You have no idea! You don't know what it means to be an SS man! We started out as the personal body guard of our beloved Adolf Hitler! SS comes from 'Schutzstaffel', Protective Echelon. We are the elite of humankind! Hitler said so! And now this! I am in the hands of these pigs!" He frowned and turned away from Thomas. Despite Lukas' arrogance, Thomas felt sorry for him.

After a short drive, they ended up in front of the local school. This school was now being used as a hospital. Russian guards carried Thomas to one of the former classrooms and opened the door. In front of Thomas were real beds with real white bedsheets on them. One of the Russian guards was helping Thomas and Lukas into the room, when a loud voice shouted, "Stop! Nobody comes into this room unwashed! Please put them into the hallway, I will be out in a minute!" Hermine, the girl in charge, had a strict regimen.

After a short time, she came out into the hallway and told the guard to bring the prisoners to the bathing area. She followed the men. She was dressed in a simple skirt and blouse with an apron tied around her slender waist. Her long, blond hair was tied in a knot, away from her kind face and her sharp formed nose. The bathing area was a shed with a huge bathtub in it. Thomas was the first candidate to hit the waves. He enjoyed it immensely. His injured leg was sticking out of the tub. Hermine had no mercy washing off any residue of lice and whatever dirt was to be found. She had new clothes for Thomas after he was clean and let the guard help him into his new bed with the real white bedsheets. Thomas felt like a baby taken care of by his mother.

Hermine watched over her patients like a hawk. She had trained all the girls that were assisting her. No lice were found in her room. The wounded men had clean bandages and the windows were always open to let in fresh air. Unruly behaviour also, was not tolerated, but unfortunately, she had no power over the daily food ration the prisoners got. It was one piece of bread a day, as big as a fist, and at midday a bowl of soup; water with something in it, and the idea of a cup of coffee. It was very thin coffee. The amount of nutrition the men got each day, just kept them alive.

Despite the good care of Hermine, Thomas' wound did not heal! He got concerned!

Hermine stepped into the room "Everybody get up! We will all go outside today! The sun is warm! We will help you to get a bit of fresh air. Thomas thought, "Wonderful!"

Lukas, the SS man said, "Wonder what that is all about? Don't trust the Russians! They have something up their sleeves!" Thomas had to smile at his roommate's grumpy attitude. Two girls helped move Thomas outside and put him on the grass with all the other prisoners from the rest of the rooms in the infirmary. Some of the prisoners found old buddies and greeted them with excitement. All the men had one thing in common; they were very skinny. The stories about each other's condition made the rounds along with how they were wounded. Thomas missed Harri. When he looked over all these former soldiers, his heart thought it would have been so good to have Harri by his side!

One of the Germans stated the fact that the War was over. "The 8th of May 1945, my friends, will be an important date in German history! On this day, the Russian army marched into Berlin and took our capital. This was the end of the War! The end of the Second World War! I must say! Germany lost! Finally, the world is at peace!" Thomas looked into the face of Lukas, whose face was red with anger.

Another prisoner spoke up in a loud voice. "What happened to Adolf Hitler? Is he in the hands of the Russians?"

The first man spoke again, "No, not at all! You know Hitler, he would never acknowledge defeat, he would rather die! And that he did! He and his girlfriend, Eva von Braun, took their own lives in Hitler's bunker." The face of Lukas turned white. Thomas could see that he was getting uncomfortable.

A third prisoner raised his voice. "You have to tell the truth about the Jews!" Thomas watched Lukas get even more uncomfortable, staring at the ground and beginning to sweat.

Looking down at the ground the first speaker said with a more subdued voice, "Yes, the Jews! Remember all those work camps they put all the Jews in? Some of the Jews really worked in there, but only a few very lucky ones. The rest of them, and I am talking about millions, I am saying millions, got killed in gas chambers. German guards let the people undress themselves and told them to go under the showers in a huge bathhouse, but instead of water, gas came out and killed them." The men around Thomas didn't know what to say. This was too much to comprehend! Germany had killed millions of Jews?

One piped up, "Are you sure about this? We heard rumours about the killings of Jews, but this sounds like an evil horror! Nobody can even think up such evil!"

Another prisoner fell in. "Except Adolf Hitler! He was like evil himself!"

The former speaker said, "But who knew about all that? Why didn't we know?"

The first man who told the whole news said, "The SS was involved. If you were an SS man, you would have known about it! My guess is that some of the officers knew something as well, but I believe very few must have known the whole story: that so many Jews were killed. There was more than only one concentration camp! I don't know how many people had knowledge of the scope of this!"

Hermine stepped outside to address the men. "Let's go back inside! Time is up!" Thomas looked to his side, expecting Lukas to be sitting there. Lukas was gone! Everybody made their way into the former school and found their beds nicely made with new bedsheets on them. But Lukas' bed was empty. For a moment Thomas wondered where he was. But Thomas had to digest the news he had just heard about how the Jews were treated by his fellow countrymen. Germany had finally lost the war but had killed millions of Jews, as well as all the other people Germany had killed in the war! "Germany is my home country! This news will be all over the world, people will be talking about us killing millions of Jews!" Thomas felt a huge weight on his heart. "I am German! Am I evil?" He didn't mind that the piece of bread was so small beside his bed. He didn't feel hungry! "What will happen to Germany now? The whole world will be angry at us!" he thought.

Hermine came into the room. She was upset. "Hm, I am sorry to tell you, but Lukas, your buddy, just hanged himself in the shed with a bedsheet. We don't know why. We are very sorry!" Thomas knew why. Lukas knew of all the evil. He might have been part of it! "He had sold his soul to the devil!" Thomas thought.

MOTHER DON'T CRY ABOUT YOUR BOY

"The stores are open again! We are able to buy as much as we want, with money." Heini excitedly exclaimed as he entered the apartment.

"Are you serious?" Otti his wife, turning towards the door replied, "No stamps, just money?"

"Yes! Just money, real money!" Said Heini, "Like in normal times! The Americans have taken over and arranged it all!"

Colour returned to Otti's cheeks, she stood a little straighter, and her eyes took on a clear visionary look. Standing in her apron by the sink she was all smiles. She turned to Emma and Sabine who were mending the socks for the family at the kitchen table, and who were now looking at her. The two little girls were watching the big girls.

Otti took charge. "Emma and Sabine, why don't the two of you and Father go shopping before the stores are empty again. Heini, you go to the butcher and try to get some ground meat. Emma, you go to the baker and try to get a loaf of good rye bread and 10 buns. Sabine, you go to the grocery store across the road and get some cans of tuna, a bag of flour and fresh vegetables. Oh, I forgot the oil and butter and eggs and if they have it, some sugar. Sugar would be so special! That will be enough for today! I can't believe it! I can actually give you some money! I have to get used to that again!"

Sabine and Heini got their bags and the money from Otti and left promptly. Emma was a bit later, because she had to change into something nice. This was an important outing!

From across the road Sabine saw the long lineup in front of the grocery store. She hurried over to be next in line. The woman in front of her sighed, "I hope there will be something left for me, when my turn comes!

Sabine agreed, "I hope so too! Do you have a big family to feed?"

"Not too many, just me and my two children. My husband is a POW in Russia. I don't know how long he will be there." Tears came into her eyes! Sabine patted her on the shoulder, trying to give her some comfort.

"Our brother is a POW in France. We hardly hear from him! I know how you feel!"

After a long wait, it was finally Sabines' turn to enter the store. Her eyes grew big! Most of the shelves were still filled with merchandise. One boy was walking back and forth from the back stockroom to the store, replenishing the shelves. Sabine hadn't seen full shelves for a long time. It was a joy! She read her shopping list to the clerk and he helped her fill the order and fit it all into her bag. She paid with real money! They both enjoyed the exchange. Sabine got everything she ask for and knowing that the next costumer would be able to get what he wanted, made her even more happy.

Filled with joy, she approached the road in order to cross over again and walk home. She had to stop! A never-ending line of military vehicles were driving slowly up the street. "This will be a long wait!" she thought. She lowered her shopping bag to the ground and got ready to wait. After a short while, a car stopped beside her.

The passenger window was rolled down and a man inside shouted, "Go, go ahead!" He was a black American soldier! Sabines' eyes got big, her face turned white, then red, her mouth fell open. The black man in the window started laughing. "Go, just go! Don't be scared!" Sabine got hold of herself, smiled back at him, grabbed her bag and ran fast across the road. On the other side of the street, she put her bag down again and turned around to see the black man one more time. "My first black man!" she thought. "Wow, that was amazing! And he was so nice! He looked so kind!"

Otti was busy helping the little girls with their dolls, when Sabine burst into the door. "You won't believe what I just saw! A real black man! And he was very, very nice!" Otti and the little girls looked at Sabine in bewilderment.

"I have never seen a black man in my life!" Otti said, a bit jealous of her daughter. The door opened again with father and Emma entering the room. Both had huge smiles on their faces and bags filled with meat and bread.

Otti was all smiles. "Empty all your bags onto the kitchen table! Let's see what we've got!" The table was full of groceries, something the whole family hadn't seen in a while. Sabine didn't forget the two lollipops for her little sisters. They squealed with delight.

Mother made sure that all the groceries found their right place in the cupboards. Afterwards she made a weak coffee. Normally coffee would be a Sunday treat only, but today, with all the goodies and the fresh apple cake Emma had bought at the bakery, it was a day of celebration. Sabine told the story about the black soldier to Emma and father.

"Oh, I have never seen a black person!" Emma said with a frown. She was also very jealous!

"Heini, why are black people in America!" Otti asked, "Don't they live in Africa?"

"The Americans used to make black people slaves," Heini replied. "They got them out of Africa. People made a lot of money selling them so they could be used as slaves to work in their fields or do their house work and so on. But the Civil War changed all that and now black people are free and integrated, as far as I know."

Sabine pondered out loud, "I wonder if now, after the war, the Jews are going to be accepted and integrated as well? I wonder if Sarah, my school friend, is going to move back to Luedenscheid? They must have released all the Jews from the work camps by now!"

Heini winced. "I am not so sure about Sarah, dear Sabine! I never told you, but people are talking about the killing of the Jews. Rumours are going around that a lot of Jews were killed in those concentration camps. I don't know how many are still alive. For them, I believe it will take a long time to get accepted in our society. Hitler has spread so many lies about the Jews. It will be------- Bang! Bang!

Somebody was pounding on the door. A loud commotion could be heard in the hallway. Father emptied his coffee cup and went to the door. On the other side of the door stood the owner of the apartment building surrounded by a group of American soldiers.

"Hi Heini, I am sorry to barge in so unexpectedly! The American army has taken over my buildings. They need the whole complex for their army to stay for a couple of days. Everybody has to move out right away! I hope it won't be long until you and your family are able to move back in."

Heini's face turned white, he had to swallow. "Where can we go?" At that moment a friend of father came up the stairs and made his way through the group of soldiers.

"Heini, our school basement is still a designated bunker with all the beds in there. You and the other families can use it. You have washrooms and the home-ec kitchen is all yours to cook in as well." The man was the custodian of the school.

Mother, who overheard it all, said, "Thank you so much! We will pack our things right away and come up to the school." The two little girls started crying. They got scared with so many strong men in the hallway. "Hush, hush you two, it will be alright!" Mother put her arms around them to comfort them. "Emma, Sabine, pack your things! Emma, don't pack too many clothes, this will take just a couple of days. After you've packed, you can help me with all these groceries and the things for the girls. Heini, please get the little wagon from the basement. It will help us to bring all our stuff up the hill to the school."

The whole family made their way up the hill. Father pulled the loaded wagon, the others carried bags with items they would need for the coming days.

Mother cringed. "I wonder what our apartment will look like after a bunch of soldiers have lived in there?"

"We better be prepared for the worst. Men can be rough when there is no woman around!" Father replied.

Sabine shouted, "Look, what is happening there?" The family looked in the direction she was pointing. A crowd of people had jam-packed the shoe store. It was mayhem!

"People are looting the stores!" Father sighed. "The Americans gave permission to loot all the stores, except the essential ones."

"How awful!" Emma said in disgust.

"Yes, this isn't a good thing, but on the other hand, the stores didn't have a lot on their shelves anyway!" They reached the catholic school and made their way to the basement. A warm welcome greeted them from their neighbours who were there before them. Every family had their own corner with beds. The little girls found their neighbourhood friends right away and began playing with them.

"I think we will be all right for a couple of days." Mother said.

Three days passed before the owner of the apartment building came into the school to tell them that the Americans had moved out. "Let's go home!" Heini said confidently. The packing started again, and the whole family walked down the hill back to their home. They entered the building and began climbing up the stairs.

Mother froze. "I have never seen the stairs as dirty as this! Now I am getting scared about our place!" They reached their suite, and Mother slowly opened the door.

The kitchen was first. It was a big room. The floor was covered with mattresses.

"This doesn't look too bad!" Father exclaimed. They put their bags down and everybody made their way through the kitchen toward the bedrooms.

"Oh no!" Emma started crying when she saw her and Sabine's room. Hundreds of cigarette butts littered the floor. The glass plates that used to cover the night tables were now broken and in pieces. Emma's sewing machine had been used as an ash tray as well. The wooden, once shiny top had black burn marks all over it. Emma's hands started shaking. "My sewing machine is ruined! Look what they did!"

The rest of the family examined the machine. The belt to turn the wheel was still on, the foot pedal not harmed, and even the needle was still in place. "It will work just fine, don't make such a fuss!" Sabine told her, shrugging her shoulders.

"They must have danced on top of those night tables!" Otti cried. All the furniture had black marks on them, undoubtedly from cigarette butts.

The family was shocked! With a deep breath, Otti composed herself. "Alright girls, put your aprons on, we have cleaning to do!" They started shuffling around. "Heini, please open the windows wide, it smells horrible in here. And please get rid of those mattresses in the kitchen." After a day of hard work, the family sat around the kitchen table for their evening dinner. Things looked and felt a lot better.

Thomas had been at the school-turned-hospital for over a month now. It was July, and he appreciated the good care under the watchful eyes of Hermine. After Lukas, the SS man took his own life, Ulrich became the new bed neighbour of Thomas. Ulrich and Thomas developed a good friendship by helping each other. Ulrich had lost his right arm and experienced a lot of difficulties getting used to having only one hand. Thomas' new life was difficult with only one properly functioning leg. So, Ulrich did some walking for Thomas, and Thomas lent Ulrich a hand if he needed one. The wound on Thomas' leg still wasn't healing, which was worrisome to Thomas!

"Did you ever hear about Canada?" Ulrich pondered one day. "Do you know you can buy a huge piece of land in Canada for only five Dollars? But you have to promise to remove the trees and use the land to grow wheat or what not."

Thomas laughed, "You must be kidding! Five Dollars! That sounds like a fairy tale! Why would they give their land away for nothing!"

"They have so much land! Canada is the second biggest country in the world! The forests are humongous! They have so many lakes, I don't know if anybody ever counted them. The Rocky Mountains are huge! The prairie is never ending! If you fly over Canada, you will hardly see a house or a city. It is a vast land!" Ulrich pulled a piece of newspaper out of his pocket and gave it to Thomas.

Thomas read out loud. "Looking for hard-working people to build our agriculture…" He was impressed! "Do they have airplanes in Canada?" he asked.

"If somebody has so much land, he needs an airplane to spray the crops with fertilizer and so on. The land is way too big; you can't do all the work by hand! My family has a farm, a large size peace of land, but a field in Canada is as big as the total land we grow our crops on. And one farmer has more than just one field," said Ulrich with a proud face.

"I would love to be a pilot in that plane for the crops! When this prison time is over and my leg is healed, I am going to make my pilot certificate and head to Canada. It sounds like a great country! I know I have to learn English. What else is important?"

"Ha-ha, you've got the Canada bug! You will not be disappointed! I have seen photos of that country. It is spectacular! They don't want me with only one arm! You have to be healthy in order to get accepted! A very important thing to know, if you go to Canada, is this song." He started singing with a proud voice, sounding confident holding all the notes in their right places. All the prisoners in the room got a little concert.

"Oh Canada! Our home and native land!
True patriot love in all thy sons command
With glowing hearts, we see the rise, the true North strong and free. From far and wide O Canada. We stand on guard for thee.
God keep our land glorious and free.
Oh Canada! We stand on guard for thee.
Oh Canada! We stand on guard for thee."

After singing, Ulrich had tears in his eyes. I love that song! It has so much power and gives you hope! Thomas was touched as well. The whole idea of going to Canada seemed to be good. It would be a totally new start for his life! He would be able to forget all about Hitler and the horror done to the Jews. A new country would be just what he needed. A new dream ignited in Thomas' heart.

The door opened and Hermine came in. Her eyes were red. She must have been crying! Everybody looked at her with concern on their faces! She composed herself and said, "I have bad news for all of us. The Russians are going to close this place and are going to bring you to a real prisoner of war camp. I am truly sorry! Trucks are already waiting outside for you and will bring you to the train station. That is all I know! I have no idea where you are going. It was a joy and honour to serve you! We will miss every one of you!"

Everybody was in shock! The girls who always helped Hermine were standing nearby ready to assist the wounded men. All the girls' eyes were red from crying. "Was this the last time that a German girl would take care of him?" Thomas wondered. The men packed their things and some gave a hug to Hermine. It was clear to everyone that her care for them had been exceptional and they would miss her dearly! Some of the prisoners had already started a relationship with one of the girls and exchanged information with a last kiss. It was a sad bunch sitting on the trucks and waving goodbye to the girls.

Down the road, a train was waiting at the station. A Russian opened the door of a train car and motioned for the prisoners to climb in. The cars were lined with rows of beds, in bunk bed style, with a second bed above the lower one. In one corner was a huge pot filled with water, which was for the prisoners to share during their trip. To prevent the water from spilling, the Russians had put a page from a newspaper on top. Thomas was very skeptical about the idea at first, but he found out that it worked! When the train started moving, no water spilled over the edge.

The prisoners had no idea about their destination. Siberia was a scary guess! The stories about Siberian prisons made their rounds. "Hopefully not!" Thomas thought. "There was not one good story from this cold Russian area up north!"

The train drove on for hours! All of a sudden, it came to a stop. "Was this a train station?" Everybody wondered. "Was this already the new camp?" Some men were hopeful. Men climbed out of their beds and opened the sliding door of the car carefully. They looked right into the faces of German people standing behind a horizontal bar at a train crossing. The train Thomas was in had come to a stop right at this spot. The people waited, expecting the train to keep going at any moment. Russian soldiers surrounded the train to prevent the prisoners from running. More and more people gathered at the crossing, forcing them to come to a halt against their will. The prisoners exchanged some words with the people waiting there, but soon the people started grumbling about the train blocking their way. The mood of the people turned sour!

A young fellow prisoner, who had a lot of difficulty moving, climbed out of his bed and made his way to the door. He put himself right in the middle of the huge entrance, holding on to the door frame. His face was pale and haggard. With his deep blue eyes, he looked into the faces of all the bystanders, took a full breath, and started singing in a soft deep voice.

"Mama, du sollst doch nicht um deinen Jungen weinen
Mama einst wird das Schicksal wieder uns vereinen.
Ich werde es nie vergessen, was ich an dir hab besessen.
Dass es auf Erden nur eine gibt, die mich so heiß hat geliebt,
Mama, und bringt das Schicksal uns nur Kummer und Schmerz
Dann denk ich nur an dich, es betet ja für mich, oh Mama dein Herz."

"Mother, don't cry about your boy! Soon we will see each other again!
I will never forget what a good mother I have.
I know that on earth no one loves me as deeply as you! If life will bring me lots of worries and pain,
I know your heart will be always praying for me!..."

Nobody, either in the train car or the people standing outside of the crossbar, was able to hold back their tears. The young man walked back to his bed and inhaled deeply. His eyes were filled with tears as well.

Finally, the train moved on. The people standing at the crossbar were still and quiet as their hearts held on to this precious moment. They waved the soldiers Good Bye!

This time, it didn't take too long for the train to come to a stop again. An official shouted, "Final stop, everybody out!" The men in the car were relieved! This was not Siberia! 'Sorau' a German town in Ostbrandenburg was written on a sign. The prisoners were hopeful when they got off the train and followed the Russian soldiers. The huge hall of the train station with its high aluminum ceiling became the new home for the prisoners of war. It was filled with at least 150 beds, the beds stacked three high, triple bunks, very close to each other.

Ulrich and Thomas walked into the hall, hoping to get their beds close to each other. They got lucky! Thomas was right beneath Ulrich. This was now their first real prisoner of war camp! A lot of Russian soldiers walked around and German Red Cross nurses tried to look after the wounded. The blankets smelled horrible, the mattresses were old, but were OK. A small piece of bread was their only meal for the night but at least the water was plentiful.

Night time came and the men settled down to sleep. "Not again! Oh no! I've had it!" All over the hall men groaned in disgust. The beds were not only full of lice but bed bugs were also appearing on the mattresses. All over the hall the popping of the bugs could be heard. Thomas tried his best to get rid of the bugs in his bed. "Plop!" Some fell down from Ulrich's mattress onto his. This was no fun!

Thomas didn't know how many times he woke up that night from being bitten and getting itchy spots. He was tired and very hungry in the morning. After a while, somebody from the kitchen came into the hall with a huge bag made out of sackcloth. Out of it came a piece of bread as big as a fist for each prisoner. "For today!" they were told. This was the only bread for the whole day! At lunch the kitchen crew gave out a bowl of soup; water with something in it. That was it for food. On top of the food the men also got a bit of a tobacco ration. Ulrich and Thomas didn't need all their tobacco so they gave it to the heavy smokers in exchange for bread. This changed their daily food portion for the better.

They were surviving, but unfortunately, after some weeks, the heavy smokers were starting to die. Thomas thought, "Their mother would cry!"

Thomas noticed that Ulrich would fold his hands every night at bedtime and asked about it. "Ulrich, do you pray at night before you sleep?"

Ulrich got red ears. "Ha, did you notice that? Yes, I pray the Lord's prayer every night. My mom taught it to me when I turned 12 years old."

"Why the Lord's prayer? Is that better than all the other bed time prayers mothers teach their children?"

"The Lord's prayer is the prayer Jesus, the Lord, taught his disciples to pray. My mom gave her life to Jesus when she was very young. She told me. "If the Lord Jesus tells us a prayer, it must be the best. I love my mom. She is the best! Do you know the Lord's prayer Thomas?"

"We learned the Lord's prayer in religion at school. But I don't think I would get it together again. Tell me the words?"

Ulrich smiled "Sure, no problem!

"Our Father which art in heaven, Hallowed be Thy name.
Thy Kingdom come. Thy will be done
on earth as it is in heaven.
Give us this day our daily bread.
And forgive us our debts, as we forgive our debtors.
And lead us not into temptation, but deliver us from evil;
For Thine is the Kingdom and the Power and the Glory
For ever and ever. Amen"

"I will have a hard time remembering that!"

"I have some tricks I use to help me!" Ulrich replied. "At first, I think about the fact that God takes so good care of me, I thank Him by saying that God is in heaven and His name is holy. Then I remember all the wrong decisions I've made in my life, and I say that His Kingdom come and His will be done. It makes me feel better to know that he is in control. My hunger tells me to ask for my daily bread. My shortcomings, like bad thoughts, lying, and whatnot, make me ask Him to forgive my sins, and I also forgive the people who sin against me. Praying like this will keep me from becoming bitter against all the Hitler people. It is easy to remember to ask for his protection from evil, especially during war, and now as a prisoner. And the end of the prayer is easy, because I know that he is the King and rules the world. That makes me feel good!"

"Wow, you sure thought a lot about your prayer! Hmm, I'll have to think about it too. I like it a lot. If I could get a piece of paper and a pencil, would you be able to write it down for me?

Ulrich smiled. "No problem Thomas!"

A Red Cross nurse came to Thomas' bed. "Hi, how are you doing? Could I take a look at your leg?" Thomas was glad about the attention to his leg and showed the nurse. She carefully removed the bandage. "Hmm, for how long was this wound been open?"

"I got shot on April the 21" of April." Thomas replied. "It will be two months now!"

The nurse looked into his eyes. "Thomas, that is a long time for a wound not to heal and close up! I wonder what the reason is? Maybe try to put more weight onto your leg. This will increase the blood flow, and that might do the trick." She put a fresh bandage on and went to the next prisoner. From then on, Thomas practiced walking with the help of a stick and was able to put more weight on his leg.

The next morning someone came in and announced, "The barber is waiting for you by the entrance. Everybody has to get a haircut today!" Thomas and Ulrich looked at each other. Both of them liked their hair very much and didn't want it to be butchered by somebody who didn't know what they were doing.

"Let's wait and see!" Ulrich comforted Thomas. "If the first of the boys look good enough, then we can go as well." So, Thomas and Ulrich let others be the first in line, and watched them come out after their haircuts. "Oh no!" The first men with the new hair cut were the three officers who didn't have time to help Thomas after he got shot and not able to get up from the ground. All three came back from the barber's corner completely bald. Thomas had to laugh. "Serves them just right!" he thought. But it didn't look promising for the rest of the soldiers! Ulrich and Thomas waited for more candidates to come back from the barber. Again, all of them were bald!

"That is it! I am not going!" Thomas said, turning around.

"Me neither!" The two stayed as far away from the barber as they could until the hall was full of bald men, except for Thomas and Ulrich. To avoid the looks of the Russians, they slipped deep under their blankets. Finally, the barber packed up his things and the danger was over. Ulrich and Thomas smiled at each other. They had made it!

Since Thomas could walk better, He and Ulrich went outside a lot. Thomas wasn't able to walk far, as his leg got swollen after a bit. The main reason for going outside was hunger. Thomas and Ulrich were skin and bones, like all the other prisoners.

Time went on and it was already autumn. One day, Thomas and Ulrich came to an area with trees, with acorns lying on the ground. Thomas got a great idea. "You know Ulrich, at home we took the acorns and fed them to the pigs. The pigs got fat and chubby. Why don't we roast them over a fire and get fat as well?"

Ulrich replied, "Ah-ah, what a good idea! Pigs eat a lot of leftovers from people, why can't we eat pig food?" Both men looked around for something to put the acorns on in order to roast them. Thomas found a metal mesh from a fence. That would serve the purpose! They made a hole and circled it with rocks and started a fire with all the dead wood that was lying around. The acorns roasted nicely over the fire. They smelled good and they looked good! Once they turned dark and crispy, Thomas decided they were ready to eat. Another fellow prisoner, who was attracted by the smell, joined the two and they sat down on the grass with a pile of roasted acorns beside them. All three of them started to eat.

Ulrich took a break from chewing. "Not too bad! It could be worse! As long as we all get fatter and stronger, ha-ha!" With stomachs full for the first time in a long while, they made their way back to the hall. The three were in such a good mood, that they were even cracking jokes with the Russian guards. "A full stomach makes you feel good!" Thomas thought.

It was time for bed, and the mood of the three scaled down a bit. All three met at the washroom at the same time, all having the need to relieve themselves at the upper and lower parts of their body. The good feeling turned into a really bad feeling, spiralling downwards into a real sick feeling. "I am sorry guys," Thomas moaned. "I guess it wasn't a good idea! I am so sorry!"

Ulrich replied, smiling under pain. "I forgive you, Thomas. I am glad to know that we are not pigs. I was wondering if our dirty clothes, which we haven't washed for months now, would turn us into pigs. It is good to know that we just smell like pigs, but that we are not pigs, ha-ha." For three days the three couldn't eat a bite. They were too sick, but they kept their bread ration wrapped in a handkerchief, only passing the soup on to the heavy smokers. After their stomachs felt good again, they had enough to fill their stomachs for a couple of days.

During the time when they were so very sick, Thomas stayed in bed all day. He took the sheet of paper with the Lord's prayer written on it out of his pocket and studied it over and over. The words "They will be done" made him think a lot about his future. "Is my leg going to heal? Will I really be able to go to Canada? Would that be the will of God? Hmm!" The other line made him think as well: "As we forgive our debtors." Am I able to forgive my little brother for wanting to kill me with that axe? To forgive my friend who tricked me into the army? I don't know. The guys who were so nasty to Harri and me after Harri lost track of them and then made us run over the open field to get the water... can I forgive them? The Russian who shot me in the leg, should I forgive him?" Thomas had to chew on it a bit longer. As for now, every night before he went to bed, he prayed the Lord's prayer. It made him feel good, and he felt that God held his life in his hands. That was a good feeling!

TO GOD BE THE GLORY

It was October 1945. A rumour was going around that the city of Sorau would become part of Poland and the Russians would have to get out. The prisoners wondered, "What will happen to us?" On the 5th of October a Russian soldier in his sand-coloured uniform with a pipe hanging from his mouth stood in front of the prisoners. Breaking out in a smile he said, "Everybody listen! Get ready to walk to the German border tomorrow morning. The border is the river Neisse, 40 kilometers away from us. It will be a long, hard walk! We know that some of you are not able to walk that far so you can stay behind for another two weeks and then a truck will come and take you to the border. The walk starts tomorrow at 5 am."

One of the German officers asked, "What will happen to us at the border? Will we be able to cross over into Germany? Are we going to be set free?"

The Russian's smile got even bigger, "Yes, once you are on German soil, you will be free! The prisoners all started talking at once."

"We will be free! I can go back to my family! Wow! I can't believe it!" On and on throughout the hall, the voice of hope could be heard.

Ulrich was as happy as everybody else, "What do you think, Thomas? We will be free tomorrow!" Thomas face showed a slight smile but also concern. "Oh, I am sorry! To walk 40 kilometers is too much for you! I am sorry! Are you going to wait two more weeks for the truck?"

Another one of the prisoners chimed in. "If I were you Thomas, I would try to walk with us. I don't trust the Russians to keep their word! Two weeks is a long time! Anything can happen in two weeks!"

Thomas said, "Just what I was thinking! Who knows what is going on in two weeks! I want to get free as well! I think I'll try to walk. I am getting better every day. I'll use two sticks. That will help me to not put too much weight on my injured leg."

Ulrich said, "We will be with you! And, they have to give us some breaks during the walk!" So, it was decided. Thomas would go with the others the next day towards freedom! At night in bed, he worried about his decision. Would he be able to make it? Would he be a burden to the others? But what would happen if the Russians didn't keep their word to pick up the wounded in two weeks. That would be so much worse!

The morning of October the sixth started early. At 5 AM the whole group of prisoners, Red Cross nurses, and the Russians on their horses, started the journey towards Germany. The kitchen gave each prisoner his piece of bread for the day and one can of condensed milk. Thomas started walking with a stick in each hand and tried to put only minimum weight on the injured leg. Ulrich was by his side, and the two started walking, dreaming of better times, their hearts filled with hope.

The first kilometers were manageable for Thomas. The Russians on their horses had their whips in their hands, and rode back and forth along the long line of prisoners shouting to them to go faster. Thomas was not the only one who had trouble walking. As it turned out, nobody trusted the Russians to keep their word. Men with all kinds of injuries walked with Thomas and the others. After the first kilometers were over, the leg with the injury started to hurt. Thomas bent down to look at it. It was swollen, especially the knee. He relied even more on the sticks to move forward. He was determined to go to freedom. After the first half of the walk the group was given a lunch break and the men were able to rest beside a brook. Ulrich and Thomas sat down on the grass and Thomas took out his piece of bread. When he looked at it, he saw that the outside was full of blood. "Hm, where is the blood from?" he said.

Ulrich's expression got serious, "Look at your hands! Your hands are bleeding! Nurse, could you come over here and help Thomas with his hands?" Thomas looked at his hands. Yes, they were bleeding. The nurse knelt down beside him and put some bandages on them

"Your sticks are too rough, Thomas, they're scraping off your skin, but with the bandages you'll be able to keep going." Ulrich went to the brook to fill up the water bottles of the two.

"Here is your water Thomas, you can do it! Freedom is at the end of this march!" After the short break, everybody had to get going again, onward towards the river Neisse where, on the other side, freedom awaited them.

The walk was getting harder. Thomas had to rest more often, and Ulrich waited patiently beside him. Finally, Thomas said, "Ulrich, please do me a favour and just keep walking. I feel sorry for you because you always have to wait for me. It would make me feel much better if you would keep going and catch up with the rest. I am not the only one walking slow. Don't worry about me!" Ulrich was reluctant to leave Thomas and let him go by himself, but he agreed to Thomas' request and went on ahead. Thomas felt better. He didn't like to be a burden.

A Russian on his horse came closer to Thomas and shouted at him to speed it up. Thomas took hold of his sticks and tried to walk faster. Ulrich was now further and further ahead of him and the rest of the wounded. The pain in his leg got worse. The swelling kept growing. "Will I be able to make it?" he thought.

One hour later Thomas had no strength left. He collapsed onto the ground. Sweat was running down his cheeks. He was done! He stretched out on the ground and closed his eyes "I don't care anymore! Just let me die here!" he thought. As he was getting closer to passing out, he got a flashback from the train ride towards Sorau; "Mother don't cry about your boy!" It was the song, the young slender boy with that wonderful strong voice had sung. In Thomas' heart a new resolve took hold. "My mother will not cry!" Opening his eyes, he spotted the Russian with his whip coming towards him, which gave Thomas more motivation. He got up on his feet determined to continue his journey. The Russian soldier rode beside Thomas for a while. Respect and compassion emanated from his eyes toward Thomas. That fact gave Thomas even more strength. "I will make it! One step at a time! I will do it!".

The sun was already down when Thomas and the other wounded prisoners reached the bank of the river. Ulrich was glad to have his buddy beside him, sitting in the grass. Thomas was spent, but so happy and very proud of himself, that he had made it.

The Russian on his horse spoke to the group. "Congratulations! Your whole group made it! We will rest for the night on this side of the river. Tomorrow you will have your freedom. On the other side of the river, the German side, there will be people to assist you with your release papers, and after that, you will be free to go." His horse turned around, and he joined his fellow Russian soldiers.

Thomas and Ulrich got settled in for the night. It was October and the nights were cold. Nobody had a blanket, so everybody moved close together to be warm. The Red Cross nurses had finished taking care of the wounded and came right into the middle of the men. "Please, take us into your middle!" they pleaded, "We know the Russians. They will molest us if you don't protect us." The German prisoners huddled all around the nurses and soon, one after the other, succumbed to their exhaustion and fell into a deep sleep. Thomas was one of the first to fall asleep. It was almost like passing out. He didn't notice the Russian soldiers walking right into the midst of them and pulling the nurses out, who resisted with all their might to no avail. He didn't hear the cries or the weeping of the nurses through half of the night. After the Russians let them go, the nurses crawled back into the arms of the German prisoners. Morning came, and their tears dried up.

Thomas woke up in the morning, cold to his bone. He sat up and noticed Ulrich coming up from the river with both of their water bottles over his shoulder. "He must have filled them!" he thought.

Ulrich looked into Thomas' face. "How are you? Are you able to walk over to the other side and get your papers done?"

Thomas smiled. "You bet. Let's go to freedom! Let's go! Let's get the papers filled out!" The two walked beside each other over the bridge to the other side. German officials were waiting at tables ready to help the German men with their papers. The two had to stand in line until it was their turn.

Free! Finally! Thomas and Ulrich embraced each other. Their hearts were filled with hope and joy. Ulrich said, "So, what's next? I have to go by train to Goerlitz and from there with another train to my hometown. Don't your parents live near Goerlitz as well?"

"Yes!" Thomas said, "We can travel together until we arrive in Goerlitz. My home is not too far from there, but we have to walk to Cottbus first, and that is still a long distance from here. I don't know if you want to keep walking with me. You would be so much faster walking alone!"

Ulrich replied, "Let's walk together! That is a lot more fun, and I might need your hand, ha-ha." Both men started the long walk towards the city of Cottbus. It was another long, hard day, but there were no Russian soldiers on their horses with whips in their hands. It was a good day.

Thomas did a lot of thinking during the walk. This would be the last day for him and Ulrich to be together.

"Ulrich, you told me that your mom gave her life to Jesus. What does that really mean?" Ulrich answered, "I have the same question, Thomas. I am just praying the Lord's prayer because she told me to, and it makes me feel good. I know that God exists and that he provides for me and protects me, but I don't know how I can really connect with him. I can tell you one thing: after everything I have witnessed during the war, I will ask my mom about it! That is a sure thing!"

Thomas said, "I don't think that my Mom would know the answer to my questions! We hardly went to church, but we always believed that there is a God. I'm hungry!"

Ulrich said, "Me too! It would have been nice if they would have given us some bread for our trip home. But it won't be too long, only another day, and we will be home." The two walked on. The distance to Cottbus took them all day. At the end of the day, they were able to see the city in the distance and their hopes rose. Getting closer, it became clear, that this city was not really a city anymore. The houses all over town were in ruin. Not one house was intact and there was not a person in sight. It must have been a terrible bombardment. Ulrich said, "I hope the train station is still there!" The two made their way over debris toward the station. It was still standing and more importantly, the tracks were all in a good shape.

Thomas looking around said, "Lets look for a house with a roof on it, the night will be cold. We need shelter!" They spotted one house with a good part of the roof still on it and made their way towards it. They entered the house, carefully stepping over more debris. They could see a room further in that seemed to be in good shape. Coming to its doorway, they spotted a woman beside two young girls who were cowering on the floor. The woman and the girls had their woolen overcoats wrapped tightly around their slim figures. Their faces were pale. A scarf covered each of the girls' hair. The woman looked at the two men with fear in her eyes. Ulrich said to her, "Is it alright with you if we spend the night here? We have to take a train to Goerlitz tomorrow. We were prisoners of war and are now free."

The women, not looking too happy, replied, "Of course, anybody can sleep in here! This is not my house, but for your own sake, don't come too close to my girls, they have lice!" Thomas said, "Don't worry. All we want is sleep! We walked all day without any food, and we just want to get home." He turned away from the woman and looked into the face of Ulrich. Ulrich was shaking, trying not to laugh out loud, tears streaming down his cheeks. Thomas had to quietly laugh as well. If anybody had lice in this room, it would be them.

The woman got up from the floor, her face had changed into a smile. She understood the situation of the two guys in front of her. She pulled two sandwiches out of her bag and gave them to the men. "Here you two. I guess I can trust you! I am sorry for not being so nice. My girls and I are fleeing to the west. I have to protect the girls. These are bad times!" Thomas and Ulrich thanked her. They both had a real sandwich with lard in their hands, something they hadn't tasted for a long time. "Give us today our daily bread' Thomas thought. God provided! Before falling asleep Thomas thought about his mother and his two little sisters.

Would they still be at home? Did they have to flee as well? He fell asleep.

Both men woke up around the same time. They discovered that the woman and her girls were gone already. They hurried to get themselves ready as well in order to catch the train. After reaching the station, they didn't have to wait long and the train to Goerlitz arrived. This train was a normal train for passengers. It was a treat the two would enjoy. The sight of normal people, not just soldiers, was a pleasure for their eyes. A mother was sitting together with her children. An older couple sat on the next set of seats. Thomas and Ulrich tried to stay away from everybody as far as they could. Both knew they smelled bad. The people in the car watched the two with pitiful eyes. Everyone had heard by now that the Russians had released their prisoners of war.

After a good hour-long ride, the train stopped in the town of Weisswasser. There would be a two hour wait for the next train to come, which would then bring them to the city of Goerlitz. Ulrich suggested, "Let's go and try to get something to eat." They walked away from the train station and found a field with corn, not far away. A lot of corn was still on it! Both men didn't wait a second to pull off a cob. It wasn't cooked, but it was real food, not only for pigs, like the acorns, but for men as well. Sitting down beside the field, Thomas peeled off the cob for his buddy Ulrich and handed it over to him. With corn in their hands, they had a good time. It felt good to have a full stomach again and on top of it, to be able to go home. Thomas could almost taste the good soup and the good bread his Mom would lovingly prepare. "Would she have enough flour and sugar for a cake to celebrate his return?" he wondered. Happy, laughing and joking, the two climbed up into the next train, destination Goerlitz.

The train approached the city of Goerlitz, and it looked alright. Most houses were in good shape. The two agreed to look for the next train to their home town right away and then say their goodbyes. The breaks of the train made a loud squealing sound as it ground to a stop at the station. Both men got out of the car, looking around for the next train they had to take.

An official of the communist party with the hammer and sickle emblem on his collar put himself in front of them. Thomas and Ulrich stopped and looked at him. He had a dangerous smile on his rectangular shaped face. Thomas and Ulrich looked around the train station. There were more men like him standing around and obviously waiting for other former prisoners of war.

The man in front of them looked at Thomas and Ulrich sternly. "May I see your release papers please?" Thomas and Ulrich handed him their papers and waited. They looked into each other's eyes, worried! The man said, "You have to stay in quarantine for four weeks before you are allowed to join the rest of the population."

Joy and hope were dispelled, worry, and a crushing sadness, filled the space. Another member of the communist party led the two to their new quarters. It used to be a former barracks for the Hitler Youth, but was now being used by the communist party as a quarantine building. Thomas and Ulrich found their beds, pretty much the same kind they had at their last stay in Sorau.

In the afternoon, a leader of the communist party of Goerlitz addressed them. "Welcome to Goerlitz! You are in the eastern part of Germany, the part under Russian control. I am one of the leaders of the German communist party. We are working very close together with our Russian counterparts. Russia has declared Hitler and his followers as dangerous criminals. You have fought in Hitler's army. You are criminals yourselves! You have no rights during this time of quarantine! Your future is in the hands of the communist party. This part of Germany will be cleansed from the wrong teachings of your former idol, Adolf Hitler."

Thomas and Ulrich looked into each other's eyes. They were overwhelmed by what they had just heard. To have said no to Hitler and to have avoided being a soldier would have cost you your life, and now they were being punished for just keeping themselves alive.

Finally, in bed, Thomas pulled the blanket over his head and just wanted to sleep, to shut out all thoughts and all emotions. He had been on the mountain top and now in the deepest valley. His emotions were all over the place! "Maybe I should have killed myself right when they drafted me?" he wondered. He overheard Ulrich crying in his bed and then he heard an utterance of disgust from him, "Oh no! Not again!" Thomas noticed it as well. The blankets were full of lice, and this time, bed bugs as well!

After Thomas had popped enough of those little creatures so he would have some peace for a while, he closed his eyes. Tears ran down his cheeks. A great sadness filled his heart. Like every evening lately, he started to pray the Lord's prayer. "Our Father which art in heaven hallowed be

Thy name. Thy Kingdom come. Thy will be done on earth as it is in heaven. Hm, …..Thy will be done! My life is in God's hands. God has the earth and the heaven in his hands!" A quiet peace came into Thomas' heart. He fell asleep.

The next morning was the start of a very dark day, not only because of the low-hanging clouds, but the exhaustion of the previous long days, with unimaginable physical and emotional pain, and of always living on the edge of breaking down, had taken its toll. Never mind the joy of freedom being crushed by the doom of another imprisonment, together with the accusaton of being labeled a criminal.

Ulrich came during the morning hours to tell him the details of their dilemma. He said, "The allies have divided Germany into four sectors. We are in the Eastern part of Germany that now belongs to Russia. The rest of Germany is open and free, but the border around the Russian sector is closed. You will not be able to go to your home. Your hometown is on the other side of the border. Actually, your town was taken over by Poland. This is a totally different country now. Those are the facts! I am so sorry! How are you? You don't look good!"

Thomas had only one word. "Done! I am done! I can't get up today! I am done!"

"Just rest Thomas, you're not missing anything!" And Ulrich left.

Thomas stayed in bed all day, thinking again and again about the horror Hitler had done to Germany under his rule. Making people like Thomas a criminal by forcing them into the war. He remembered what the guys in the school hospital told him. Hitler had gassed millions of Jews. He was so shocked about it at the time that he had put it into the back of his mind. It was now front and centre. Hitler gave orders to kill an unbelievable number of people, mainly Jews. Thomas wanted to push it back again, but it was right before his eyes. He pictured the trains filled with living Jews taking them to the concentration camps. They would be told to take a shower, to undress, because they had to wash up, then to stand right under the shower head and turn the crank open. Gas came out. Living people collapsed into dead people. Just like that! One group after the other!

Thomas cried again. He fought for that guy! Bleeding for the wrong cause! Shame washed over him in full force, and cold guilt penetrated his soul. He didn't dare look into anyone's eyes.

A middle-aged doctor dressed in a white coat came to Thomas and asked, "How are you doing? I would like to examine you." He looked Thomas over and was shocked to see his swollen leg and the blisters Thomas had all over his hands and feet. "Did you walk the 40 kilometers from Sorau to the border like all the rest of the prisoners?"

Thomas said, "Yes! And the next day 20 kilometers from the Neisse to Cottbus, in order to catch the train."

The doctor was shaking his head. "How did you do it Thomas? That is impossible with an injured leg like yours! You must have been out of your mind! You could have collapsed right there on the way!"

Thomas replied, "I actually did, but I got up again."

Affirming Thomas, the doctor said, "Heads up to you Thomas! You are a hero in my eyes! But now, you have to rest. The swelling in your leg has to go down, and the blisters on your hands and feet have to heal up. The blisters are full of pus! I will cut them open and put on a bandage so they can heal up. I would advise you to stay in bed for at least three days!"

"Thank you, doc. I am not planning to go anywhere, ha-ha!" The doctor went to the next man close to Thomas. He was very young and was having epileptic attacks. After every seizure he had to throw up the little food he received in this place. Thomas was very sorry for him. Watching the guy throw up and suffer dampened his own appetite. Since they gave out even less food than in Sorau, it was a good thing.

Thomas thought about what the doctor had said. "You are a hero in my eyes!" In his mind he looked back at the 40 kilometer walk and knew that it was not his own strength that brought him to the river Neisse. He knew it was God who helped him on his way. He remembered the closing lines of the Lord's prayer, "For Thine is the Kingdom and the Power and the Glory forever!" To God be the Glory! God had given him the strength!

After three days had passed, Ulrich came to Thomas' bed. "How are you buddy? You have now been in bed for three days! You must be starved! Are you getting better? How are your feet and hands?"

Thomas replied, "I am getting better, and yes, I am starved! This little piece of bread we are getting each day is not enough to live on. We will all die in here!"

Ulrich laughed. "Finally you're getting your spirit back! Yes, we will die with this little bit of bread. Here is half of my sandwich which I got today when I was begging."

Thomas gladly took the sandwich. His eyes grew big. "Begging? You are begging? Where and how?"

Ulrich replied, "Begging is the only way to keep us alive! Everybody is doing it! We are allowed to go into town, so we go and beg for food at the houses. You better start begging too. You have to live!"

Thomas had to think about that. "Begging? I have to go begging? I don't know how to do that?" The next day brought some sunshine into the barracks. It promised to be a warmer day than the ones before. "Today is the day!" Thomas decided. He got up and was ready to go and beg for food. He was scared! What would people think of him?

With his hands and feet still rapped in bandages and using his sticks he walked out of the barracks toward the first houses of the city of Goerlitz. He stopped in front of the first house. "What should I do now? What does somebody say when they beg? Please would probably be a good word, hmm?" Thomas knocked on the door. The door opened, and an older man stuck his head out. "You are already the third guy asking for food! We don't have much ourselves! The man shut the door and left Thomas standing there.

Thomas sat down on the steps. "This wasn't a good start, but at least I didn't have to say anything, ha-ha." He walked on further into town and knocked at another house. The door opened and a young woman with long brown hair falling over her shoulder that framed a beautiful oval face, appeared in the doorway. Thomas asked, "Please, do you have a little bit to eat?"

The young woman spoke kindly, "Why don't you sit down on the stairs! I am in the middle of cooking something.

I'll bring it out for you in a minute." Thomas' heart jumped for joy! She was going to give him something to eat! He sat down on the stairs and waited. It didn't take long and the woman came back to the door.

"This is for you!" she said, giving Thomas a plate with food and a fork to eat with.

Thomas looked into her eyes, "Thank you so much!" The lady went into the house again, and Thomas looked down at his plate. He couldn't believe his eyes! Two boiled potatoes, with the peel on, and garnished with a bit of cheese and green onions on top. It looked so beautiful! It looked like a feast to Thomas. Maybe life wasn't so bad after all. He enjoyed every bite of it. "Just like at home!" he thought. At night before falling asleep he prayed the Lord's prayer again. He stopped at "Give us our daily bread," Silently he said "Thank you God for giving me my daily bread today!" Thomas had a good night's sleep.

Thomas' hands and feet had healed up. He was able to go begging everyday from then on. All the others did it as well. Over time the citizen got to know the men. They felt sorry for these undernourished, former soldiers, but they themselves also had very little to eat. The war was just over and the economy at a very low point. Especially in the east sector of Germany, there was very little to eat, but the people shared what they could with these poor fellows.

The four weeks in the barracks were almost over. The doctor looked at Thomas' leg again, as he had done many times before, and now said, "Thomas I am worried about your leg! After you are released tomorrow, please go to the hospital right away. You can tell them that I sent you. Your wound is still open. The time from April until November is way too long for a wound to stay open. They have good doctors in that hospital! Wish you well!" Thomas decided that after his release he would do just what the doctor had said, but first, today, he needed something to eat.

He walked a bit outside of town into the countryside. On his left was a nice house, which he planned to try out first. He got closer but stopped in his tracks. Over the door was an emblem with the hammer and sickle, showing that the people living there, were communists. He was thinking that it would be better to keep going, when the door opened and a middle-aged man came out of the house. He asked Thomas what he wanted and started a conversation. A girl in Thomas' age joined them, and all three had a good talk about their families, the village Thomas came from, the job he learned, and so on. At the end, the man told his daughter to fill Thomas' bag with food. He said, "Feel welcome to come back whenever you are hungry, we'll have more for you!"

Thomas replied, "I thank you so much. You are very kind! Too bad I didn't meet you before, but I am moving out of the barracks tomorrow morning. I have a bad leg that won't heal up. They told me that the hospital here in Goerlitz has good doctors who will be able to help me. So, I am going to go to the hospital tomorrow."

The man and his nice-looking daughter looked at each other with a frown on their face. "Oh, what a shame! We just got to know each other! How about if my daughter visits you and brings you some food?"

Thomas' ears got red as he said, "That would be very kind of you! Thank you very much! I better get going now! Bye, bye!" And he left the nice people.

"I guess he wants to have somebody to marry his daughter!" Thomas thought. He found himself a nice place to eat and had a good dinner. Tonight would be his last night in the barracks!

Coming back into the barracks he found Ulrich sitting on his bed, with his head down. "What is wrong with you? You can go home tomorrow! You will see your parents and siblings! You might even get a cake and coffee! Why are you so sad?"

"I am not really sad, Thomas, I am scared! I am looking forward to seeing my family, but this will be the first time they will see me without one arm. They don't know! Do you understand? This will be a shock for them. I am scared!"

"I understand that!" Thomas said, "I would have the same fear if I would meet my parents. But I do believe they will be over the moon just to have you back, doesn't matter one or two arms. They will love you to pieces, don't you worry! The sad thing is, that I will miss you! But I am happy for you!"

The next morning Thomas got up early. Ulrich was already dressed, sitting on the edge of his bed, waiting for Thomas to wake up. He was eager to catch the first train out of Goerlitz to his home town. "Thomas, can you do up my shoe laces for the last time, please?"

"It will be my honour," Thomas replied, and knelt down to do up his friend's bootlaces. When he looked up, he discovered the eyes of Ulrich tearing up.

"We might never see each other again!"

"I know where you live. You never know!"

"I wish you the best, Thomas. I hope you will end up in Canada and fly your airplane! Take care, my friend! I have to go catch the train!"

I WANT TO LIVE

Sabine was crushed! She opened the door to the apartment and walked into the kitchen. Her face was in a frown, she could hardly hold back her tears. Mother looked into Sabines' face and asked, "What happened? What is wrong?"

Sabine couldn't hold her tears back anymore. "I was in Halver this morning because yesterday, our neighbour, Mrs. Berhaut told me that Erna was looking for me at the school where we stayed, while the Americans were using our building. Erna was looking for me to ask me back to work for her again. When Mrs. Berhaut told me that, I walked right away down to Halver, to tell Erna that I would love to come back and work for her."

"Na, that is no reason to cry!" Mother said, "So, what is the bad part?"

Sabine spoke again. "The bad part is that Mrs. Berhaut overheard somebody say that Emma and I got a job offer from the hospital, and she assumed that I would be working in the hospital by now. Because Erna really needed help, she hired another girl. Erna and I, we both cried! She would have really liked to have me back! I am so angry that Mrs. Berhaut lied to her!"

Mother replied, "Oh, I am so sorry for you! But don't be so hard on Mrs. Berhaut. She shouldn't have said that you worked in the hospital, but I don't believe she is evil and wanted to harm you. It is more a misunderstanding! How are they doing in Halver? Did their store get looted as well?"

Sabine excitedly answered, "No, mom, you won't believe this. Remember the two prisoners of war from Russia who were working in the shop, and the two other prisoners who got a sandwich every morning that I made for them? Those four men protected the store, day and night. They got themselves some weapons and stood guard day and night in front of the store, until the looting stopped. I am so happy for Erna and Guenter! The two were always so good to everybody! They gave shelter to people who were bombed out. I remember a lot of nights when Erna and I were preparing sandwiches for the people who just got homeless. Erna and Guenter deserved to be protected! Anyway, I guess I'll accept the offer from the hospital now!"

"Good for you!" Mother said. Sabine walked into her bedroom, where Emma like always, was sitting in front of the sewing machine.

Sabine asked her, "What are you sewing today?"

Emma replied, "The little ones each need a new dress. I have some fabric left over that will look pretty on them!"

"Good for you! I decided to accept the job offer from the hospital! Are you going to join me? Should we go to the hospital together?"

Emma jumped up from her chair and threw her arms around Sabine. "Yeah! I would love to! You didn't have to do this just for me!"

Sabine smiled. "Sorry, I didn't do it just for you! I went to Halver to get my old job back, but because of a misunderstanding it was taken already. I would have rather worked for Erna! But I guess the hospital will be fine as well! I heard they are very busy in the hospital with all those wounded soldiers. They can use a lot of hands to help them. I just hope that I'll be able to work on the floor with patients. That would be a lot of fun!"

"I'd rather work somewhere else," Emma replied, "not with people. Sick people throw up or need help with going to the washroom or even worse, they die! I'd rather stay away from all that stuff. Are we going tomorrow?"

Sabine, with a smile on her face, said, "Sure! Why not!"

Dirty, smelly, and full of lice, Thomas stood in front of the Goerlitz hospital. He approached the reception desk and asked for directions to the floor the doctor at the barracks had told him to go to. "Second floor and then to your right." he was told. The secretary was holding her nose, when Thomas finished seeing her. Thomas knew he smelled bad. He had said good bye to Ulrich and both had laughed about their dirty clothes, the horrible smell and the lice. Ulrich was on his way home. His parents lived in this section of East Germany.

Thomas worked his way up the stairs. Stairs were difficult! He couldn't avoid putting weight on the bad leg. It hurt and it took a long time to get up this one floor. A nurse was coming down the stairs, more jumping than walking. "Hi, how are you? Can I help you?" She looked into the eyes of Thomas with a lot of compassion. Thomas told her his destination and she replied, "That is funny! I work on that floor! Why don't I just go with you and help you to settle in!" She gave Thomas enough time and room to make it up the stairs and led him to the lead nurse.

The lead nurse asked Thomas his name and the name of the doctor who had told him to come here. She called the nurse, "Nurse Olga, this is Thomas our new patient. Please help him with the bath, free him of the lice and give him fresh clothes. I'll tell the doctor to look at him. Thomas will get the free bed in 209."

Nurse Olga led Thomas to a washroom with a real bathtub. Olga let the warm water run into the tub and asked Thomas to undress himself. By now with all the previous nurses and treatments and baths, Thomas was used to doing this even in front of a nice-looking girl. Olga had very thick dark brown hair that was braided down each side. Her green eyes were a good match to her white, china-like, porcelain, skin. She was the sporty type with a slender build. "OK Thomas, jump into the waves! I'll leave you alone for awhile. Enjoy the water." Thomas was in heaven! A real bath, time to enjoy it, and a nice young lady! So many good things at the same time! He soaked in the warm water and washed himself, using a lot of soap. Olga came back after a while with a special shampoo against lice and helped him with his hair. After Thomas was dried off, he put on a new outfit and was led by Olga to room #209. Olga opened the door and Thomas looked at 12 beds standing beside each other with the headboards against the wall. This was so much better than the bunk beds in Sorau and at the barracks. Thomas said "hi" to everybody and walked to the empty bed. It was wonderful! Real bedsheets, no lice!

At lunch another nurse came and gave everybody their soup. It tasted okay, but the portions were small. The other men told Thomas that the food was just enough to keep one alive. All of them had family or friends who would supply them with extra food. Thomas didn't have any friends or family in this town. He wondered, "Maybe the daughter from the communist house will keep her promise and bring me something to eat?"

The doctor, a young fellow with a skinny build and blond short hair, came into the room together with the lead nurse. He was here to take a look at Thomas' wound. "Hi Thomas! I am Doctor Wenkel! Let me see the wound on your leg!" Thomas put the blanket aside and the nurse unwrapped the bandage. Dr. Wenkel looked at the wound for a long time. "Hm, this wound is still full of debris from your tibia bone. We have to clean it out in order to give it a chance to heal. How about the day after tomorrow? We have surgery on that day." Thomas was very thankful to hear the doctor's suggestion to clean out his wound. Of course, he agreed to it.

The day of his surgery came, and to his relief, Thomas was told that he would get sedation for this procedure. They put him under, and Thomas didn't feel a thing! When he woke up, he was taken to his room again, wondering what the doctor would tell him about the surgery. It only took a couple of hours until Dr. Wenkel visited. "Thomas, you are lucky! We got all the debris out! My guess is that your leg will heal in no time. The surgery was a success!" Thomas smiled and took a deep breath of relief. He would be able to heal. He would be able to keep his leg! Pictures of the endless prairie, the huge Rocky Mountains and the countless lakes in Canada appeared in front of his eyes. He was filled with hope again!

He started to make plans for his future. At first, he thought, "I have to reach my parents. I have to know if they are stuck in Poland or if they are in the free West, but wherever they are, I am going to freedom, and will start working in order to get money to go to Canada. I wonder if I will be able to make my real pilot's license there. Of course, I'll have to learn English as soon as possible!" Thomas dreamed on and on. He talked about his dreams to the other men in his room. As it turned out, he was not the only one who had Canada on his heart. Canada seemed to be the hot ticket in Germany after the war.

Two days after the surgery the pain in Thomas' leg, instead of easing up, got worse. On top of that, he developed a fever. When Olga measured his temperature, she was very concerned and called the doctor right away. With long strides Dr. Wenkel came into the room, followed by his assistant. "Hey Thomas! What is going on? Let's take a look at your leg!" Nurse Olga took the bandage off and both doctors bent down to have a better look at the wound. The two looked at each other with worry in their eyes.

Dr. Wenkel looked into Thomas' eyes. "Thomas, this isn't good! This is actually very serious! You have a sepsis down underneath your knee! Nurse Olga, I'll give you a cream to put on Thomas' leg right above the septic part. This will prevent the sepsis from affecting more of the leg. Thomas! It's time to fight! You will do it! Stay strong!" The doctors left the room. Nurse Olga left as well but came back in shortly after with a pot of cream in her hands. She looked Thomas right in the eyes and said, "Thomas, we will get rid of it! You are strong! We will help you! I am going to put this cream on and a new bandage, and I believe that you will get better!"

"You are strong!" Didn't Thomas say exactly the same words to his little brother when he had his high fever and then shortly after died of pneumonia? His little brother was a real strong, little boy, and he died! Thomas quickly fell into despair, thinking about these things. He knew very well that he wasn't strong at all. He had no strength to fight. "Will this be the end? After all the other times I could have died? Is this it?" he thought.

Towards the evening, the fever got worse. He was tired! Before he slept, he said the Lord's prayer, and again, he stopped at "Thy will be done!" He thought, "God! My life is in your hands! I am not strong, but you are mighty! As far as I know, You made the mighty mountains! You made the beautiful, strong horse, You created the trees, the flowers, the little birds! God, You created men! My life is in your hands! You decide if I live! I want to live!" Thomas fell asleep.

From then on, the doctors and the nurses made every effort to save Thomas's life. He was seen by the surgeon every day. The first day the doctor put a drainage into the infected area in order to get rid of the pus. The drainage was cleaned out every day and his bandage were changed daily as well. Every time the doctor and nurses worked on him, they sedated him, so he didn't have to endure the pain. The staff had made a firm decision not to give up on Thomas and his leg. Thomas made his own decision, by eating everyday at least some of the food they put in front of him. Eating was now an effort instead of a pleasure.

The door opened, and in the doorway stood the daughter of the communist father. She came with a bundle full of food, just as she and her dad had promised. Thomas smiled at her, but he wasn't even able to sit up, because he was so weak. The girl looked shocked. "What happened to you?"

In a very weak voice Thomas told her the story of the surgery and his sepsis. It was hard for him to talk and she noticed it. She didn't stay long and wished him well. Too bad! Thomas hardly touched the food.

This condition of Thomas went on for weeks without any change. The lead nurse gave orders to put Thomas into a private room. She said that Thomas was in no condition to cope with so many people in his room. Thomas was thankful but he knew that to be alone in a room meant you might die. Time went on. One day nurse Olga came into the room. Standing beside his bed she said, "I have bad news for you and for us! Dr. Wenkel is being replaced by another doctor. Dr. Wenkel refused to join the communist party and so is being transferred to a building were people come to get rid of their lice. Instead of doing surgery, he'll have to wash people's hair! I am very sorry for him! I am sorry for you too! The new doctor will not see you every day! He is a different type of man!"

Thomas' voice was very weak. "Thank you Olga! Thank you for all your effort!" The nurses had a lot of pity for Thomas. They liked him and did their best to take care of him. Often, they brought good food from home and Thomas made a special effort not to disappoint them. The fever and the pain didn't ease up. It was torture without end! Sleep was hard to come by! At times he was so exhausted that he passed out and slept a bit. The night nurse always kept close watch over him. One night she couldn't endure his suffering with all that pain anymore. She didn't have any orders, but thought she was doing a good thing for Thomas and gave him a shot of morphine. Thomas felt cold and it got dark around him. "That's it!" he thought. He was too frail to cope with morphine. His heart threatened to stop beating. The doctors and the nurses fought all night to keep Thomas alive. Thomas survived!

The next morning when nurse Olga came into the room, she was very angry at the night watch! "Sorry Thomas! This was close! I am glad you made it! The nurse meant well, but morphine was too much for you! I am here to cheer you up. Would you like to marry me? Just for fun?"

Thomas managed a smile. "Just for fun? Sure! I would love to!" Olga pulled two cheap rings out of her pocket, and put one ring on Thomas' hand and the other ring on hers.

"Ha-ha, we are engaged, Thomas. You and I are engaged! How does that make you feel?" Thomas smiled at her. He had a nice, warm, fuzzy feeling. Olga was very nice. Days later, Olga came into the room. "Thomas, guess what? Today is Christmas Eve!"

Thomas was shocked. "Already! I've been here for six weeks now!" Olga stepped beside his bed and put a little bit of Christmas baking on his night table. "Here is something to nibble on! My Mom baked it! Thomas smiled at her. Another nurse brought a very small Christmas tree into the room and put it on his night table. It had two stars made out of straw and a dark, red ribbon on it. One of the branches was holding a candle holder with a small, white candle in it. The tree was very small, but Thomas loved it. At the end of the day, when it got dark outside, a nurse came into Thomas' room and lit the candle. "Frohe Weihnachten" she said to Thomas. Thomas looked into the light of the candle and took a bite of the baked goods from Olga. He chewed slowly, cherishing the moment. Thoughts about his family arose in his mind, of past Christmases with a huge tree and lots to eat, and the little train set he got one year. "Where is my family? I know they think about me and wonder where I am!" Tears ran down his cheeks.

FINAL DECISION

"This is a wonderful room!" Emma exclaimed. Emma and Sabine were standing in the doorway of their new room at the hospital. Both were very happy! This was a new start! Each of them had their different work positions. Emma had a job in the hospital bakery and Sabine was hired as a helper on the surgical floor for men. Both jobs came with a modest salary, a room for the two to live in, and all three of their meals for the day. "Oh, the best!" Sabine thought, "a uniform!" It was a grey dress with a white collar and a white apron. They each got two sets of them. "No worries about what to wear anymore!" Sabine thought. She loved it! Emma complained that grey was not her colour and made her look a bit pale, but she was very happy to be in the baking shop, away from patients and all their problems.

The two had spent the first night in their new room and their first day of work was about to start. Sabine got up before her alarm went off. She couldn't wait to find out what her new job was all about. She had to be in the dining room at 6:45 AM for the daily meeting. As Sabine arrived, the nurse in charge gave them the orders for the day and other work updates. Sabine was welcomed and introduced to the others. Finally, she was able to make her way up to the floor where her future lay.

The patients on this floor were men, mainly those injured during the war. Dr Wilms, the chief doctor in charge, was a well-known specialist in dealing with amputated limbs. Almost every man on the floor had at least one limb missing.

Sabine walked along the long hallway with doors, she couldn't count, there were so many. It was still early and quiet. She found the room for the nurses and knocked on the door. A middle-aged nurse in her blue uniform dress, with a white nurses' hat, white collar, and a white apron, opened the door. She had a round face and very blue eyes, and she smiled. "You must be Sabine, the new helper the administration promised me an eternity ago."

Sabine had to laugh. "Yes, I am Sabine."

"Praise God! My name is Nurse Cefie! I am so happy that you are here! We can use every hand! Sorry, but I have no time to talk to you, we are already behind! Why don't you come with me and I'll show you the drill?"

Nurse Cefie and Sabine went down the hallway where she showed Sabine the linen closet. Together they piled the bed sheets and other equipment onto the cart and both made their way, pushing the cart in front of them to the first room. The room was semi-dark. The curtains were still drawn in front of the windows as the patients tried to get a few more minutes of sleep. Nurse Cefie walked briskly to the window and opened the curtains, which flooded the room with light. "Oh no!" was the response from the eight men lying in their beds. The men opened their eyes slowly and one after the other spotted Sabine standing beside Nurse Cefie. Herr Becker, 'Mr. Big Mouth', whistled and said, "What is this, a new beauty? Welcome to our humble world!"

Sabine blushed a bit and said, "Good morning my name is Sabine! Nice to meet you!"

A choir of voices said, "Good morning, Sabine!" Nurse Cefie and Sabine looked at each other and smiled.

"This will be funny!" Sabine thought to herself. From then on, she hardly had time to think anymore. She and Cefie not only had to make all the beds of the patients and wash the patients that were unable to do so themselves, they also had to kick the rest of the men out of bed and remind them to wash up. The room was filled with life! After they finished that room, they moved on to the next one and did the same routine with those patients and so on it went. More teams were doing the same work in other rooms.

After all the beds were done, the patients were to receive their breakfasts. Sabine was ordered to join the kitchen crew. She could hear their loud voices already from afar. She stepped into the kitchen. "Good morning, everyone, I am Sabine, the new help on this floor!"

"Yeah!" everybody was cheering. "My name is Liese, we can use another hand!" Liese was a girl around Sabines' age with thick blond hair braided towards her back. She turned around, facing a slightly older woman standing in her blue apron by the kitchen counter. "Frau Henschel, should I carry the breakfast together with Sabine into the rooms today?"

Frau Henschel smiled and said, "Of course, you can teach her how it works! Great idea!" She was busy putting the margarine and plum sauce onto the slices of sourdough bread. Every patient would get one slice of bread. The coffee was not real. It was made out of grain. Liese and Sabine each received a tray filled with the breakfast portions and walked down the long hallway to their first room.

Liese opened the door. "Guten Morgen meine Herren! Good morning to you men!" The face of every man lit up to see the young girls with breakfast in their hands. The two went from room to room. Sabine got to know all the rooms and the patients. She was totally famished and tired after breakfast had been carried out to all the men. Finally, she and the other staff were able to get a bite themselves. Frau Henschel had already made enough sandwiches for everybody. The staff got the same amount to eat as the patients. After that, Sabines' morning was filled with washing the patient's night tables, bringing full bottles of urine to the huge sink in the special washroom and washing them out, helping patients onto the bedpan, and of course, cleaning up. She thought that she had walked a lot of kilometers that morning, it was busy! Frau Henschel was again in charge of lunch. She needed some help to peel the many cooked potatoes. Today's lunch was those cooked potatoes with some vegetables. Liese and Sabine served the patients again, collected all the dirty dishes, washed the dishes, and brought out coffee together with a small biscuit.

Liese said, "Come Sabine, we have our break now! I'll show you the dining room where we get our 'Mittagessen' (lunch)." The two went downstairs to the dining room which was already full of staff from all the other floors. Liese seemed to know almost everybody and introduced Sabine. The two found a free table and got the same lunch as the patients on their floor. Sabine was happy when she was able to go to her room to have some rest. She lay down on her bed and was asleep right away for one hour. She had to be back on the floor by 4:30 pm to help with 'Abendbrot', the evening meal.

Frau Henschel had again prepared one slice of bread for every patient, but this time with cheese on top. After the patients had their food, the staff was able to eat theirs in the kitchen. The dirty dishes had to be washed again, the urine bottles had to be emptied, as did the bed pans. All the patients had to be prepared for their night sleep. At eight o clock, the workday for Sabine was over. She was totally out of energy when she opened the door to her room.

Emma was already in bed. "You won't believe how hard I had to work! I had to stand the whole day! That is way too hard for me!" Emma complained.

Sabine looked into her eyes. "You will get used to it! The first day is always the worst! I had to walk all day! You have no idea how long those hallways are! But we have great jobs, we will be fine! By the way, did you get any bread?"

Emma's mood brightened at the question. "Yes! We have to cut off all the ends of the bread loaves. The ends are being thrown out for the pigs to eat. I was able to rescue some. They are in the bag on the table."

"You're a lifesaver!" Sabine said. "I will eat some tomorrow morning before I go to work. It takes a long time until we get anything to eat. Patients are always first! But I love my job! The nurses and the other staff are all great and the patients are very nice as well! But I am tired now! I'm going to bed! Good night!"

Over time Emma got used to her job as did Sabine. The thick ends of the wonderful sourdough bread loaves that Emma was able to rescue from the pigs, proved to be a welcome addition to the lean diet of Sabine's whole family. Otti cooked bread soup in any variation she could think of. The family sent a letter to Emil with a photo of the whole family during that time. Emil was still a prisoner of war in France, but he was able to write back how surprised he was to see that his family was so well fed and looking as normal as ever when most of Germany was starving.

One day Sabine walked down the hallway to ask Nurse Cefie for her orders. Standing beside her was a new nurse. She looked like a country girl. She had round, red cheeks and her hair was tied in a bun. "Good morning!" said Sabine.

Nurse Cefie turned towards the newcomer. "Sofie, this is Sabine, our help! You will be able to learn a lot from her! Sabine, this is Sofie. Today is her first day as a student nurse! I know you will be a great help for her! Why don't you two make the beds and wash the patients together?"

"Alright!" Sabine said.

Turning towards Sofie she said, "Let's get started. We have lots to do.

Opening the first room, Sabine called out to the patients, "Good morning! I hope you had a good nights' sleep!" She pulled the curtains to the side of the window and the usual morning complaining about the light ensued and the routine started. Sabine introduced Sofie to all the men, who in one chorus chimed, "Hi, nurse Sofie! Nice to meet you!" Sofie's already red cheeks turned a shade deeper red.

Sabine said, "Herr Becker, could you please get up and wash yourself at the sink? Sofie and I are going to make your bed!"

Herr Becker said in a voice, drooling with pity, "Dear Sabine, I am not feeling so well today! I have great doubts that I will be able to walk to the sink all by myself! Please would you be so nice and let me hold on to one of your beautiful shoulders, so I will not fall on my way to the sink?"

Sabine had to hide a smile and said, "Herr Becker, I am very sorry to hear that! I will contact the doctor right away! He will give you one of his life empowering shots with the extra long and fat needle into your back side! I will do that now immediately!"

Sabine was just reaching the door, when Herr Becker called out, "Oh! All of a sudden, I feel a lot better! Funny how that works sometimes! Ha-ha" Sabine laughed as well.

Later on, the same day, Sabine was cleaning the night tables, when Sofie came in, holding a container with thermometers in her hand. Nurse Cefie had told her to do the daily pulse and temperature check of the patients. Since the day was full of emergencies, Sofie would have very little time to do it. Nurse Cefie told her only to check the temperature of the patients who looked like they had a fever. The thermometer had to be put under the armpit and stay there for a couple of minutes. That would take up a lot of time. Sofie had no idea how a person looked like with a fever, so, she asked the men, "Does anybody here feel a bit feverish?" The whole room erupted in laughter.

Herr Becker joined in too. "Yes, please come over and feel my forehead! I am feverish everyday!" Sofie's cheeks turned red again and all the men only had their pulse checked.

Christmas had passed for Thomas without any changes. His days were filled with pain, fever and fatigue, but he didn't give up. He nibbled on his food every day, fighting for his life. The doctor came to his bedside one day, sitting down for a serious talk. "Thomas, the sepsis in your lower leg is eating itself upwards! It is growing! We can't save your leg anymore! It is over! We still have the chance to save your knee! This is very important when you have to wear a prosthesis. The lower leg has to come off, otherwise you will die!"

Thomas' eyes filled with tears. In a soft voice he said, "Okay! This is the final decision then! Cut my leg off! Thank you, doctor." After the doctor left the room, Thomas turned on his side and cried! He thought, "Germany has lost the war and I am losing my leg! I better stop thinking about why this is all happening."

Two days later, on the 21st of January 1946, the nurse came into the room and took Thomas to surgery. Thomas was shocked to see Nurse Olga lying on a stretcher. She smiled at him. "Don't worry! I am fine! I have your blood type! I will give you some of my blood during the surgery. We nurses do that once in a while! Especially when we are engaged to a patient, ha-ha!" Thomas was touched! Another nurse gave Thomas an anesthetic which put him out.

When Thomas woke up later on in his bed, it was like nothing had happened. He was wondering if his leg was really cut off. He pulled his blanket away and was able to see what happened. His right leg ended ten centimeters below the knee. Just gone! He didn't feel any pain, he didn't feel sad! He was confused!

From then on Thomas' condition improved! The fever left him and it became easier for him to match his strength with his will to live. His weight was down to 40 kilograms at that point. A nurse with a strong build had a lot of fun lifting Thomas out of bed and carrying him around a bit. Thomas was okay with this. Besides his normal appetite, humour came back into Thomas' life as well. He could laugh again. He was back in his old room with the 12 beds. All the other men were good company. Life had Thomas back again!

The bed beside Thomas was empty and a new patient was admitted. The newcomer and Thomas looked at each other and Thomas felt a jolt of joy in his heart. "Michael! Hi Michael! What a surprise to see you here!"

The man looked deep into Thomas's eyes and asked him, "Do I know you from somewhere?"

Thomas said, "I am Thomas! Thomas Wenzel! I am from your town in the Riesengebirge!"

The other man's face turned into a horrified expression. "Thomas Wenzel? What happened to you? You look terrible! I am sorry, I didn't recognize you right away!" Thomas knew he looked horrible, not at all like himself. He was not offended. He told him his story in a short version and the man understood. After the emotions of both men had calmed down, they caught up on everything that happened during the last year. Unfortunately, Michael didn't know anything about Thomas' family. Michael's own family was stuck in Poland and both men were wondering if their families would have to leave their houses and move to the west. Since Michael was able to walk and move around, he made trips outside the hospital and came back with food from the farmers. He offered to help out with the pigs in the hospital and got more food for himself and Thomas. Unfortunately, the time with Michael was very short, because he was getting healthy very fast and soon left the hospital. Thomas appreciated the good time he had with an old friend.

Thomas was still holding on to his Lord's Prayer at bedtime and couldn't believe how much God cared for him. During the time with Michael, he gained some weight and strength back. He was now strong enough to walk with crutches.

Today was the 15th of April 1946. Thomas turned 19 years old. Since he had been in the hospital for almost half a year, the nurses considered him part of the family. They celebrated with him. One of them even gave him a bowl of real German beer soup. Thomas enjoyed it very much.

A few days later Thomas awoke in shock from what felt like a lightening bolt spiking through his leg. He grimaced in agony as an intense sharp pain pierced his right, lower leg. Sweat ran down his cheeks, his body drenched, he sat up in bed throwing the blanket to the side. He gazed at his leg. It looked okay. It was still cut off at the point it was before, but the pain came from the area where there was no leg anymore. What? It hit him! Phantom-pain! The doctor had told him about it. How cruel is that? You don't have the leg anymore, but you get the pain instead!

The door opened and Nurse Olga and Lidia entered the room. Olga looked at Thomas with concern in her eyes "Thomas, what is going on? You are totally wet! What happened!"

Thomas wiped his forehead with his handkerchief. "I just had my first phantom-pain! It wasn't good, to say the least!"

Olga said, "I am so sorry Thomas! I heard from other patients how cruel it can be! I hope you don't get them too often! Why don't you go outside onto the balcony into the warm sun? Lidia and I are going to put new bedsheets on your bed. We have to get the bed beside you ready for the new patient anyway."

Thomas got out of bed and grabbed the crutches that were leaning against a chair. "Are we getting a new patient today?"

Lidia turned towards Thomas with a huge smile on her face. "Olga is determined that you and the new patient are related! His last name is Wenzel, the same as yours"

Thomas forgot all about his pain and laughed. "Ha-ha, people with the name Wenzel are all over the Riesengebirge where I am from. It would be a real miracle if the new guy would be related to me! Ha-ha."

Olga looked at him with a serious face. "You never know!" Thomas made his way towards the balcony. He opened the door, where the warm air engulfed him. It was May! The trees, the meadows were all in their best green. Early spring flowers added their beauty to the picture. It was a wonderful, rich landscape to look at, but Thomas couldn't enjoy it! His heart, his mind, was troubled with his fate of going as a cripple through life, instead of reaching his dreams of becoming a pilot, of immigrating to Canada, and marrying a wonderful looking woman. None of his dreams would become reality! He knew that! He grieved! It was hard to let go! He turned around to go into the room again, his beautiful warm, brown eyes downcast, his gentle face, surrounded by the thick, black hair, bent down in defeat. He opened the door to step inside.

That same moment as he stood in the doorway, the door at the other end of the room opened up. Thomas looked at the worn-out boots, a dark brown, very worn pants, a checkered blue shirt, a face... that face? Thomas' face turned white! He had to hold on to his crutches! "Papa?" he said out loud. "Papa!" Both men made it to the middle of the room and met in a long embrace. Thomas relaxed and thought, "Home!" Tears streamed down both faces. The other men in the room cried as well. Nurse Olga, who was watching the whole scene, cried and laughed with them.

"Thomas, I knew it was your father! It had to be! I knew it!" She was jumping up and down. Tears still in her eyes, she left the room.

August took a step back and looked at Thomas, "My boy, what happened to your leg? Let's sit down and tell me your story!" Thomas and his Dad sat down on his bed, and Thomas began. August listened intently. He was angry about the two guys who tricked Thomas into the war. He could just picture the situation of being surrounded by the enemy with no way out. He was hurting with Thomas when Thomas told him about how he got shot in the leg. He also cried when Thomas told him the story about the young guy on the train who sang the song about the mother who shouldn't cry about her son.

He wiped off his tears and said, "You have been through a lot of suffering Thomas! I am sorry for you! If your Mom would know all of this, she wouldn't stop crying! But I am here now! I'll take care of you! I heard from your Mom, that they are afraid of being pushed out of our house at any time by the Polish people. We don't know where our future will be. Mom knows that you became a prisoner of war. She knows that I am stuck here in the East."

Thomas looked at his Dad. "What happened to you? Why are you in the hospital?"

August replied, "I was a prisoner of war with the Russians as well. After being released, I found a job on a farm. The food at the farm gave me a skin disease. I hope the doctor will be able to help me with it! We will be fine Thomas! I'll take care of everything! I have lots of experience with trading and organizing things!" The face of August started glowing with pride. He kept talking.

"One time in prison camp I found an old rusted knife beside the kitchen at the barracks. I picked it up and looked around for something to sand it down with to its former glory. The knife looked almost like new after my treatment! So, I went into town and traded the knife for a bottle of vodka. You know how much the Russians love their vodka! I went with the vodka to another house and that man gave me an old saw for it. I went to work again and polished up the saw until it looked decent. With that good looking saw, I went to a farmer who had lots of pigs, but was in need of a good saw. So, I got a whole little pig for it. Me and my friends at the camp had a great night of roasting the pig over the fire. Boy, it was good eating!"

Lying beside each other the two had plenty of time to tell their stories of the war times. August was able to leave the hospital every day and went out and about to gather food for himself and Thomas. Thomas and his Dad had lots to eat and more of Thomas' strength came back to him. Nurse Olga arranged for a private room for the father and son. Thomas didn't know how to thank her for all she had done for him.

Trudy finished helping little Otilia to put her dress on. Both went into the kitchen where the rest of the family was sitting around the table. Everybody got their bowl of flour soup with a piece of butter in it. Otto, the grandpa, was talking about his plans for the day. Grandma Milli looked out the window. "My, I miss those animals! Too bad we had to butcher them all!" The family had decided to eat all of their animals before the Polish people would come and take them away from them. A loud knock on the door startled them. Trudy and the rest of the family looked into each other's eyes! All of them were thinking the same thing. "Is this it?"

Trudy went to the door, opened it, and saw three officials standing in front of her house. The one in charge said, "Guten Morgen Frau Wenzel! Could we please talk for a moment?" Mother knew what this was all about and with a sad, defeated voice asked them inside. The whole family gathered around the three men fearing what they had to say. One of the men opened his mouth. "Dear Frau Wenzel! You know that this area, Schlesien, is now in the hands of the Polish people. I am sorry, but I have to ask you to leave your house in one week's time and to move to the West of Germany. I have inquired for you and found a city still willing to take in some refugees. The name of this city is Luedenscheid. Here are your papers for leaving the Polish zone and entering Germany." The men got up from their seats. Trudy received the papers and led the men to the door. Nobody said a word!

Mother told the children to go outside to play. Finally, the tears came running down her cheeks. "All the hard work to build the house! All the labour to entertain the summer guests and have them make good memories in our area. The grave of our little Ludwig is here. All the good times we had with our children in this house! Thomas won't be able to say goodbye to the house! This is too much!" Otto and Milli were crying as well!

Milli, wiping her eyes with the end of her apron, said "We lived our whole life in this place, in the old house. August was born here! He won't be able to see it anymore either! What an awful day!"

"We knew this would happen!" Otto said, "Let's look forward and think about what we will be able to take with us on the train. We have to be smart about it! We can only carry so much! I might be able to sell a couple of things we can't take with us! At least we will have the money!"

Regina, the older of the two sisters, hadn't gone outside and listened to all the talk. "Mama, what will happen to my cat? Can we take her with us?"

Trudy looked at her. "Don't you worry about your cat! The new people will love her! She is a good cat!"

Little Otilia looked from behind Regina's back. "Will the new people take care of my bike? Opa just put oil on it?"

Trudy took the face of the little girl into her hands. "They will love your bike! And as soon as we are able to buy a new one, you will get a new bike!"

One week later, with loaded suitcases and bags filled with food, the Wenzel family stood at the train station, waiting for the train going West. None of them had any idea where this city of Luedenscheid was, how it would look like, if there were any mountains or even a forest. With many thoughts and questions in their hearts in suspension, they embarked together on an unknown future, and boarded the train.

GOING TO LUEDENSCHEID

Sabine was drained and famished. It was early in the afternoon and she longed for her lunch. "I hope there is still some food left in the dining room!" she thought. Sabine opened the door and made her way to the counter. The lady behind the counter was still keeping some potatoes and vegetables warm in the pots. Sabine was relieved and happy! It didn't matter that it was carrots again. It was food and she was hungry! With a full plate in her hands, she turned around to look for a good table to sit at. There was Inge! She still had this fragile body and blond hair like always. Sabine spoke to her. "Inge! What are you doing here? Do you work here in the hospital?

Inge, who was sitting at a table, started to smile. "Sabine, it is nice to see you! Yes, I got a job on the women's floor. I am a helper for the nurses!"

Sabine smiled back at her. "I am a helper on the floor for men, mainly for surgeries. There are a lot of former soldiers with amputated limbs. We have our hands full, but I love it!" The two started having their lunch together. "So, how did you and your family survive the war? I haven't seen you since school!"

Inge stopped putting her filled fork towards her mouth. "We were okay, like most people in Luedenscheid! The only one who suffered was my brother. I believe you know him! He is a bit older than I am."

"Did he have to join the war?" Sabine asked.

Inge, still chewing her food, continued, "He couldn't be a soldier with his thick glasses. Remember? His eyes are really bad?"

"Right!" Sabine replied and put another fork with carrots into her mouth.

"We were hoping to be able to stay together as a family during the war, but then, one day there was a knock on the door, and a SS-officer wanted to talk to my brother. He gave him a paper, explaining that he was being drafted to bury Jewish people."

"Do you mean the Jews who died in the workcamps?" Sabine gasped.

Inge put her fork down and replied with a sad smile. "Workcamps? Which planet do you live on Sabine? Those were concentration camps, designed to kill millions of Jews! Haven't you heard about that by now?"

Sabine looked down at her half full plate in shame. "I am sorry! My Dad said something like that one time and I did see headlines in a newspaper that was lying on the side table of a patient. But to be honest, I never really believed it. I put it all to the back of my mind. The whole thing sounded too horrible to be true!"

With a stern face Inge looked into Sabine's eyes. "It happened for real Sabine! The Jewish people were shipped like animals in train cars jam-packed full. At the camp they kept some healthy-looking ones for a while to do hard labour and the rest had to go under the showers."

"What do you mean, showers?" Sabine asked.

Inge explained, "Once they were undressed, they had to step right under the shower, and out of those shower heads came poisonous gas, not water. It was very strong gas! They died in seconds right under the shower. Naked as they were, their bodies were thrown onto a truck and driven outside of the camp to long trenches. This was the place where my brother had to work. He had to take care of the bodies. The bodies had to be laid side by side and he had to cover each layer with lime. They are not sure about the numbers yet, but they are talking about millions of Jews being killed throughout Hitler's Reich."

Sabine put her fork down, her eyes filled with shock. "Millions? Millions? I am so sorry Inge! I didn't get truly informed! I guess, I really didn't want to know all that evil. This is just not believable! This is horrible! How is your brother now?"

"My brother would pray to God that whole time, that it would stop, but it went on and on. He lived in a nightmare! A lot of nights he had to sleep right beside the trenches, his hands dirty, his mind guilty! Just picture that! His life is marked by this! He has repeated nightmares about it. Real horrible dreams! He feels so guilty, because he was part of this horror, but if he would have refused the job, he would have been a deserter and would have been hung on the next tree! I have to stay with him and leave our bed room doors open at night, so I am able to hear him scream when the nightmare comes. Our life is actually a nightmare because of it!"

Sabine with a very serious, defeated face looked into the eyes of Inge. "Inge, I will pray for you and your brother. God is good! I am very ashamed of our country, Germany! This is unbelievable! We have to pray for our country! We have to ask God to forgive us. I've lost my appetite and I am very tired! Thanks for telling me all this, I need some time for myself. Take care Inge!"

Sabine took her half empty plate in her hands and got up. She went to her room and fell down on her knees in front of her bed. "Lord Jesus! Please forgive us? Please forgive Germany? The Jews are your chosen people! I am so sorry!" She layed down on her bed, but couldn't find rest.

Thomas and his Dad, August, had a good time together at the hospital in Goerlitz, but the problems with Thomas' leg weren't over. He wasn't able to fit into a prosthesis because the wound at the apex of his cut-off limb, didn't heal. The wound was still open after weeks. Thomas and his Dad got worried about it. One day the doctor came in for another serious talk with Thomas. "Thomas, your wound is a problem! It should have healed by now! So, we have to do more steps in order for you to be able to use a prosthesis to walk. We have to cut off another piece of your leg. Unfortunately, we have to cut right above the knee."

August, listening in, got up from his bed. "He won't have his knee? That would mean he would not be able to bend at the knee, and Thomas would always limp when he walks!"

The doctor's forehead wrinkled up, "I am sorry! Yes, that is the way it would be! He might have to use a cane to walk as well."

Thomas looked at the doctor, his eyes tearing up. "Thank you so much for all the good things you have done for me! I need a bit of time to think about this!" The doctor left the room.

Dad started walking back and forth in their little room. "Not in my lifetime, Thomas! They will not take your knee off as well! There has to be a better way!" The two had a bad nights' sleep.

The next day, August got a letter from his wife. Trudy told him, that they were being evicted from their house and would move to a new city named Luedenscheid in the western part of Germany. Thomas and his Dad were not surprised about the eviction, and were relieved to know where their family would be. Dad got up. "Thomas, we will go to the West! The doctors in the West are much better than the doctors here. We will get you a good doctor in the West!"

Thomas was not as enthusiastic as his Dad, "How are we going to go to the West Papa? We are stuck here in the East! They won't let us out!"

August with a smile on his face said, "Just watch me son! We will go to the West!" August told the doctor the next day that he and Thomas would try to go to the West and get a second opinion on his son's leg. The doctor wished him well. From that day on, August was gone for most of the days. He was busy doing his trades and networking. One day he finally said, "I have enough!"

"What do you have?" Thomas asked.

Dad smiled, and with a twinkle in his eye, he said, "Enough bottles of vodka. The Russians love their vodka!"

The next day, August walked to the office of the General in charge of giving out permission for people to go to the West. The guard in front of the office of this important

General asked August for his written appointment with his boss. August with a big smile looked into the guard's eye. "I do not have a written appointment, but I will give you this!" Out of his bag he pulled a bottle from his stash of vodka. The guard had a smile on his face and let August pass.

August knocked on the door of General Vladimir. After a moment, a harsh voice called him in. August carefully opened the door. He looked at a general sitting behind his desk in his uniform, with a lot of medals hanging down his full chest. The hair of General Vladimir was unwashed and uncombed. His beard which could have been two weeks old, still had the leftovers from his last meal sticking to it. His mouth was drawn downwards. As his right hand was holding his obviously hurting head, he barked out "What do you want from me? Do you have an appointment?"

August knew he had come at just the right time. This General had a severe hangover!

"General Vladimir, I don't have a normal appointment. I thought that you might like this instead?" August pulled his first bottle of Vodka out of his bag and watched the eyes and the rest of the face of the General come to life. August kept on talking. "My son, the only son I have, needs a doctor in the West! His amputated leg just doesn't heal and the doctor in the hospital here can't help him anymore! My dear General, do you have a son? Do you know how much it pains you to watch your son suffer?" Another bottle made his way onto the desk in front of the General.

The eyes of the General started to shine and his body straightened up. "I know what you mean! I have a son myself! But my hands are tied! Our government doesn't give me permission to give you papers to leave the East!" He looked at the bag August was holding in his hands and August understood. Another bottle made its way onto the desk in front of the General. "Of course, we could arrange that I would be at the train station tomorrow at the time when the train goes off to the West. I could tell the guards to let you jump on."

August, showing the General that there were more bottles in his bag said, "You will not regret your decision! See you tomorrow!' And he left.

Nurse Olga was in tears when she heard about the planned departure of Thomas and his Dad. She liked Thomas so much! The other nurses were sorry as well. Thomas was already part of their family! He had been in the hospital for so long, he would be missed. Father and son had a restless night before rising and getting ready for the trip. Olga gave them a small bundle of food to take along. Thomas felt bad about hurting her feelings, but he didn't want to stay in the East. He wanted to be with his family. He wanted to be in the free part of Germany, and he longed to have his leg fixed once and for all!

The two, August, with a small bag over his shoulder and Thomas hobbling behind on his crutches, made their way to the train station. As expected, a few soldiers guarded the place and approached them right away, asking about their reasons for being there. August told them about the permission from the General, but the soldier in charge had his orders. No papers, no travel! It was as simple as that!

Thomas started to worry, but his Dad told him not to give up, that it would be all fine.

Sadly, the first train to the West drove into the train station and left without Thomas and his dad. Both sat on the bench, Thomas in worry, August clutching his bottles of vodka, in hope. Around the corner came a pitiful looking General. His hair was worse than the day before and he smelled horrible! His eyes had trouble staying open! He was in bad shape! He gave Thomas and his Dad a wave and started talking to the commander of the soldiers. The next train to the West rolled into the train station.

August and Thomas could see that the soldiers were having a heated discussion with the Generals, whose voice was getting louder and whose face was turning crimson red. After a while the commander seemed to soften up. The General approached Thomas and his Dad and told them to jump onto the train into an empty car. August gave the General the promised bottles of vodka and they then turned to quickly get on the train. The General also turned and in a miserable and dejected state, and in a semi-stupor, headed back to town.

The soldiers heard loud noises. They had another problem to take care of and went to the front of the train. All of a sudden, the wide door of the train car was pushed open, and the face of a priest looked at August and Thomas, who were now sitting on the floor. The priest, with an urgent demeanour, spoke quickly. "Fast, nobody is looking right now! Come into our train-car! I overheard the conversation between the commander and the General. You two will never make it over the border without papers. I can help you. Come!"

Thomas and August slipped out of their car and entered the train wagon that the priest showed them. This car was already filled with people. The priest told them to sit down beside the rest and explained, "I have permission to take my flock out of the East into the West. I have a list of all my people from the authorities, I will simply put your names on my list and you tell everybody that you belong to my flock."

When everyone had found a place on the floor the priest took his paper out of his bag and asked Thomas and August their names. He made an effort to write the names just the same as the other names on the list. After he was done, he said, "Welcome to my flock!" Everybody had a good chuckle! The train started to roll towards the West.

Thomas and his Dad made it over the border to their first city in the free West. Helmstaedt was the name of the town. The western soldiers at the train station were very nice and helpful. Everybody had to get out of the train and undergo a treatment against lice. This time it was fast and painless. The Red Cross nurses had a huge syringe-type looking device with which they sprayed lice killing powder into the sleeves and trouser legs. The hair got an extra treatment. A nice Red Cross nurse came to Thomas and asked him about his leg. She looked at it and gave him a fresh bandage. Father and son were impressed by the treatment they received in Helmstaedt. Another train arrived at the station and everybody had to board. This time it was a real train, for passengers, with real seats. August and Thomas enjoyed sitting on a bench and being able to look out the window onto the West German landscape. Both men took a deep breath of relief. Freedom was real this time!

The train stopped in Warendorf. A soldier shouted, "Alles Austeigen!" The city's administration was prepared for their coming. After everybody got off the train, a soldier led the group to a place that used to be a horse farm before the war. The stalls for the horses were now turned into places for people. Every family was assigned its own box. These stalls were clean and filled with lots of fresh hay.

August had to laugh about the whole idea. "I hope nobody will neigh during the night, Ha-ha!" They were told that everybody had to stay here for a couple of days.

August got busy again! The problem with the priest was that he and his flock were going to the wrong place for them. August and Thomas had to travel to Luedenscheid, and August was determined to make that happen. He visited people and made trades again all day long. During those days, Thomas visited with the other people, especially with the priest. He wanted to show his appreciation to him for taking them out of the East.

One day, the priest entered the box where Thomas was sitting on the hay and asked him, "Thomas, do you know the Lord Jesus as your personal Saviour?"

Thomas was all ears! "I wondered for a long time about that! I don't know how I am able to get close to God! I pray the Lord's Prayer every night, but I don't really feel like I have a relationship with God!"

"Praying the Lord's Prayer is a very good start!" The priest said. "You actually have the important sentence right in it! It says, 'And forgive us our debts, as we forgive our debtors.' You have to ask Jesus to forgive your sins. God gave his only begotten Son to die for us on the cross so we would be saved and united with God! Jesus is the way! You can't meet God with all your dirt, your sins. You have to be washed in the blood of Jesus to get clean and be able to face God!"

Thomas looked at him in disbelief. "Is this the only way somebody can be with God? It is so awkward to have Jesus die for my sins!"

The priest smiled. "This is the only way! This is the way God the Father designed for us. Thomas, you know how it works for a new child to be born? The egg has to meet the sperm. There is no other way! God designed it that way! When you ask Jesus to forgive your sins, and you turn away from your old sinful ways, you will be filled with his presence! The Holy Spirit will give to you the assurance of the presence of God in your life! You are born again! There is only this one way!" Thomas thanked the priest for all the good things he had done for them and promised that he would think about what he had just heard.

August came into the box that night with a bright smile on his face and new papers for him and Thomas in his hands. Thomas didn't ask how he did it, but he had an idea. The next morning Thomas and August said Good Bye and thanked the priest and his flock. The two climbed into a train going in the direction of Luedenscheid. On their way they had to switch trains and were now sitting on the last train to their new home. Another man who was also missing a leg joined the two and asked how they were doing? Thomas told him about their trip and his long story with his leg. The young man smiled. "You are going to the right place! The hospital in Luedenscheid has this famous doctor, Dr. Wilms is his name. He is an expert! I was under his care! I am very happy with how things went with my leg. I will get a prosthesis very soon and nobody will even know that one of my legs is missing."

Thomas got a jolt of joy and hope in his heart. "How do I get in touch with this Dr. Wilms?" Soon Thomas had all the information he needed to get in touch with this doctor. Was this God again?

'Luedenscheid'- The train stopped right in front of the sign. Father and son looked at each other and smiled. The family had written them their two addresses. August asked a person how to get there and was told that his parent's place would be the closest. Father and son walked up the incline of the Friederich Strasse, which was the next street coming out of the train station. They didn't have to walk far and reached the apartment very soon. August and Thomas looked at each other with a big smile and August knocked loud on the door. Otto, the grandpa, opened the door just a crack and looked with a curious face into his own sons' eyes. A huge smile appeared on his face, as his ever-present pipe fell out of his mouth. He opened the door wide and he yelled, "Milli, come fast! August and Thomas are here! August and Thomas are here!"

Otto and August were tied in a hug when Milli reached the door. "Let's get inside! I want to hug them too!" Milli's tears were streaming down her face. She pushed her husband away from her son and gave August a long hug. Otto already had Thomas in his arms, and then it was Milli's turn. It took a while until they finally made it inside their room.

The three men sat down at the table while Milli got busy preparing some sandwiches. They already knew about Thomas' missing leg, but had so many questions and stories of their own to tell to Thomas and August. August had to put a stop to it after they had finished off the sandwiches. He and Thomas still had a long way to go to the place were Trudy and the children lived. They said their Good Byes for now and started walking towards the new home of the family.

It took them almost one hour to reach the place. August asked a person if the house he was looking at was the right place. Yes, it was! August was not happy. His family lived in a barracks made especially for refugees like his family. A barracks! He didn't like that! "This is not a place for my family!" he muttered.

Thomas and August found the door with the name Wenzel on it and knocked. Quick, light steps made their way to the door. The door opened and a young girl with black curly hair and a skinny build looked at them. She stared at August and Thomas for a moment and then shouted out loud, "Mama, Papa and Thomas are here!" Trudy flew to the door and embraced her husband and son. Tears of relief freely ran down her cheeks.

August couldn't believe his eyes when he looked at his wife. "What did you do with your hair, Trudy?

Trudy's hand stroked over her short hair as she laughed. "I knew you wouldn't like it! But we got lice on our way to Luedenscheid, so, I cut it short. It will grow again." Turning to Thomas she said, "Thomas it is hard to see you on crutches!" There were more tears in her eyes. "I knew that the doctor had to cut it off, but seeing it now is hard. I am sorry son! But at least you and Dad are alive! How many men didn't make it home! But you did. Thank God for that! Let's go to the table! You must be very tired and hungry!

Thomas told the story of how he got shot in his leg. He had to repeat it over and over again, so that his sisters could know all the details. Tomorrow young Otilia would have a great story to tell her friends at school. Thomas had to laugh with his sisters. It was so funny and it was a good thing to be able to laugh about his missing leg. At night, when everybody was in bed, Thomas had a quiet moment to himself. He had to sleep on the sofa in the big kitchen, but all he felt was, "I am home!" Tears ran down his cheeks. He let his feelings go. After such a long time and all he had gone through, he was finally... Home!

Father had big plans for the next day after breakfast! He was going to work his miracles at the administration responsible for the housing of refugees. August went out and got busy! Thomas had a day of rest, catching up with his family. His mother had to cry a lot when she heard his stories with all the suffering in the woods surrounded by the Russians and the time as a POW. When August came home in the afternoon, he had a lot of information, which he didn't know before. Every family, doesn't matter if you were a long time resident of Luedenscheid or a refugee, was only allowed to live in two rooms. If somebody was living in a house with more rooms, they had to share their place. This was very hard for the owner of a house, but opened up a lot of rooms for refugees. Dad was busy every day looking for a better place for his family and finally found one in a 'rich people's villa. The people still had two rooms left and let the Wenzel family even have their furniture. The location was one of the best in Luedenscheid, close to the Stadtpark (City Park). The family felt blessed! August had done it again!

Thomas didn't sit around idle during this time either. He went up to the Luedenscheid Hospital and asked for an appointment with Dr. Wilms. He got an appointment for the next day. Dr Wilms understood exactly the problem with Thomas's leg. He said he didn't blame the other doctor who suggested cutting off more of Thomas' leg in order to have the wound heal. He would have done the same himself, had he not just recently invented a new method to salvage the leg. Dr. Wilms explained his idea to Thomas who agreed to it. The doctor left, leaving Thomas full of hope. Thomas would be admitted to the hospital the very next day.

THOMAS & SABINE

Thomas pushed the hospital door open. His wet hand slipped off the handle, but he made it inside. The water was dripping down from his jacket. He felt his hair, it was wet all the way to the scalp! Thomas had walked in the rain to reach the hospital. With both hands working the crutches, he couldn't hold an umbrella. People had told him an umbrella would be the number one item you needed in Luedenscheid because the city received a lot of rain. From the North Sea and going south there was a long stretch of low land, of flat countryside. Luedenscheid was on the first rise in elevation and built on top of lower mountains in the centre of Germany. Any clouds coming from the North had to rise into a higher colder air mass and then released their water on the Luedenscheid area. Inside the hospital Thomas was standing in front of a huge sign designating all the different floors in the hospital. Thomas found out that he had to go to the second floor. So, he started going up the stairway, leaving a wet trail behind him. His nose smelled the disinfectants. Everything looked clean. He felt like a wet cat coming into a clean house. Holding on to the railing, jumping one stair at a time, he made it to the next floor.

An energetic looking nurse walked towards him. "Good morning! Can I help you? Are you looking for something? Are you the Herr Wenzel we are waiting for?"

"I am Thomas Wenzel! I am supposed to be admitted today! Dr. Wilms told me to be here in the morning."

"Nice to meet you Herr Wenzel! I am the head nurse on this floor! My name is Nurse Cefie! Come with me to your room. I'll make sure you get a towel to dry yourself off with." Nurse Cefie walked in front of Thomas towards room # 215. She opened the door and Thomas looked at six beds. All except one were filled with men close to his age. Another nurse was checking the pulse of a patient. Nurse Cefie, walking in front of Thomas, announced, "Good Morning everybody! Herr Thomas Wenzel is your new bed neighbour. I hope you're all going to have a good time together!" She turned towards the other nurse. "Nurse Sophie, could you please help our new patient dry himself off and get into his nightgown?"

"Yes, of course!" Nurse Sophie replied.

Thomas smiled at Nurse Sophie. "Thank you very much, but I'll take care of myself!" He took the towel he was given and got ready for the day bed.

The door opened, and Liese entered the room with a tray in her hand. "Good morning, Herr Wenzel! I have breakfast for you! The rest of our patients got theirs already, but we kept yours, just in case!"

Thomas smiled! He found that very nice and thoughtful. "Thank you very much!" Liese put the tray with the food in front of him and left. She walked as fast as she was able to and burst into the kitchen where Sabine was busy washing the dishes. "Sabine! Sabine, you won't believe it! This new guy in 215 is gorgeous! His hair is strong and black, his face is so nice. I don't know his eye colour yet, but I know you will love him!"

Sabine dropped the sponge she was doing the dishes with and held her middle. "Ha-ha, this is the third time in one month that you told me the same story! He will be just like everybody else!"

Liese crossed her arms in front of her chest, standing there with her feet apart and a face which was very serious, "Don't worry! You will get to know him! This time, I am right! I just know it!"

"You better take the dishtowel in your hand! We have lots to do!" Sabine teased.

Beside Thomas's bed was Egon, another patient whose leg had been amputated as well. Thomas and Egon hit it off right from the start. Egon had only high praise for Dr. Wilms and his assistant Dr. Voelkner. "They are specialists! They know what they are doing! You will see it for yourself!" The door opened and Liese came into the room again and took the tray with the empty dishes away from Thomas' night table. While she was doing this, she looked for a long time into Thomas' eyes. After she left, Egon laughed. "What was that? Is she sweet on you?" Thomas had to laugh as well. This was funny. Liese seemed to be a funny person.

Liese came jumping up and down into the kitchen, the dishes on her tray barely survived. "His eyes are a wonderful brown! Brown like chocolate pudding!"

"Aha" was all Sabine had to say.

Nurse Cefie came into room 215 with some papers in her hand and sat beside Thomas's bed. She had to finish the admitting papers. She asked a lot of questions and told Thomas that the doctor would see him tomorrow. It was all fine with Thomas. He liked it here! The men in the room were not so sick. They talked and joked a lot. Most of them had an injury from the war and great hopes to be able to live a normal life after they came out of the hospital. Thomas had a good time with them.

The day went on and Thomas had some time to gather his thoughts. He looked out the window. It was a grey, rainy day. His Dad would be all wet at his new job, going from door to door collecting money from the subscribers of the local newspaper. It was a dream job for his dad! Thomas smiled just thinking about it. Every man he knew had to start his job at 7am and work until 7pm. Dad started at 9am and finished at 5pm. This short workday gave Dad plenty of time to do his personal trading and other business on the side. The job actually helped him with his own plans, because he met a lot of people during the day. People were the key for Dad's business!

The door opened to room #215 and a young woman with gold blond wavy hair which surrounded a face like an angel and, with a perfect slim and wonderful figure in that pretty, clean uniform dress said, "Dinner is ready! I hope you will like it!" She went from bed to bed to deliver the dinner for the patients. Thomas' heart stopped a beat. "Did the sun come out? The room seemed to be in a bright light? Why is it so warm in the room? Is somebody playing a wonderful tune?" he thought.

Sabine came toward his bed, "Guten Tag Herr Wenzel! My name is Sabine! Welcome to our floor! I hope you will enjoy the food!" She put a full plate of potatoes and vegetables, a glass with water and the cutlery in front of him.

Thomas' cheeks got a bit red, but he managed a very quiet "Thank you!" Sabine left the room.

Egon and the rest of the men erupted in laughter. "Thomas, you are in over your head! Sabine is a great woman, but we have to warn you, we call her 'The Fortress'. You are not the first to be enamoured by her. We are not in her league! I tell you!" Thomas smiled in order to hide his mixed feelings. He paid attention to his food. It was the safest place for now. He was confused!

Sabine walked with fast steps toward the kitchen. Liese was waiting, smiling like a teacher to a student. "Na, was I right? Is he gorgeous?" Sabine's face turned a bit red. Liese jumped up and down. "I knew it! I knew it! He is the one! Finally, a man Sabine likes! I was afraid that it would never happen!" The rest of the kitchen crew had a good laugh!

Frau Henschel came to Sabines' rescue. "Sabine, you better get the next tray! We have lots to do!" Sabine took the tray and left the kitchen. She was confused!

The following day, Dr. Wilms, a man in his forties with some grey hair showing at his temple, and his assistant, Dr. Voelkner, a bit younger, came into room 215 to look after their patients. Both examined Thomas' wound, looked each other in the eye and smiled. Dr Wilms turned to Thomas and said, "Thomas, you are the perfect candidate for our new skin transplant method. We call it the 'handle plastic'. You are the second patient we are going to perform it on, so, it is brand new! But don't be scared! Doesn't matter what will happen, we can't make it worse than it is already. You can only win!"

Thomas looked into the eyes of Dr. Wilms "You almost got me scared, ha-ha."

Dr. Wilms got serious and explained, "You will have a couple of surgeries. In the first surgery we are going to cut a piece of skin in a rectangular shape off from the inner part of your good leg. This cut will be at the exact height of the wound on your right leg. The key is that we don't take it completely off, but leave both the upper and lower ends on, in order to keep the skin alive with blood. The two longer sides will be sewn together, so the whole thing will look like a handle. After this first step, you have to rest for a couple of weeks, until your skin grows back underneath the handle on your left leg. During that time, the wound on your right leg will be prepared with alcohol bandages, so it will be very clean for the transplant."

Thomas said, "Sounds like I will be in here for a while!"

Dr. Voelkner smiled and replied, "Don't you worry about that! We have great nurses and good food in these meager times! You will like it here!"

Dr. Wilms kept going. "Now comes the second step of the surgery. One end of the handle will come off your left leg and be sewn onto one end of your wound. Both legs will be put together into a cast for two weeks, so you won't be able to move them. The new skin has to grow onto one side of your wound. After this is done, we get you out of the cast and remove the second end off your left leg. The handle will be cut open and the whole piece of skin will be sewn right on top of your wound. You will have brand-new skin covering your wound, strong enough to withstand the pressure from the prosthesis. So, tomorrow will be step one! See you in surgery!" Both men left.

Egon, who was listening in to the whole conversation, said, "Man, that sounds complicated!"

Thomas, with a furrowed brow, agreed. "Yeah, you are right! Dr. Wilms put a lot of thought into that one! I trust him! I believe he knows what he is doing! I had to stay in hospitals for months on end already. I guess I am used to it. The food looks alright to me and the people are great as well! As long as I will be able to wear a prosthesis at the end, that is what I want! I would like to be able to work as a technician. That is the job I learned!"

Egon's eyebrows went up. "You are a technician? Do you know what the city of Luedenscheid is all about? This town has almost as many factories as it has families! One joke is that every family in Luedenscheid owns their little factory! They are manufacturing small metal things like buttons for furniture, screws, and so on. To be a technician in Luedenscheid is like being a baker in Bakers town! Ha-ha."

The door opened, and again, the room was filled with pure sunlight. Thomas enjoyed the warm feeling Sabine gave him when she was present in the room. She didn't look like a 'fortress' to him. She was his sunshine! "Guten Abend! The "Abendbrot" is here! I hope you will enjoy the sandwiches with real cold cuts today. Unfortunately, Herr Wenzel will only get a clear soup. He has surgery tomorrow." Sabine put the plates down in front of every patient and gave Thomas his soup. She looked into his eyes saying, "Enjoy!" and left. Thomas got a bit red again and had to suffer the laughter of the whole room, again.

The next day, Nurse Cefie and Nurse Sophie pushed Thomas with his bed into the surgery area. Thomas was waiting with other patients in the hallway after the nurses wished him well. Another nurse pushed him into the surgery room where the doctors were waiting for him. "Hi Thomas, this is the start of your healing! We are excited to do the first step today! It will be all fine!" The doctors got ready and the nurses prepared Thomas. Surgery was on!

In the afternoon, after Thomas woke up and got his thoughts straightened out again, the doctors entered the room and Dr. Wilms spoke. "Thomas, it all went well! Now the new skin has to grow underneath the handle and after that we can do the second step." Thomas felt good, he knew he was in good hands.

It was Sunday, the day where visitors were allowed in the hospital. Some patients had their family gathered around their beds. Thomas was waiting. The door opened and a small head with curly black hair and a beautiful, fine face, looked into the room. It was his little sister Otilia searching the room with her big brown eyes until she detected Thomas in his bed. She ran towards him, followed by her older sister Regina in her blue Sunday dress and with the same strong black hair as Thomas. The parents were the last ones to enter. The sisters found a spot on his bed and mother and father had chairs to sit on. Thomas tried to explain the handle plastic surgery to his family, but it was too complicated for little Otilia. Thomas lifted the blanket off his legs in order to show her the first step of the process. The eyes of Otilia got very big. "Now they damaged your good leg, Thomas! You will never be able to walk again!" The whole family had a good laugh. Her mind was set! Tomorrow in school all the children would hear that the other leg of her brother was now damaged as well. It was funny!

August had some good stories about his trades and finally, Trudi unwrapped a big piece of cake she had baked. Thomas started to eat while she was telling him. "Right close to the house we live in is the city park. This park has all kinds of trees. I walk there every day. I already found some mushrooms and other plants and herbs like we used to have in our forest. I started to dry the leaves and pretty soon I will be able to make my tea again." Her face was all smiles!

Thomas said, "Oh, that would be good! I am so looking forward to that!" The colour of Trudy's tea was gold and the aroma was rich. She knew exactly which plants were good for a healthy tea.

Time went by fast and the door of the room opened. "I am sorry, but the visiting hour is over! All visitors have to leave!" Sabine closed the door. She had seen the family of Thomas! "They look nice!" she thought. Why was this so important to her? She didn't know why this seemed to matter.

The following Sunday, Sabine had the day off. On days like this she loved to attend the service at the Christuskirche (Christ Church). On her way over she thought about how special Sunday mornings were! People seemed to be more happy and more relaxed. A lot of the people she met on her way even greeted her, which was not the normal thing to do in Luedenscheid. When she reached the church, she opened the huge wooden door and looked across the pews already filled with parishioners. "Oh, there is Inge!" she told herself in a very quiet voice. She found a seat right beside her. "Hi Inge!"

"Hi Sabine! Good to see you! We got the same Sunday off. That is great!" Turning to the man beside her, Inge said, "Willi, this is Sabine!" Turning towards Sabine, she said, "Sabine, this is my brother Willi!" After her introduction, they had to be quiet as the pastor came up to the podium and the sermon started. During the sermon, Sabine found herself looking at the stained-glass windows of the church a lot of times. The sun shining onto the glass made the colours vibrant, so beautiful. Besides admiring the windows, she was able to follow the encouraging words of the pastor who seemed to know his Bible and his Saviour well. The pastor blessed the congregation at the end, and everyone emptied the church.

"Don't just run-away Sabine! I have to talk to you!" Sabine smiled and turned towards Inge and her brother. "Do you remember what I told you about the nightmares Willi had from his horrible experience during the war?" Sabine looked at Willi and felt uncomfortable, but Inge kept talking. "It is alright, Sabine. Willi knows that I told you about it, and he wants me to tell you the rest of the story. So, the nightmares kept coming more frequently, every night, sometimes more than once."

Willi looked at Sabine and said, "I was afraid of going to sleep and so sorry for Inge that she got woken up so often."

Inge took over again. "So, Willi decided to talk to our pastor about it. It was the best idea ever! The pastor had heard horrible war stories from other men before and wasn't surprised when Willi told him his story. The pastor knew right away what to do. He and Willi went to Jesus! They gave the whole horrible memory into the good hands of the Lord. Willi asked Jesus to forgive him and cleanse him from all the evil, and the pastor blessed Willi in the name of Jesus. Willi was forgiven, and the power of evil left him. From that day on, the nightmares were gone! The two of us can sleep in peace! Willi is set free from this horrible past! We are so happy! Willi is now a normal man and could even get married."

Sabine gave Inge a big hug and smiled to Willi, "This is a great story. I am so happy for you two. You made my day!" Sabine walked home to her family for the noon meal. Otti, in her apron, was busy cooking at the stove.

"Hi Sabine! For a change, we don't have bread soup. I am cooking a delicious pea soup, and we will have some good wieners with it."

"Sounds great! You make the best pea soup in the world! It sure smells good in here!"

Otti went to the window. "I better open the window to get some fresh air in here!" She opened the window and noticed a bald, skinny man standing in front of the house, who was looking at her. "Sabine, you should see this poor man on the sidewalk. His clothes are all in tatters, his head is bald. He is a sorry looking guy. I wonder…" Otti heard the man say, in a rough sounding voice, "Mama!"

She tried to get a better look at the man and fumbled. "Emil? Emil is that you?" Emil broke out in a huge smile and waved at her.

Otti turned around to the others in the room. "Emil is here! Emil is here!" Otti, Heini, and Sabine, ran down the stairs and met up with Emil in front of the house. Emil almost fell over from all the hugs! "Come upstairs, let's go to our apartment!" Heini said. They closed the door behind them and took a good look at Emil. His face was almost like a skull! The skin draped tight over the bones. When Otti hugged him, she could feel every rib in his chest. It didn't take long, and it was clear to everybody, that Emil was in dire need of a bath. He smelled bad.

Sabine grew worried. "I wonder if Emil should take a bath right away, before we eat, I am worried about lice!"

Emil agreed, "You should be worried! These lice have been with me for the last years. I am so used to scratching myself and killing those creatures."

Heini volunteered. "I'll get the bathtub from the basement. Do we have hot water Otti?"

"Oh yes! Plenty! I put the big pot on to wash the dishes with after dinner! Emil will be fine! Sabine and I will get busy with the dinner and you can help Emil with the bath! Please take this special soap Sabine gave us against lice and use it liberally!" The huge metal bath tub was placed in the middle of the kitchen and Emil found himself sitting in nice warm water, with Dad helping to get rid of the lice and clean from all the dirt he had collected over the last time. Sabine took Emil's dirty clothes right away and threw them into the outside garbage.

Emil was almost done when the door burst open and the two young daughters, Walli and Gerdi came in. Walli blurted out. "What is that? Who is sitting in our bath tub?"

Otti came right over to the two little girls. "This is Emil, your brother! Remember Emil? He is back home from all those years as a prisoner of war. Emil your brother is back!"

Gerdi, the younger one, said a very shy, "Hi Emil!" And Walli did the same. The girls had very little memory of their big brother. He was a stranger to them.

Otti tried to break the awkward moment. "Why don't the two of you wash your hands and let Emil finish his bath. After dinner we'll celebrate with waffles and coffee. Too bad that Emma has to work today and can't be with us."

"Waffles, yeah!" The two got busy cleaning their hands and gave Sabine a hand setting the table. Emil was clothed in his father's pants and shirt. It was all way too big for him. A belt was needed to keep the pants from slipping down. The family sat around the table. Soup was just what everybody needed. Emil ate double what the others had. He was starved!

"So, son, let us hear what happened in France!" Heini started.

Emil's face got serious. "A lot of lice, very little food, and hard work! To put it into a nutshell!" The family listened intently to the stories of Emil's years in France.

Sabine was standing at the huge sink filled with dishes from all the patients on her floor. There were a lot of dishes today. She had to work hard. Liese helped her by drying the dishes and putting them away. Thomas was walking back and forth on his crutches along the hallway. He had all his surgeries behind him. It was all good! Dr. Wilms promises were coming true! This doctor was an expert! Thomas watched as Sabine worked so hard. He leaned against the post of the doorway to the kitchen. "Would you like my help? I am able to dry dishes!" he offered.

Liese got a bright smile on her face. "Oh Thomas, please, we have so much today! You can dry the dishes, and I'll put them away and prepare the coffee." Thomas came into the kitchen and leaned against the counter. Standing on his one good leg, he took the dishtowel from Liese and started drying the dishes. Sabine smiled at him. She didn't know if she got warm because of the hot water in front of her, or the presence of Thomas standing beside her.

"So, Thomas, how is your wound now, after all the surgeries?" Sabine inquired.

"Very good! It is healing!" Thomas remarked. "Dr. Wilms said that if it keeps healing that well, I will be released in a couple of weeks."

Sabine got a bit sad. "What are your plans after you are able to go home?"

"First, I have to wait for the new skin to get really strong and healthy, so it will be able to withstand the pressure of my prosthesis. With the new prosthesis I will be able to walk normally and work as a technician like any other normal man."

Sabine got excited. "You are a technician? That is the most needed position in Luedenscheid! By the time all the factories are up and running again, they will look for a man like you! You have a great future in this town!" Both kept talking and working. From this day on Thomas helped with the dishes every time Sabine was working. It became a new normal for the two. Both enjoyed it a lot.

"I have this Sunday off!" Sabine told Thomas while they were doing the dishes.

"What are your plans?" Thomas asked.

"I love to attend the service at the Christuskirche on Sundays. The church has a very good pastor. I love to hear him preach and I like to sit in church and look at the painted glass windows, especially when the sun shines on them. It is spectacular. The colours get deep and rich."

"Hm, would you mind if I ask Dr. Wilms today if he would give me permission to join you on Sunday? I would love to go to a church and hear a good sermon!" Thomas stated.

Sabine's face got a bit red. "Sure! It would be nice to have company. I would love it!"

It was Sunday, and Thomas and Sabine walked together across the marketplace of Luedenscheid. It was called the 'Marketplace' for now. The old name 'Adolf Hitler Platz' was gone. The people were relieved about that. The two took a long time to walk to the church. Thomas was slower with his crutches. They passed the windows of the stores. Since it was Sunday, the stores were closed. At 2pm Saturday afternoon, the stores closed for the whole weekend. Thomas told Sabine that his wish for now would be to own a bike. It would be much better for him to get around after he had his prosthesis.

"I would love to have a bike too! I only rode a bike once, from my brother, and went down the stairway with it. He never let me go on his bike again! Ha-ha," Sabine laughed.

Thomas had to laugh as well. "My little sister at home always wanted to have my bike too. I didn't like that either! Ha-ha"

Sabine got serious. "How did you get shot in your leg?"

Thomas started his story. "We were surrounded by the Russians in this wooded area by Spremberg. We tried a lot of times to break out of it and get behind the enemy lines. On one of those attempts, I got shot. The funny, stupid thing was that we had to shout a loud 'Hurrah' before starting to cross this dangerous field and then I got shot!"

"Why did you have to shout 'Hurrah'?" Sabine asked.

"The officers believed it would take our fears away."

Sabine looked Thomas in the eye. "Did it?"

"Not totally, only at the very moment when we said the 'Hurrah'! After that, the fear came back in full force." Thomas countered. "Nobody was that stupid! We all knew the enemy had us in their sight! We had good reason to be scared, but if you get an order, you have to obey it!"

The two stood in front of the church. A lot of people had already made their way in. Thomas and Sabine followed them inside the church. The benches filled up, and Thomas and Sabine found themselves on a bench right in the centre of the church. Sabine looked to her right and spotted Inge and her brother sitting not too far from them. Inge made a face like a question mark, seeing Sabine sitting with a man in church. Sabine had to smile.

The organ started playing and the pastor came onto the platform. Thomas looked at the stained-glass windows. Sabine hadn't exaggerated; the windows were beautiful! He loved them, but most of the time, he had to look at Sabine. He couldn't believe his luck to sit beside such a beautiful woman. He was wondering what God was doing in his life.

The pastor started the sermon. "John 3:16 says as follows: 'For God so loved the world, that he gave his only begotten Son, that whoever believeth in him should not perish, but have everlasting life.'" He kept talking about the cross, where Jesus died for our sins. He was concerned about the people listening, if they would understand what he was talking about. He said, "I see some young men sitting in the benches. How many of you have fought in the war?" Thomas and four other men put up their hands. "How many times did you on the battle field look death in the eye? How often did you run towards the enemy with a loud "Hurrah" and find yourself alive on the other side?" Sabine and Thomas looked smiling at each other. The pastor spoke on. "My guess is that the army did a good job in teaching you how to handle a weapon, how to march in unison, and all the other skills you needed to have victory over the enemy, but did they ever teach you how to have victory over death itself? I am talking now to everyone. How many times did you look into the eye of death and get away with it? You survived? Please take one minute right now; think about the moments when you were close to death and you didn't die. Just one minute, right now!"

The church was very quiet. People had their eyes closed and concentrated on what the pastor had asked them to do. Thomas remembered the many times he was saved by God during the fight in the Spremberg woods. He thought that the shot in his leg could have been a shot in his heart. And later on, during the time as a prisoner of war, he could have died of starvation, and the time in the hospital in Goerlitz when he was so ill. The doctors actually expected that he would die.

Sabine remembered as well. She thought of the train with the munitions in Halver being bombed. It could have been much worse. And the time the American soldiers were riding into Halver and she was hiding behind the bushes in the dark. That could have been bad! And of course, the time she was sitting in the train going home to Luedenscheid and they came under fire. If she wouldn't have left the train in that tunnel, she would have been dead like all the other people.

The minute passed, and the pastor kept going. "Did you remember moments close to death? Do you believe that Jesus saved you right at that moment? Then please take another short minute and thank him for saving your life!" It was quiet as everyone said they're thanks to God in their mind. The pastor started again.

"I ask the soldiers if they taught you in the army how to conquer death? Of course not! All of us have to die one day! We don't have victory over death! But one person did! His name is Jesus! He died on the cross and rose again on the third day. He conquered death! He didn't do it just to show us how mighty he is! He did it in order to conquer death for us! His death on the cross paved the way to the Father, to God! We will live forever with the Father in heaven because of the death and resurrection of Jesus. Though he died on the cross, Jesus is alive. You are able to talk to him today! You can ask him to forgive your sins and accept his death on the cross personally for you! He loves you! He died for you! Do you want to accept the forgiveness of your sins through his death on the cross today? You personally? If you do, please get up from your seat and show to Jesus and the whole world that you really mean it."

People in the church got up from their seats. Thomas felt that every word the pastor had said was just for him. Thomas was serious! He meant it! He rose slowly from his seat. The moment he was fully up, he felt a shower from heaven coming down on him, washing him clean of all his sins. It was good!

He opened his eyes and noticed that Sabine was standing right beside him. "This is good!" he thought.

The pastor spoke a special blessing for all the people who were standing. Now everybody got up and sang one more hymn, and the service was over.

Thomas and Sabine remained standing and looked each other in the eyes. Thomas was mesmerized by the beauty and sparkle of Sabine's green eyes. "Do you believe that you and I will have a future together?

Sabine looked up into Thomas's wonderful, warm, brown eyes. "I believe!"

About the Author

Karin Zielke was born and raised in Germany. She currently lives in Canada with her husband, and has two sons. Karin has enjoyed visiting her hometown, Luedenscheid, in Germany, and learning and writing about the history she is connected with.

A Heartfelt Thanks

My first heartfelt thanks go to both my Mom and my Dad, who wrote down their war stories for their children. You gave me the bone structure of this book. I look up to both of you! You are my heroes! Praise to the Lord Jesus himself, who let you live and survive through all that time. He is God! He is good!

Thanks to God Himself, who gave me time, and a great husband, to help me with writing this book.

Jeremy Tynedal was also a great help with editing my 'wobbly' English. Thank you, Jeremy!

Reading Ken Follett's trilogy 'The Century' gave me the push to write this. His books also reminded me of the killings of many disabled people during the Hitler regime.

The webpage of the 'Luedenscheider Zeitbilder' provided important data and information for the chapter "Luedenscheid Under Attack".

Pastor David Jeremiah told the story about the father and his two daughters talking about death in a radio show I listened to. The story is in the chapter "Surrounded".

Numerous internet articles gave me important dates for many of the stories.

Manufactured by Amazon.ca
Acheson, AB

13093287R00173